Lyra

The Greek Mysticals: Book One

By Sam Miller

First Printing, 2019

Ebook ISBN 978-1-7338742-6-7

Paperback ISBN 978-1-7338942-0-5

www.facebook.com/SamMillerAuthor

Dedication

Thank you to all who have supported me and stood by me during this process. Especially my family who has had to put up with me! A special thanks to Lacie, without you I would have never finished this book and been inspired to write the rest of this series. Thank you!

Contents

Prologue

A low groan fills the tiny room. The sound bounces off the walls and the woman lying bound on a small twin bed, glances around furiously, hoping it wasn't too loud. She lays in silence before breathing a sigh of relief and relaxing against the uncomfortable bed. Her light red hair fans around her and her gray eyes lock onto the ceiling in thought.

She knew this was the beginning. The beginning of the end of her life but also the beginning of her children's. Another soft groan falls from her lips as her stomach tightens in another contraction. Her face screws up and her eyes shut in concentration, trying not to make a sound. Everything depends on her keeping quiet and not alerting her guard she is in labor. The contraction subsides for now and her thoughts drift between her unborn children and the love of her life: Felix.

She should have known when she met him, they could never work being who they are; being *what* they are. But the mate bond never lied. They were meant to meet, meant to fall in love, meant to have these babies; Liliana wouldn't change a single thing.

Thinking back to almost a year ago, she remembers meeting Felix at the beach that day. How scared she had been, a part of her knew then what would happen. It was her destiny to meet him. Having his children was written in the stars and dying in childbirth was always how she was meant to die. She could live with that as long as her children survived.

Liliana glances around the dark room, her eyes landing on the small window to her right. It's the only way she can tell the time of day. A long stream of bright light flows through the dusty, smudged window and falls upon the dirty floors. It's probably around midday if she had to take a guess.

Lucky for her, she was allowed one walk a day, and she hadn't used it up yet. This just might work out. Ana braces herself for the next contraction and this time, not a sound escapes her lips. She can do this; she has to.

Contraction subsiding, she calls out, "Hey! I'm ready for my walk now." The room remains quiet and then the sound of heavy boots against the earth reaches her ears. She knew he was out there.

The door opens revealing Marcus, a cruel man who guards the small home. His dark hair shaved close to his head and his black eyes stare at her in hatred. He volunteers to watch her, just to see her suffer daily. He looks at Liliana tied up on the bed and a cold smile tugs at his mouth. Seeing her dirty and bound always made his day, and thoughts of her would flow at night when he was alone in his bed. Not that he would admit that to anyone but himself.

Leaning against the door, his eyes travel her body and settle on her round stomach in disgust. While he found the feisty red-head attractive, the thought of her carrying those nasty hybrids leaves a bad taste in his mouth. If it was up to Marcus, she would be dead by now and so would those abominations. He glares at her belly before dragging his eyes over her breasts and into her gray eyes. One would think her eyes would be drained by now, lackluster, but they are the same as when she was brought here months ago: strong. Marcus still has hope he can beat that out of her before she dies. He comes closer and peers down at her.

"You can go for your walk now if you give me a kiss first," he says, looking down at her lips and puckering his own. Liliana turns away in revulsion. This isn't the first time he has suggested sexual favors from her, and like every other time, she shuts him down.

"I'm sure Felix would love to hear that," her voice rings out clear as her eyes stay trained on the wall across from her. There's a small, dingy table littered with takeout boxes and only one chair, the other is in a broken heap by the wall; where it's laid since another guard broke it weeks ago. Marcus inhales and chokes out a laugh.

"That pussy won't do anything. He leaves you here every day. What kind of man leaves the woman he claims to love, who is pregnant with his children? A pussy, that's who," Marcus growls out and spits on the floor. Despite his tone, his hands reach into his pockets and fish out the key. He unlocks her slowly, hands lingering on hers as he twists the key in the lock. Liliana can't suppress her shiver of revulsion as his skin touches hers. He finally lets her go and takes a step back, allowing her the freedom to get up by herself. At one point this was a relief to Liliana, but now this is torture at almost nine months pregnant. She struggles to her side and slowly escapes the bed. Her back cracks as she sits up and a sigh of relief exhales from her mouth at finally being off her achy back.

"Will Felix be here today?" Her voice is even as she asks Marcus, standing on her feet and swaying a little. Her stomach tightens, and she quickly turns away from Marcus and breathes quietly, she can't have him know the truth or he will never let her out for a walk.

"Later. He's bringing your lunch in about an hour. You gonna give me a show today? I'll give y'all a few minutes alone as long as I can join in," he asks, hands dropping to her waist. She roughly pulls away from him and almost falls back onto the bed before she leans against the headboard. Marcus laughs and walks back towards the door and Liliana follows him silently. Sometimes it's best to say nothing, especially when she's in a hurry to get outside and into the woods.

Walking into the bright light, her hands come up and block her eyes. Marcus grunts and slams the door shut behind them and walks a few feet away, where he has a round table and a chair set up in the grass. Playing cards are spread out along the rough wood and he continues his game of solitaire as he sits down. He doesn't even blink at Liliana as she hurries into the trees surrounding the property. Marcus knows she can't escape; they brought in a witch to set up a ward around the property, Liliana couldn't take a single step past the circle no matter how much she wanted to. It also drained her of her powers, rendering her human in the small space. At least they didn't keep her locked up in the house all the time and allowed her the chance to walk every day.

Liliana walks out of view and leans against a nearby tree out of sight. She doesn't wait there long before she is traveling west, towards a grove of hollow trees along the ward border. Having seven months to explore the woods, she knows the perfect place to labor where Marcus won't hear her. Every step she takes, her contractions build, and she feels wetness seeping down her legs.

Finally, she reaches the hollow trees, and she rushes to one that's just along the line. Liliana braces herself against the tree and squats down, pushing with everything she has. Her body isn't ready to push yet, but she knows she has little options. Marcus will come looking for her in an hour and she needs to give birth to both babies and hide them before he comes for her. Their only hope is her getting back to Marcus before she bleeds out and telling Felix where to find them. While their relationship may be forbidden, someone must be looking down on them in favor; so far everything is turning out perfect.

Liliana pushes for what seems like forever. She has no way of knowing how long it's taking and there is so much blood beneath her; already she is tired, but she has to keep going. Reaching down, she can feel the first babies head. Excited, she bears down and pushes with everything she has. Despite her pain, she's able to reach down and catch her baby.

It's a beautiful baby girl, with patches of light red hair sticking to her head. She looks just like her mother. Liliana smiles down at the little babe and kisses her forehead before tugging down her dress away from her breast and bringing the little one up to nurse. She knows she doesn't have much time to spend with her daughter but wants to give her the best start in life she can.

"Thank the Goddess! You are so beautiful," Liliana says, staring down at her little girl. "I'll name you Lyra, after my favorite constellation. May you look up at the stars and know I will always love you. You will be vibrant and full of life, no one will bring down your spirit."
The tiny infant doesn't so much as open her eyes as her mouth speaks, she drifts to sleep in her mother's arms, feeling love and contentment.

Knowing she can't waste any more time, Liliana finishes delivering the placenta and reaches into the hollow tree, pulling out a few shirts she was able to store there. They will have to be enough to keep Lyra warm for a few more hours. Carefully, she wraps the baby up and with one last glance at her beautiful face, she lays her gently inside the tree. Feeling another contraction hit her, Liliana braces herself against the tree to ride it out before waddling away.

Blood trails behind her and she has to stop multiple times from the pain. Liliana starts to second guess herself, maybe she should have hidden both the twins together? No, she shakes her head. It might have been easier on her, but she wanted to give them both a chance at life, and that meant keeping them separate; there was less of a chance of them being discovered if they were apart.

Breathing through her next contraction, she has to stop again. Black spots dance before her eyes and her body sways a little. She can't make it to the other spot. Looking around, she spots a fallen log close to her, and she shuffles over to it carefully, blood pouring out of her. She's losing too much, too fast. She falls as she reaches the log and stays on her knees as she pushes again. She has to have this baby fast; she can't die out here without seeing Felix again. Liliana needs to tell him where to find the other baby and she wants to see him just one more time before she dies. Determined, she ignores the pain and bears down.

"What are you doing?" She hears behind her. Tears stream down her face, she's too late, and she knows it. This baby doesn't have a chance now that Marcus has found her.

"Please help me. I just went into labor and something is wrong," she sobs. She can't let him know she already had Lyra. Without a word, Marcus walks over to her and takes her into his arms, carrying her back to the small, one-room hut she has spent the last seven months living in.

"Of course, something is wrong. Did you think your babies would survive? That you would? This was always how it was going to end. Lucky Felix, he's just in time to witness this," Marcus laughs, "He can watch you die." With long strides, they reach the hut in no time. Liliana's eyes are shut and her body aches.

"Ana!" Felix's voice reaches her ears, and she pries her eyes open, needing to see him. He's standing by the front door of the hut and his brown eyes show his deep worry for her. Whenever he visits, he always keeps his emotions locked up tight. He never wanted to worry her, but she knew he was scared and in denial. He thought he could fix this somehow- that they could live a happy life together with their babies. That's not their destiny though.

"She went into labor in the woods," Marcus says, handing me over to Felix. "I found her almost passed out." Felix looks down at Liliana and kisses her cheek before walking into the hut. The bed might not be the most comfortable but there was no way she was standing up anymore, she needed to lie down. Felix lays her down and settles in beside her on the tiny bed.

"What can I do?" He asks her. Marcus, surprisingly, waits outside the hut and allows them some privacy. This is the first time they've been alone since they were caught all those months ago and Liliana lays her palm against his dark cheek and brings him in for a wet kiss. Neither of them cares they are crying; they enjoy the touch of the other for a second before pulling away. Liliana pulls his head down and brings her lips to his ear.

"Listen, I had a baby in the woods already," she says as Felix pulls away and looks at the door, knowing Marcus shouldn't hear this.

"Are they alive?" He whispers in her ear, just loud enough for her to hear.

"Yes, I put her in a hollow tree along the west side of the property. Find her Felix. Take her and run away, please." She whispers, tears leaking down her face.

"I will. I promise. For now, I'm staying with you. Maybe I can somehow get this baby as well? I can take down Marcus and run away with all of you."

"I would love that, but it will not happen, at least not with me. I love you, Felix," she says, leaning back and looking into his eyes. "But I'm not going to survive this. I've lost too much blood and I'll just slow you down. You take our babies and you get them out of here. Don't you dare look back."

"I can't just leave you," he says, tears rolling down his face. In the year Liliana has known Felix, he has never cried; not even when they were found a few months ago or at any point since they have held her captive. Never. But now he's openly crying.

"It's okay. I've known for a long time now that this is how I would die. I can be at peace if you can get our babies away. That's all that matters now. Keeping you and them safe. Can you do that for me?" Felix looks into his mates eyes and nods. He doesn't want to believe that she will die but even he can't deny that she is losing too much blood. The scent fills his nose and he can't do anything to save her.

Liliana moans and sits up, pushing down as hard as she can. Felix supports her and whispers words of encouragement in her ear. Neither of them notices Marcus walking back into the room and watching them. He's always wondered about their relationship, how they could be so in love. He's watched them for months, but they were never very emotional, always hiding it so others didn't see. Now he can see they love each other, and a pang of guilt hits his heart. Nothing he can change now. What's done is done and even if he had wanted to help them, no one has ever survived this before. Only two other pregnancies like this have ever existed, and both ended in death for the mother and her babies. He stands against the wall and watches the scene unfold.

With one last push, a baby is born. Marcus steps closer as Felix lets Liliana relax against the bed and goes to his child. He lifts the little boy into the air and stares down at his tiny face, pale and covered in blood. He places the baby on Liliana's chest and her eyes open briefly to look at her second child. She whispers, "Phoenix," before her eyes roll back into her head. Marcus steps forward and takes the baby before she can drop him and Felix stares at his wife's face.

"Wake up Ana! Please baby," he cries in anguish. "I need you."

Marcus looks down at the little baby and his heart clenches. Despite his tough guy act, he felt bad for the couple in front of him. "He isn't even breathing," he breathes out. Felix's head whips away from his wife and he looks at his son. He's right, the babies chest isn't moving, and color isn't flooding his pale cheeks as it should. Felix sobs looking between his dead wife and son.

His face tightens, and he hurries out the room. There is nothing left for him there. He could cry all day in that room, and nothing would bring them back, he had to get to Lyra. Someone he could save. The only person he had left in the world. Pushing his emotions down for the moment, Felix runs outside and into the forest, heading toward the west and trying to sniff out the path his mate had taken. He picks up on her scent and follows it through the trees.

Coming upon the grove of hollow trees, his eyes search the ground for any sign of disturbance. Seeing blood on the ground, he walks to the tree right along the border and reaches inside, grasping the bundle with both hands and carefully lifting it. He half expects to find a pale, unmoving baby inside and he closes his eyes before looking down. His eyes lock with a pair of deep gray. Lyra is tiny with light red hair and long eyelashes; she looks just like her mother. The baby is wrapped in a few shirts and her eyes are staring up at her father in wonder, he's the first person she has laid eyes on.

Felix lets out the breath he had been holding and tucks Lyra into his chest and looks around before running as fast as he can. He can't stop by his old place to grab anything, there's no time and there's a risk someone will see them. He has to protect her with everything he has. Lyra is all he has left.

Chapter 1

Lyra

The cool, crushing blue water pushing against my warm skin is a relief. It's like I was made to be in the ocean, it caresses my skin and my hair floats around me. I propel myself to the surface and take a deep breath, looking up at the sky. Floating on my back, I gaze up at the stars; the sun hasn't risen just yet.

Dad says my mom used to do this: just lay in the water and stare up at the stars. She was obsessed and would point out all the different constellations to my dad. Apparently, that's how she came up with my name: Lyra was her favorite constellation. Looking above and to the right, I spot it. It looks like a harp. It's the only constellation I know. Dad showed it to me as a young child and whenever I look up, I always seek it out. Seeing it makes me feel connected to my mom, knowing she looked at the stars and loved them so much that she named me after them. I can almost feel her joy, her happiness when I look up at them. Maybe that's how she felt looking at the stars, or maybe how she felt knowing she was pregnant with me and my brother.

Closing my eyes and breathing in a lung-full of air, I dive under the water and swim down as far as I can go without drowning. Down here I feel at home. I open my eyes and look around, my eyes adjust easily to under the water; I can see better here than above, at the moment. My eyes land on the rock floor below me, and the fish swimming left and right. They don't even flinch when they see me swimming with them, either they are used to me or don't see me as a threat to them. Flashes of light blue and browns flow around me, it's not as colorful here as it is in the Gulf of Mexico, but I love it all the same.

Kicking myself to the surface again, I look to the horizon. The sky is turning a lighter shade of purple and blue, with yellows and reds mixed in. I know it's time for me to head home now that the sun is peeking out. With one last glance at the never-ending sea, I turn towards the shore and swim inland.

The sand is grainy against my feet and sticks in-between my toes; I pay it little notice though and trek towards my home. This is probably the first house I've considered a "home" in a long time. We've moved so much over the years that usually we never stay long enough for me to call a place "home." The little yellow house with dark blue shutters is in front of me within minutes. It has a small back porch that wraps around to the front and lots of windows. It's a perfect little beach home and I almost wish we could stay here forever, but I know dad will want to move soon enough.

I quietly walk onto the porch and into the house, entering the kitchen. All the lights are still off, and I quickly flip the coffee switch on my way towards the hallway leading to the bed-rooms. I don't even bother turning on lights; no need to wake dad up earlier than he needs to be when I can see relatively fine. I'm used to walking around every morning and late at night after a swim in the ocean.

In my bedroom, I walk right into the connected bathroom and finally turn on a light, making my eyes flinch at the brightness. Once my eyes adjust, I make sure I have a clean towel hanging by my shower and strip out of my baby blue bikini. I throw them in the hamper and hop into the warm shower to rinse off the salt.

After a quick wash, I step out of the shower and throw my hair into a towel to dry off and walk to my closet. I pick out a silver tank top I know will bring out the color of my eyes and a pair of jean shorts that show off my curves. I look into my bathroom mirror when I'm done and reach into a bin on the counter, fishing out a hair tie I fix my still damp hair into a high ponytail, the light red hue shines in the fluorescent light and the ends are already curling. I turn left and right, examining myself and shrug. One would expect a redhead to be pale but I'm a light tan, it offsets my silver top and gray eyes. My shorts mold to my curves; doesn't matter how much I diet and exercise, I just can't get rid of my hips, or my ass. Not necessarily a bad thing, I guess. All the guys at school seem to find me attractive enough- even if I don't bother wearing makeup.

Sighing, I walk back into my bedroom and glance at my bedside clock: 7 am. If I don't leave soon, I'm going to be late for school. Thanks, dad, for making us live so far away from civilization. It takes me almost forty minutes every day just to make it to school, and that's if there's no traffic. Yay. I slip on a pair of gray flip flops that are by my bed and head out of my bedroom, planning on grabbing an apple for breakfast and a cup of coffee to go. The kitchen light is on when I walk in and dad is sitting at the kitchen island sipping his coffee. The light reflects off the countertops, making the blue flecks stand out.

"Morning hun," he mumbles into his mug, eyes still half closed. Dad gets up early every morning, I would think he would get used to it at some point but not so far.

"Morning," I say, grabbing my thermos by the sink and filling it with coffee. I add my cream and sugar and pop the top back on before striding over to the island to hug dad goodbye.

"Can you stay for a sec?" He asks, giving me a one-armed hug.

I nod, grabbing an apple from the counter and biting into it. The juice flows out and runs down my chin a little. Dad sees and with a small laugh, grabs a napkin from the counter and hands it to me. I wipe my face and look at him, "What's up?"

"I'll be on the water for a few days. Hoping to catch enough fish to be off next week for your birthday." Dad is a fisherman. He also works on boats, cars, fixes up homes. He does just about anything he can to keep a roof over our heads and food in our bellies.

"You don't have to do that, dad. You don't need to overwork yourself just for me. We can stay at home and grill some fish. Or go to Sharky's and share a pizza," I say, hoping he will go along with one of my ideas. My birthday isn't a big deal to me. It's a little weird celebrating the day of my birth when my mom and twin brother both died the same day.

"Nice try. You only turn eighteen once, kiddo. I plan on having the whole week off and taking a trip somewhere. I was thinking of heading inland and spending a few days near Asheville, up in the mountains," he says hopefully. Which is weird for him, usually he likes being away from people and doesn't trust easily. We've lived on Cedar Island for four years now, it's always been small towns along the coast. We've moved a lot and I'm not sure why, but every few years dad just up and quits wherever he is working and moves us somewhere new. I try not to complain too much. I'm not a fan of people either and I don't make friends easily. He always picks places close to the water, and that suits me just fine. I've been swimming since I was a baby, at least that's what my dad says.

"Yeah dad, let's go someplace packed with people. Just what I want to do for my birthday," I mumbled sarcastically. "Please dad, let's just stay in. Mira has already mentioned dragging me out tomorrow. That'll be enough for me for a year." I know I'm begging; I even pout a little. I just don't like going to new places.

"I already booked the hotel," he says, looking apologetic. He looks older than I have ever seen him. My dad is a decent looking guy of Hispanic descent. He has dark brown hair, buzzed close to his head and deep brown eyes. Many women have tried asking him out, but he's never been interested. I think he's still in love with my mom. Not that he talks about her often, just once in a blue moon. I know that they met on a beach in Texas and it was love at first sight. They dated for a few weeks before eloping. Two months later they found out my mom was pregnant with twins. My dad doesn't mention much after that. I do know my mom was overjoyed to be pregnant and loved me and my brother more than herself. I also know I look just like her, same red hair and gray eyes. Not that I've seen a picture of her or anything, either dad doesn't have any or he hides them. People always ask if I'm adopted because I don't look Hispanic at all. My mom's genes must have been strong. "Are you even listening to me?"

Looking up, I realize I must have zoned out. I do that sometimes when I'm thinking about my mom or my brother. Dad is staring at me perplexed. Probably wondering why I haven't flipped out about him booking a hotel for my birthday without discussing it with me first.

"Sorry dad, just thinking about finals this week. You know I'm going to be late for school, right?" I grumble. Dad flinches back and his eyes drop to his empty coffee mug. I might have been a little mean. Oops. "Dad, I didn't mean it like that. You know I love talking to you! Can we talk later, when you get back? You can tell me the details of our trip then."

His face lights up, eyes crinkling in the corners as he smiles. He sets down his 'best dad in the world' coffee mug and stands up. He's wearing a button-up Hawaiian shirt, khaki shorts, and sandals. Oh, and socks. Yes, my dad wears socks with his sandals. Even in June. Sometimes I wonder if I'm adopted too.

"That would be great! It's a little mountain town, not a lot of people. I know you'll love it!" He says smiling. "Miss Lynn knows I'll be gone until Sunday, so she might call or come by to check up on you. If you need to, go stay with her until I get back. I know how you feel about being home alone."

Actually, I love to be home alone for the most part; not that my dad cares. He's always worried about me staying home while he goes on his boat. To him, I'm still his little girl who's scared of the dark. I haven't stayed with Miss Lynn for almost two years now; since I turned 16 and got my license. She's a very sweet older lady but there's something off about her. The way she looks at me sometimes makes me feel like a monster. Or something special. I can never tell with her. Either way, it creeps me out and I tend to avoid her if I can.

Besides, dad has been going on fishing trips for my whole life. I don't remember much from when I was younger, but I do know he used to take me with him until I started school. After that, he always went on fewer trips. When he did, I would stay with my Aunt Karen.

Aunt Karen isn't my dad's sister, or my mom's for that matter. She's an African American woman in her forties, with long dreads. I haven't seen her in about a year. She used to travel around with us when I was younger and helped my dad raise me. I've asked dad before how he knew her, he just said they met when he was younger, and she was a friend of his. We see her at least once a year, usually around my birthday. She's off traveling the world and has her own family now. Last I heard, she was living in Georgia with her husband and two kids.

I think she's the reason we haven't moved in a while. About eight years ago, she met her husband when we moved to Louisiana. When it came time for us to move, she decided to stay with him, and they got married. It was hard on my dad raising me alone for two years when we lived in Florida after that. He didn't trust anyone else to watch me and even pulled me out of school for a year to home-school so I could go with him on his fishing trips.

That was probably the best year of my life, but also the loneliest. It was nice not having to go to school every day. I woke up when I wanted, went to the beach when we weren't on the boat. But I had no one to talk to but dad, and he was always worried about me. Finally, he decided it was time for a change and moved us here, to Cedar Island. He knew Miss Lynn and trusted her enough to watch me while he was away. We've been here ever since.

"I'll be fine dad, but I'll go see if her if I need too. Love you!" I swiftly give him a hug and a kiss on the cheek, feeling a light stubble underneath my lips. "And dad. Shave. For the love of God." It just doesn't look right on him.

"Maybe I will. Maybe I won't. Hard to shave on a boat sweetie," he says laughingly. I swat his arm and laugh. I love my dad. He's a bit overprotective sometimes, but he is the most important person in my life. I don't know what I would do without him. "I love you kiddo. I'll leave some money on the counter for food. Make sure to eat something! I swear you're eating less and less these days... Drive safe. Do I need to call the school and let them know you'll be late?"

"Nah, I have Mr. Wright first and he's pretty cool with me being a few minutes late. See you in a few days. Be safe!" I yell, jogging out the door and grabbing my bags on the way out. I doubt I'll need my backpack today; I could always turn my book in early I guess.

Tomorrow is the last day of finals, and Friday is pretty much a free day. Then I'm off all next week until next Friday, which is graduation, giving me plenty of time off during my birthday week. Not that I want to do much for it. I'm perfectly content staying home with my dad and hitting up the beach every day. It's so quiet here on the Island, barely 500 people live here, and more than half is a wildlife refuge. It's like having a huge forest wall between our little town and the rest of the world, with the ocean on the other side of us. But I guess I can give dad a little trip. He seemed pretty excited about going.

Running down the steps, I throw my backpack and my purse in the passenger seat and slam the door to my SUV. Dad bought me a used 2006 Ford Escape, a beautiful dark blue color with leather interior. What more could a high school senior ask for? Sure, it has some miles on it and occasionally needs fixing, but dad can fix just about anything.

Sighing, I prepare for the long ride to East Carteret High School, where I've gone for the past four years. Dad was nice enough not to have us move during high school. I was even able to make a few friends this time, Mira and Ryan. Mira has red hair like mine, but hers is much darker and she is pale. I don't know how anyone who lives on the coast could be that white. Ryan is a typical surfer dude, shaggy blonde hair and dark green eyes. I'm pretty sure he has a crush on me, but I'm not interested. I'm not interested in any of the guys I've met.

Ever since I was little, I always felt like someone special was waiting for me. It was just this sense that told me I was meant for someone, and they were meant for me. A soulmate. Sometimes I have dreams of him. I never remember his name or face when I wake-up, but the feelings he gives me in the dreams carry on when I wake up. They leave me breathless and aching for more. Most nights I wake up with my underwear drenched. It's those times that I wish I could have a casual fling with someone to relieve some tension, but I can't do that knowing someone is out there waiting for me.

I tried explaining it to Mira once, and she just laughed. She thinks I read way too many romance books, which I do, but I won't settle for anything less than someone who makes my heart beat fast and my breath to quicken. I want to look at them and know that is the person I want to spend the rest of my life with. That's not too much to ask for, right?

Chapter 2

Lyra

Parking in front of the small, one-story building, I hightail it to class. I have two minutes to spare before the bell and I can't believe I actually made it to school before eight. I don't even notice the other classrooms as I rush by, my focus only on my first class.

I rush inside just as the bell sounds. Score! I walk past the other filled seats and head to my spot by the back window. No one bothers to look at me except a pale, redhead with bright blue eyes sitting by my seat. As I walk past, she smiles at me, showing her teeth. Today she's wearing a light pink, cap sleeve dress. Her arms are crossed, and her eyebrows are covered by her long bangs.

"Finally! Way to almost be late. Did you head to the beach this morning?" She teases.

"Is that even a question?" I laugh. I go to the beach every morning, even when it's snowing outside. There's just something so calming about the water. "You know I go every day, Mira."

She laughs and Mr. Wright looks over at us with a raised eyebrow. "Is something funny ladies?" He asks, his eyes narrowed, and lips pinched. Despite his facial expression, I know he isn't actually mad at us. Mr. Wright has to be the nicest teacher at school. His eyes hold a sparkle behind his thick-rimmed glasses. He's in his late fifties and already has a bald spot surrounded by gray hair. His long sleeve button-up shirt is a light blue today and tucked into his black slacks. No matter how warm outside it is, he insists on wearing his best clothes.

"Now that everyone is here, and quiet," he says, eyeing me and Mira. We simply smile back, and he lightly shakes his head. "We can start. I know the final was yesterday, but I haven't had a chance to grade them all yet. I'll have those grades back to you by Friday when I see you next, or you can email me if you are concerned. I expect everyone passed though. Lucky for you that means I have nothing for you to do all class. Feel free to study if you'd like, read a book, or you can talk quietly amongst your-selves. I can write a library pass for anyone who would like a quieter place to study."

Everyone cheers and starts talking at once. Some pull out cell phones to text their friends, a few pull out books to read, some get up for a library pass. I turn to Mira and she starts talking immediately about boys, her plans for summer and what comes after. I tune her out for the most part. Sometimes I wish I could still be that quiet girl that no one talks to. Then I could just sit in the back of the room and read a book quietly or go to the library and be alone.

"Are you listening to me?" Mira asks. I smile and nod at her, actu-ally trying to pay attention to her words now. She continues on talking and I sigh inwardly. It's going to be a long day.

***

Walking out of school, I find a nice place outside to eat my lunch. It's beautiful out, and I couldn't resist eating out here in-stead of the crowded lunchroom. Mira and Ryan will most likely find me.

Opening up the little bag I grabbed at the cafeteria, I pull out a carrot and bite into it. The sun is shining down on me and there's barely a cloud in sight. Perfect. The only way this could be better is if I had sand underneath my butt and clear water in front of me. Closing my eyes, I just enjoy the warmth of the sun and the wind playing with my hair.

Hearing voices, my eyes pop open and I see Mira and Ryan walking towards me. They don't look the happiest to be outside. Mira is wobbling in her high heels, the stilettos sinking into the moist earth, and Ryan is shielding his eyes from the bright sun; guess he forgot his sunglasses again. I almost feel bad dragging them out here, but honestly, they could eat inside if they wanted. No one has to eat with me, I'm perfectly content sitting here on my own. Don't get me wrong, I love my best friends and they are great to be around, but it's also nice to sit in silence every once in a while and enjoy the weather in peace.

"There you are. Didn't see you inside so we figured you would be out here," Mira says, plopping down beside me with a nasty look at the ground. I'm sure she's worried about her dress getting ruined. Ryan smiles before sitting down on the other side of me. He's wearing black shorts and a fitted green t-shirt that matches his eyes. All the girls at school drool over him and I definitely see what all the fuss is about. He's lean, with a swimmers body and his blonde hair is just long enough he can tie it back. We've been friends since sophomore year when he moved here from California. We both love the water and swim together often. He's on the swim team but I can't be bothered with all that. Swimming is my passion, not a sport.

"It's just too nice outside to be in. Hope it's okay," I say while taking another bite of my lunch with a loud crack.

"At least it's seventy-six degrees out," Ryan says then glances down at my bag of carrots. "Is that all you're eating?"

"Uh," I say, looking down at them and back up. "Yeah. Is there something wrong with eating carrots now? I didn't realize that was a problem."

"Nothing wrong with it," Mira soothes. "You just usually eat more is all. Are you on a diet or something? You don't need it." Great both of them are ganging up on me now.

"Not really, no. I just haven't been hungry lately. Maybe my stomach is shrinking or something." They do have a point. Usually, I grab a tuna sandwich with a bag of chips and I'm still hungry after. I'm the type of person who can put away a whole pizza if I really wanted to. Which I have done before. A few times.

Ignoring their jibes, I try to eat the rest of my carrots before giving up. I already feel full. Maybe I'll order a pizza for dinner. I can never say no to pizza.

"Anyway, I wanted to talk to you about tomorrow!" Mira squeals. She even claps her hands and bounces in her spot.

"No please," I groan out. If I'm being forced to go on a trip with my dad, I want out of Friday night. I doubt Mira will let me though. She's so excited to go out and I know my begging will fall on deaf ears. "Can't we just have a sleepover or something?"

"No way. I hear Justin is throwing the biggest party ever! We're totally going. Your birthday is next Tuesday, and I know you won't let me do anything big for that. You have to come! Please!" Now she's pouting. Ugh.

"What if I say no?" I cross my arms and stare her down, hoping to intimidate her. Ryan laughs at the both of us, he's used to me and Mira fighting like this.

"What?" We both snap at the same time. Ryan flinches and looks startled at being the center of attention now.

"Nothing!" He says, hands raised in the air now in surrender. "We all know Mira is going to make you go, it's not like you really have a choice in the matter. You'll say no and Mira will just show up at your house and pick out an outfit before tying you to a chair and doing your makeup." He's right dammit. It really doesn't matter if I want to go or not. When Mira is this insistent on something, I give in or be tortured.

"Fine," I say. "But only because Ryan is right. Even if I say no, you'll just end up in my bedroom tomorrow night and make me wear an awful outfit."

"I would not! The outfits I pick are cute too!" Mira yells, hitting my arm and glaring at me in mock anger. "Just because I pick out clothes that actually look good on you doesn't mean they are awful."

"Are you saying I don't look good in what I pick out?" I glance down at my outfit. I thought I looked good today. Guess not.

"You look beautiful Lyra. Like you always do." Oh no. I don't like the look in Ryan's eyes. It's one thing knowing he likes me, it's entirely different when he says stuff like that. I glance at Mira, seeing her duck her head quickly, but not before I saw the pain in her eyes. She has big feelings for Ryan, and he can't keep his eyes off me. I feel awful about it, especially because I have zero feelings for him, and they would be perfect for each other. Mira and Ryan have a lot in common if he would get his eyes off my boobs and onto hers. Mira's are bigger any damn way.

"Thanks, Ryan, you're a great friend." I know I'm being a bitch, but I need to shut him down every once in a while; remind him he's in the friend zone. I haven't exactly told him I'm waiting for my soulmate, but I have mentioned that I'm waiting for the right guy to come along and that he doesn't go to our school. You would think that would be enough of a hint, but apparently not. Every once in a while, he will flirt with me like this and I'll have to make a comment and hurt his feelings.

"Yup. That's me. A great friend," he mumbles, looking away. I know I hurt his feelings, but it's for the best. I can't have him thinking I'm into him when I'm not. That would be even crueler.

"You're coming with us to the party, right?" I ask, trying to cheer him up.

"You know I will. Who else will drive you drunkies home?" He jokes. Well, maybe not about Mira. She likes to go out, drink and have fun. I, on the other hand, do not. I have maybe one beer and I'm done for the night. My dad puts a lot of trust in me and I don't plan on messing that up anytime soon. He's not like most dads who lecture their child about not drinking, having sex or trying drugs. He trusts me to make the right decisions and I know I can go to him at any time if I have any questions.

"Very funny. Like you'll be the sober one Friday night," I laugh. Ryan drinks a good bit too usually. Sometimes more than Mira, but he holds his liquor good. I'm the DD of our little group and I'm perfectly fine with that. If I ever have one too many, I call my dad and he takes us all home, no questions asked. Since he's away on a fishing trip, I'll have to make sure I keep it at one and done. "What time does the party start?"

"Eleven but since we are friends with Ryan, Justin said we could come earlier for a swim. Like nineish."

"Sounds good to me. You guys can come over to my house after school if you want. I know you will want to get ready together," I say, looking at Mira and she smiles prettily at me. I know she plans on dressing me up. Yay. "I can get a few pizzas from Sharky's too. Sound good?"

They both nod and continue eating their lunches. Ryan has a personal pizza from the lunchroom and Mira grabbed a salad. She's always worried about her weight, even though she's way skinnier than me. I eat another carrot before bundling the little bag up and placing it in my purse for later. Chugging some water, I stand up just as the bell rings signaling the end of lunch.

"How do you always do that?" Ryan asks, as he gets up and shoves the rest of his pizza in his mouth. He's pretty talented like that.

"I'm just that great," I say, before helping Mira up and linking arms with her. We stop at a trash can for them to throw out their trash and head to class. Ryan and Mira have Science next, which is right beside my English classroom, so we all walk together in silence.

"I'll see you guys later," I say. Mira and I have next class together, math, and I see Ryan last period during water aerobics. Technically, it's supposed to be only for swimmers, but the swim coach loves me and allowed me to join the class with the others. He's begged me a hundred times to join up, but I couldn't do it. I think he respected that I didn't want to make a sport out of something I love. Ryan nods at me and enters the classroom, leaving me and Mira behind. She stares off after him with a love-sick look on her face.

"He's really into you. Maybe I should hang back on Friday and let you guys go together," she says, eyes still staring at the door. I give her a shake and she turns to look at me with sad eyes.

"No way in hell. You know I'm not interested in him. I'm waiting for the right guy and too bad for Ryan, it's not him. Plus, you're totally into him. Like I'd really go out with him, knowing you'd be at home crying your heart out." She knows me better than this. I know she's upset that he flirted with me earlier but still.

"Sorry," she mumbles, looking sheepish. "I know you don't like him; it just gets to me, you know? I'm right there beside him, we have classes together and we hang out at Sharky's when you are working. Why can't he notice me?"

"Oh Mira, I'm sorry. I don't know why he's so into me. You know I don't encourage him and shut that shit down as soon as he hits on me. I've completely friend-zoned him. Maybe you just need to be more direct? Ask him on a date somewhere where I'm not going to be. You guys hanging out at Sharky's while I'm there working doesn't count as a date." I give her a hug before patting her cheek. "If he says no, he's not worth it. There are tons of guys who would go out with you. Hell, Justin would fall over himself if you so much as blinked at him once. You should ask him out on Friday at his party. I know he will say yes!"

"You're right. I'm just going to do it. I'll ask Ryan to go out, and if he says no, I'm done. I'll move on with Justin; he is pretty cute too." Her words are drowned out by the late bell ringing. Oops. We jump apart and she runs into her class while I walk into mine. I don't run anywhere. The extra two seconds to walk my ass into the room isn't going to piss off the teacher any more than me being late already. I might be a swimmer but I'm not very athletic. At all.

I take a seat in the back and pull out my purple notebook and get started with the writing prompt on the board. Now writing is something I can do. Writing, art, swimming, and reading. All activities I can do by myself. Growing up I didn't have many friends; I'm just not an extrovert and moving every few years didn't help matters.

Looking back at the board, I read the prompt again: *What are your plans for the summer? After? Are you going to college, vocational school, or getting a job?*

Great. Just what I wanted to think about. I have to be the only high school senior without a plan. Dad hasn't even asked me about it either. I'm pretty sure he wants us to move again, but he hasn't mentioned a place yet. Usually, he gets antsy after two years and starts looking. No, he just seems like he is waiting for something to happen. Maybe he wants me to pick the next place? Definitely some place by the water. I don't know how I would survive anywhere else.

Nothing is really holding us here anymore. I'm done with high school next week when I graduate. We rent our little house on a month-to-month lease. Dad doesn't have a fantastic job anywhere; fishing he can do wherever, really. I do have friends here, but Ryan is going to medical school almost three hours away and eventually will take over his dad's practice, and Mira is off to Carteret Community College for nursing. They will both be too busy to hang out with me anymore. I'll be forgotten.

Blowing out a breath, I start to think about the beach and going on an adventure. Yes, that's what I want to do. I want to travel, explore a little and meet new people. Maybe find my soulmate. I know he's out there just waiting for me to find him. He could even be looking for me right now. It's decided. I'll go with dad next week to the mountains and then I'll see where I end up next. I've been working at Sharky's since I got my license and I have quite a bit of money saved up to do whatever I want. I tried helping dad out with the bills, but he insisted I save it all.

Where should I go? I've been all along the East coast and even to California. I would love to go down to the Caribbean or maybe to Europe. I've always wanted to visit Italy and Greece one day. That would be amazing.

Happy, I start to write out a plan and completely forget the writing prompt. Who cares anyway? This is our last writing prompt; we take our final after this and then I'm done. That's it.

I'm almost free.

***

I roll the windows down and turn the radio up as I drive home. Just knowing I have a few days left of school and dad isn't home, puts me in awesome spirits. My smile is wide as I sing along to whatever song is playing and watch the world pass by.

Pulling into my driveway, I park my car and practically dance up the steps before spotting someone seated on our porch. I scream and jump backward, dropping my purse and spilling its contents all over the ground, before realizing it's just Miss Lynn.

"Goodness, I didn't mean to scare you, child," she says while looking down at me. Her long gray hair is braided today, and you can really see her face. Not a single wrinkle even though I know she's almost eighty and has high cheekbones below her gray eyes. Now, some people think I'm related to her. We have similar eyes and facial structure. Many years ago, her gray hair was a soft red. She was a beauty, but never married or had kids. Instead, she's lived in her little cottage on Cedar Island for most of her life and runs an online herbalism store.

"It's alright. I just wasn't expecting anyone to be here," I say,

29

looking up into her eyes. They strangely look like a snakes' for a second before appearing normal again. It must be the light playing tricks on me. I drop to the ground and pick everything up before putting it back into my purse. "What can I do for you?"

"Oh! Nothing dear. I just came over to check on you. Get a sense of how you are doing. It's almost your birthday isn't it?" A sense? She words things in weird ways sometimes. I shrug it off and walk up the steps, joining her on the porch. Her yellow dress blows a little in the wind and her feet are bare. A plate covered in aluminum foil lies on a rocking chair by the door, on the ground a gray thermos sits.

"I'm fine. Just coming home from school... I was going to head down to the beach for a little while before heading to bed. My birthday is next week." I'm getting that vibe again, the one where I can't tell if she thinks I'm atrocious or epic.

"Ah yes. I thought it was coming up. You are looking more mature by the day. I made some baked cod earlier and brought you a plate with potato cakes and green beans. I know your dad is away, which means you'll be ordering pizza. Again. Are you hungry?" Something about her question makes me think she already knows the answer.

"Not really, no. I just haven't been as hungry lately. Think my stomach is shrinking or I'm coming down with something," I say, unlocking the front door and stepping inside. I set my now empty backpack on the couch beside my purse before heading into the kitchen with Miss Lynn following behind me. She's carrying the plate and thermos in her hands.

"Maybe you are just craving something, and you don't know what it is yet," she says, watching me closely. Actually, that does sound right. I do find myself craving something different; something I've never had before.

"Could be," I say, not wanting to agree or disagree with her.

"Well, you're in luck. I whipped up a shake for myself earlier and made way too much. It just won't be the same tomorrow. I brought it with me in case you wanted it." She places the plate on the kitchen island before trying to hand the thermos to me.

"No thanks, I just don't want anything right now," I say before she twists open the top. It must be some type of berry shake as it has a pink color to it. The idea of berries isn't very appealing to me, but it does smell good. "I guess I'll give it a try."

Taking it from her, I sip slowly and find it does taste just like a bunch of fruit. It is good though and does hit my craving. Maybe that's what I wanted all along, some berries.

"What's in it?" I ask, taking another sip.

"Some recipe I found online. Different berries and of course an ice cream base," she says winking. Watching me intently as I sip, she smiles fondly. "I'm glad you like it. You know I have no children of my own, it makes my heart happy when you like what I make."

When she says stuff like that, it makes me feel bad about second-guessing her. I know she means well and cares for me. I just can't shake this weird vibe I get from her sometimes.

"Well, thank you for it. It is good. You'll have to write down the exact recipe for me so I can make it myself."

"Sure, just know food tastes better coming from other people. I add my love to it," she says laughing. "I'll be on my way then. You can call me if you need me or stop by anytime. I don't mind you dropping in. You still have the key right?"

I check my key ring and see the light green key still there. "Yup. I'll be fine on my own though. Promise."

I walk her to the door and thank her again for the food before shutting the door and locking it. Alone at last. The house is so silent now. Walking back into the kitchen, I lift the foil from the food and take a few bites. There's also a piece of sweet cornbread on the plate, one of my favorites. Sweet!

After eating almost half the plate and finishing off the shake, I change into my green bikini and throw a matching sundress on over top. I'll hit up the beach for a while before going to sleep.

Before I can leave, my phone buzzes on my bed. It's Mira. Oh! I completely forgot she was asking Ryan out today!

"Hey Mira, how did it go?" I ask, walking into the living room and sitting down on our sectional.

"It didn't. I tried dropping some more hints. Said maybe we could ride together to the party without you. I even suggested him and I get something to eat by ourselves, then head to your house. He wasn't interested. Either he's not into me or it all went completely over his head."

I hate to say it, but he probably just isn't interested in her. Ryan is used to girls flirting with him, he's not stupid. Man, I was really hoping he would at least give it a try. I have a feeling if he went out with her once, he would realize how into her he really is.

"New plan! You wear something killer to Justin's party." I hear her snort on the other side of the phone. I know exactly what she is thinking, *don't I always wear something hot?* "Yeah, yeah I know. You always dress to impress. Wear that blue crop top and those white jean shorts you have, navy blue bikini underneath. He loves blue. We will all go together, and you will flirt with Justin the whole night. Who knows, you might realize how hot Justin is and get over Ryan. If not, it might make him jealous at the least."

"That could work. I feel bad using Justin like that though. He's a sweet guy."

"Technically, it's not using him. You might actually like Justin if you could get your head out of Ryan's ass."

"But it's a fine ass!" She says laughing. I shake my head at her through the phone. "Okay, thanks boo! I love you. I'll talk to you tomorrow."

"Later," I say before hanging up.

I hope Ryan really sees Mira Friday. They would make an awesome couple, and it would get him off my back.

I set my phone down on the kitchen counter before walking to the backdoor and running off the porch. Breathing in deep, I take in the stellar view. We live right on the ocean and the sun is already low in the sky. Breathtaking. I could live out here for the rest of my life and be perfectly content.

Running down the beach, I shrug off my dress and dive into the water.

***

Walking inside after my swim, I strip out of my bikini and throw it over the shower rod in my bathroom. I don't even bother showering before putting on a new pair of underwear and a tank top to sleep in. I'll be back out on the beach tomorrow morning before school.

I plug my phone in and set it beside my alarm clock. Turning back towards the door, I shut off the light and climb into bed. I stayed out in the water later than I should have. I had meant to come back inside hours ago. I'm sure I'll be fine on only five hours of sleep

Rolling over, I close my eyes and try to forget the day. Focusing on school, the party tomorrow, my birthday next week. I wonder where dad wants to take me? Why the mountains and the secrecy? We've never gone to the mountains before.

As I'm drifting to sleep, my thoughts drift toward my soulmate and I know I'll see him in my dreams tonight.

If only I could remember his face.

Chapter 3

Unknown

*T*rees blur past at an alarming rate, wind shooting past me as I run through the forest. The air is humid, pointing towards the beginning of summer. A sensation prickles in the back of my head and I stop, head whipping to the right, nose in the air sniffing. Something has changed; I'm no longer alone. I realize I'm dreaming, and that realization makes my dream-scape shift around me and I search the trees, knowing she is here.

I shift into my human form, eyes peering through the trees. There. She stands by a lake not far from me. Her red hair cascades down behind her, covering her whole body. It shifts with the wind and I can just make out her white tank top and blue underwear; typical for her.

Making my way over, I strip off my sleep shirt and hand it to her. Without a word, she tugs it on and turns to me. Her gray eyes fill with happiness at seeing me and I find myself lost in her gaze. It's always like this between us, no barriers. I open myself to her and she opens herself to me.

We stare out over the lake, neither of us bothering with words. Both lost in our thoughts and simply enjoying each other. I turn and study her face as she continues staring at the rippling water. Her face is soft looking, tanned like she is in the sun often. Her red hair is curly and past her hips. It's down tonight, slightly wet still and sticking to her exposed skin. I release her hand and run my fingers through the soft texture; she turns to me and her lips twist up in a small smile.

"I missed you," she says. Her voice has no distinctive accent, no way of determining where she is from. It has a slightly lyrical tone to it and I long for her to sing to me. Somehow, I know it would be beautiful.

"I missed you too," I whisper, turning my body to face hers and grasping her waist. We face each other now, both of us examining the other.

"I wish I could remember your face when I wake up. I don't know how I can keep forgetting you."

"I'm a forgettable person," I joke. She laughs, and my chest tightens. I wish she was really here.

"You are not forgettable. You have to be the hottest guy I've ever seen," she says, voice turning flirtatious.

"You think I'm hot?" I ask, grinning down at her.

"You know I do," she says, bringing her hand up and laying her palm against my face. "I love your black hair and your blue eyes. I even love your stubble, which normally I don't like on guys. I find it attractive on you though. I would do anything to remember you when I wake up."

"I'll shave if you want me to. I have no reason at the moment."

"Don't you dare. I love it," she says, rubbing her palm against the prickly hair. I lean my face into her hand and close my eyes, enjoying her touch. Even in a dream, her touch ignites feelings in me no one else ever has. I can't imagine what it will feel like in real life.

"I'll leave it then. Where are you?" I ask desperately, already knowing she won't answer me. I hold her tightly but already she is pulling away. Fading.

"Around. You'll find me one day, won't you?" She asks me, pulling away and looking up at the night sky.

"Either I will, or you will find me. We will find each other. Can you tell me your last name at least?" I beg. I can't help it. She gives nothing away about her life when she's with me.

"One day it'll be your last name," she says simply, turning around and walking away from me and the lake. I run after her, trying to catch her before she leaves, but it's too late. She disappears behind a large tree and is gone. The trees start to shake, the earth moving below me, and I know I'm waking.

I shoot up in bed, eyes wide and clutching my sleep shirt in my right hand. My body is drenched in sweat. I glance at the clock by my bedside, way too early. She always leaves me too soon. I lay on my back and rub my hands over my face, closing my eyes and thinking of her again. I wish she would just tell me her name. I'd find her in a heartbeat if I could. One day she will be mine... and I'll be hers.

Chapter 4

Lyra

F riday morning, I peel off my PJs and grab my green bikini, throwing them all in the wash. I have enough swimsuits to wear a different one every day of the week for two weeks straight, but I was partial to my green one. Grabbing another suit, this one a gold color with metallic, silver dots adorning it, I change and grab my laundry basket. I walk across the hallway to the mudroom and dump the load in the washing machine. No point in just washing a few pieces of clothing.

Laundry started, I head back into my bedroom and grab my phone. Walking down the hallway, I flip on the kitchen light and glance around at the updated appliances. The stainless-steel fridge holds pictures of me and dad. I stop and stare at them. There's one in front of each of our old houses we've lived in over the years. Most of the pictures are of dad and me with Aunt Karen. Virginia as an infant, South Carolina and Alabama as a toddler, California as a young child, Georgia when I was eight, Louisiana is the last one with Aunt Karen when I was ten. There's only two without her, a picture of me and dad from when we lived in Florida and finally a picture of us in front of our current house, here on Cedar Island. So many different places, so many memories.

I touch each picture before turning away and walking outside to swim. This time I bring my phone with me and set my alarm for an hour from now; needing to change the laundry and actually make myself some breakfast today. I need to watch myself and make sure I don't skip meals anymore.

Setting my phone on the sand, I look up at the still dark sky. It's almost five in the morning and the sun isn't in sight yet, but the sky is a bit lighter already. I run, at full speed, into the ocean and laugh, enjoying the feel of the water closing around me. I let myself sink into the water and just relax into its embrace before propelling myself above and floating on my back. I stare up at the sky in thought, trying to remember the dream I had last night.

All I can remember is being so happy and content. I know I was with my soulmate and I think we were in the woods somewhere, but that's about it. I wish I could remember him. I've been researching lucid dreaming, in hopes of learning to control my dreams but that hasn't been working out too well. An annoying sound starts to beep and my head swings back to the shore. My phone's alarm is blaring and I'm farther out at sea than I thought, I'm surprised I can hear it this far away. I look back up at the sky and see it is, in fact, lighter than before and the sun is already rising on the horizon.

I swim back to shore and make a mad dash to the house. My feet pad lightly against the tile flooring, leaving a layer of sand in my wake. I'll have to sweep that up later. I switch over the laundry and head back into the kitchen, turning on the oven and beginning the search for our blender. I know we have one somewhere, we just haven't used it in a long time.

Finding it above the fridge and behind the unused crock-pot, I give it a thorough cleaning and plug it in. Now to decide what fruit to use. Opening the fridge, I don't see much but strawberries. I place the strawberries on the counter and search the freezer for some vanilla ice cream; we have just enough for two scoops. Slicing the strawberries, I add them to the blender with the ice cream, but it doesn't look like enough. I look in the small fruit bowl on the counter by the coffee pot and pick through it until I find a too ripe banana. That'll do. I slice it up and add it with the rest before replacing the top and starting to blend. My stomach is already growling.

Stopping the blender, I pour it into my thermos and take a sip. Good, but not as good as Miss Lynn's from yesterday. Setting the cup down, I get the ingredients out for scrambled eggs and grab some bacon. I layer the bacon on a cookie sheet and place the rest back in the fridge. I shove the sheet inside the preheated oven and set the timer for fifteen minutes. Bacon done, I set out a skillet and turn the stovetop on, before taking out a bowl and mixing eggs, milk, cheese, and a little salt and pepper together.

I don't even notice the time passing. The eggs cook easily and by the time they are done and plated, the timer beeps signaling the bacon is done. It's a little floppy, just how I like it. Placing my plate down on the table and grabbing my shake, I dig in; enjoying my breakfast for the first time in days and finishing the whole thing.

I quickly wash my dishes before heading back to my bedroom and picking out some clothes. Settling on a white t-shirt with my dads fishing logo on it and a pair of jean shorts, I change and run a brush through my hair. I don't see the point in dressing up for school. I prefer to be comfortable, especially when today is the last day and we will be doing nothing but signing yearbooks and talking about the party tonight.

Checking the time, I take my laundry from the dryer and put it away, before packing up the rest of the food Miss Lynn brought last night. I grab my phone and purse, in no rush today. It's amazing how fast I can get ready when dad isn't here.

Getting to school, I search the parking lot for my friends and spot Ryan. He's wearing jeans today and a white polo shirt. I slam my car door and rush over to him with a big smile on my face. "Hey!"

"Hey yourself, you look great today," he says, then seeing the look I give him he adds, "I mean you don't look sick anymore. That's all." Good boy. I really don't feel like having to turn him down twice in one week.

"Yeah, Lynn came over last night and gave me a shake. She said it was just fruit, but I think she had some herbs in it. Made me feel so much better."

"Really? You went to Lynn for help? You could have gone to a doctor. My dad would have come over and checked you out." Ryan doesn't like Lynn. Like at all. He's never even met her as far as I know, but whenever I mention her, he freaks out.

"What's wrong with Lynn? She's taken care of me for four years now and has always made me stuff whenever I got sick. You act like she's some freaky witch."

Ryan laughs but it seems forced. "Yeah, just like a witch. With her freaky deaky plants and special tonics. I just don't like her okay? When you are sick, you should see a real doctor. Like my dad. He would fix you right up."

"Maybe next time Ry. I've known Lynn for a long time, and I trust her," I say, shrugging my shoulders and walking towards the school. "Besides, I didn't go to her. She came over last night."

"You don't feel, like, bad around her? Like she could eat you for breakfast?" He asks, grabbing my arm and stepping into my path. His eyes search mine, looking for some indication that I agree with him.

"Not really," I say, shaking my head. "Don't be so over dramatic! Sometimes I get a weird vibe from her, but I know she has my best interest at heart. Why go to a doctor when I can literally drive two houses down and get something from her? No side effects, no insurance needed. She doesn't even charge me." A lot of people around town don't like her that's why she doesn't bother selling her herbs and mixtures local. She straight up sells them online and doesn't deal with people.

"Just be careful around her. Please Ly," he begs. His hand drags down my arm and grasps my own. I look down at our hands and back up at him. He quickly lets's go, but his face remains serious.

"Yes, Ryan. I'll be careful around the woman who has watched me for years, who still has a bedroom set up for me and who helps me when I'm sick," I say sarcastically. I don't understand his problem with her. I get that she gives off a bad vibe to people, but if she wanted to do anything to me, she would have a long time ago. She's had me asleep in her house I don't even know how many times. Completely vulnerable. It's too late to "be careful" around her now.

"Fine. Don't listen to me. I'm just worried about you. You've been acting funny lately. Spacing out and you haven't been eating. Even Mira is concerned."

"Mira is concerned about what?" She asks, coming up beside us and giving me a quick side hug. She's wearing a pink shirt today and tight jeans. I don't even have to glance down to know she's wearing high heels. She's going to break her neck one day, I swear. Her eyes register the closeness between Ryan and me, but she doesn't comment.

"About Lyra not eating," Ryan answers, looking triumphant. He knows Mira will agree with him. Great.

"Yes, totally worried. Where's my finger licking friend? You normally eat like a horse," she says, poking my soft tummy. Bitch.

"Geez. Way to make me feel fat guys," I say with a laugh. I know they don't mean it like that, but I still like to tease them. I honestly do eat a lot usually. Just not lately, but that's changing now. "I don't know what's gotten into me, I just haven't been hungry. I was telling Ryan that Lynn brought me over a shake and a plate of food last night, and whatever she put in it gave me my appetite back. I feel so much better."

Mira wrinkles her nose at the mention of Miss Lynn. She's not a fan of her either.

"Well, if it helped you that's all that matters to me," she says, smiling over at me.

I give Ryan a smirk. At least Mira can put aside her dislike of Miss Lynn and realize she has helped me. I stick my tongue out at him. I know, I'm totally acting my age.

"Real mature Ly," he laughs, sticking his tongue out at me too. Who's the immature one now?

"Since when have I ever been mature?" I joke. They both laugh and lock arms with me, one on each side.

"How do you feel your English final went yesterday? I didn't get to ask during math or when I called you last night," Mira asks, head tilted towards me. If she wasn't holding onto me, I'm sure she would have fallen by now in her death traps.

"It went great! I finished with time to spare and spent the rest of the class doodling in my notebook," I say, steering her clear of a group of kids. She really should pay attention to where she's walking.

"Good! I'm so ready for the party tonight. Are we still meeting at your house after school?" Mira is always ready to party.

"Yes, ma'am. I have to swing by Sharky's to grab pizza first. Any preferences?" I ask, turning my head to look at both of them.

"Pepperoni," they say at the same time and grin at each other.

"Speaking of tonight, can you give me a ride Ryan?" Mira asks as we walk inside the school. It's a bit crowded now to be lined up and I release their arms and walk to my locker, the two of them trail behind me.

"Yeah, I can. Why?" Ryan can be so dense sometimes. Any other girl would ask him that and he would immediately know they were flirting with him. Maybe I'm wrong about him not being interested, he always seems confused when it comes to Mira.

"You're always soberer than me and we live near each other. It would just be easier to drive to Lyra's together so you can drive me home after. Is that okay?" Plus, she has a humongous crush on Ryan. I'm sure that has nothing to do with wanting to ride with him.

"Yeah, I'll pick you up at your house after I swing by mine and change."

The bell rings and Ryan heads off to class with a wave to us while Mira and I walk to ours in the opposite direction. It's going to be a long boring day. I'm even a little excited about the party tonight. That should have been my first clue that tonight wasn't going to go according to plan.

***

No way. I'm not wearing this. I turn to Mira, who is sitting on my bed behind me, and give her a *what the fuck* look.

"You are so wearing that tonight, you look freaking hot!" She actually squeals. I don't think I've ever seen her so happy before. Must have been the ride over with Ryan. Turning back around, I look at my reflection again. I'm wearing a forest green, halter style dress made of a soft fabric. Mira insisted I try it on without a bra and wouldn't you know it actually works? You can totally see the outline of my boobs, but they look fantastic. The dress molds to my upper body, showcasing my thin waist and my wide hips, then flares out loose and ends just above my knees. Not really how I wanted to look tonight, I draw enough attention from guys as it is. I don't need to emphasize my assets, but I do look good, maybe even gorgeous.

"Really Mira? I look like I'm going on a date," I say, turning back to face her. My eyes are wide, and I have no doubt my lips are pouting a little. I really don't know if I want to wear this. "Shouldn't I be wearing an overdress with my swimsuit underneath?

"You can change at the party silly! It's all about first impressions. Walk in wearing this, change into your swimsuit and change back into this for dancing. The guys won't be able to stop looking at you." Yeah, that's just what I want. She eyes me up and down, and her gaze pauses on my face. "Just make sure not to get your hair or makeup wet. You don't want to ruin it."

Actually, I do want to ruin it. I don't know why I gave her free rein of my look tonight. She straightened my hair, then curled it (what was the point? I have naturally curly hair) and braided two strands, making a ring around my head, before braiding them together to fall dead center of my hair.

My eyes are lined with a black eyeliner, and purple eyeshadow rests along my eyelid. My already long lashes are coated in mascara and my lips are a scarlet red. I look beautiful and I know it. That's part of the problem though, I don't want to look good and have to fend off guys all night long.

"What's the point of swimming if I can't get my face wet? And there's no way my hair isn't getting soaked, it's down to my ass!" She walks past me into my bathroom and fishes out a purple hair scrunchy, coming back she pulls my hair into a messy bun like I had done this morning. Her messy bun looks 100 times better than mine though. You can still see the braids on either side of my head and a few pieces are draped down artistically around my face. I don't know how she does it so well.

"God, I hate you," I say, grabbing my green bikini and throwing it into my purse for the night.

"Nope, not that one," Mira says, tugging the suit from my purse and going to my swimsuit drawer. She digs through it for a few seconds before pulling out my dark purple suit and swinging it in the air in victory. "This one!"

I take it from her and put it in my purse without argument. This is also one of my favorites but it's thinner than most of my suits and shows a little more skin than I would like at a party.

Finally, ready for the party, I look at Mira. She took my advice and is wearing the blue crop top with white jean shorts. I can see her navy-blue halter bikini peeking from underneath her clothing. Her eyes are lined with thick eyeliner and heavy mascara, her lips are a dark maroon color. She looks great but could really wear less makeup. At least she's not wearing foundation like she usually does.

Linking arms, we walk into the living room together where Ryan is playing on his phone, sitting on my couch. He looks up as we enter, his eyes widen, and his mouth drops open with a soft gasp. I'm surprised to find his eyes aren't only on me, they are flickering between the two of us. He's eyeing us like he's never seen us before in his life.

"Wow.... You guys look great," he whispers, eyes finally lingering on Mira. Finally, he's seeing her as a woman!

"Thanks, you ready to go?" She asks, eying Ryan. He's wearing a white button-up shirt and navy-blue swim trunks, told her he loves the color blue.

"Yeah! Let's take Lyra's SUV." Ryan starts walking out the front door.

"Actually, why don't I drive myself tonight? Justin lives on the other side of the island, there's no point in you guys driving with me all the way back here before you head home." Ryan looks at me, then he turns to Mira.

"Sure. Come on Mira," he says. Yes! Who knew I would be so great at matchmaking? Locking the front door and walking to my car, Ryan and Mira are already backing out of my driveway. I quickly start my car and follow them. I can't wait to see how tonight ends!

Chapter 5

Lyra

The ride to the party doesn't take too long, not even ten minutes. It's a good thing Justin lives on the island, same as me, otherwise, we would have a much longer ride ahead of us. Justin lives in a huge, two-story home right along the refuge. It's a large lot, with trees surrounding the front and the forest to the back. The pool is on the left side of the house and everyone seems to be parking in front of it, on the lawn. The air smells of fresh grass and firewood.

Seeing Mira and Ryan talking by his car, I decide to give them some space and walk to the pool without them. I greet people along the way, but most people don't stop to chat with me. I'm not necessarily a loner but I'm not chatty Cathy either. Seeing Justin by the pool bar, I head over to say hi and to thank him for inviting me.

"Hey, Justin! Thanks so much for the invite," I say, smiling at him brightly. He looks great tonight, wearing just a pair of black trunks, low on his hips. He reaches in for a hug and I let him wrap his arms around me.

"No problem Lyra! You totally saved my ass in History this year. I wouldn't have passed without you. Plus, any friend of Ryan's is a friend of mine. Feel free to grab a drink, but you have to hand your keys over to the bartender. No one leaves drunk."

"I don't plan on drinking that much," I laugh.

"That's what everyone says," a voice says behind Justin. I look over his shoulder and see his twin sister Ann. Their mom is from Korea and their dad from Italy, both have black hair, brown eyes, and tan skin. Justin has short, straight hair and Ann has hers cut just about her shoulders. While they look alike, their personalities are as different as night and day. Justin is easy going and gets along with everyone while Ann is very reserved and doesn't talk much. And I don't think it's because she's shy either, she's always been a bit of a bitch to everyone.

"Well, I'm serious! I don't drink and drive. Dads' rules. Especially when he's not home to pick me up." Ann rolls her eyes and walks back into the house. She's not a fan of me.

"Sorry about her, she's not the friendly type," Justin says, looking at his sisters retreating form.

"Don't worry about it. I'm not always that type either," I say, laughing. It doesn't hurt my feelings when someone doesn't like me. "Is there a place people are putting their bags and clothes while they swim?"

"Not really. You can go inside, through the kitchen, second door on the left is a bathroom for you to change. There are two bathrooms on this floor and one in the basement too, top floors are off limits. People have been leaving their stuff wherever. I didn't invite too many people, maybe thirty, I don't think anyone here will steal someone's shit, but you never know." He shrugs.

"Thanks. I'll go change and put my stuff in my car. Can't be too careful," I say, walking towards the kitchen door Ann disappeared through a few minutes ago.

"I feel ya!" Justin is already heading towards the bar, I assume to order a drink for himself. It must be nice to have so much money you can afford a freaking bartender to tend your high school party. Geez.

Stepping inside, I see there's food all over the marble counters for guests to help themselves. I snag a weenie on my way to the bathroom to change. Delish. I walk into the bathroom which is all white and sparkling. I don't know how anyone could keep their bathroom so freaking clean. There's a white shelving unit, which has a few bags on it. I assume people are leaving their stuff in here, but I'm not going to risk it. I change fast and walk back out to my car, folding my dress neatly and laying it in the back-seat with my purse.

"Why didn't you come find us when you got here?" Mira says from behind me. "We were looking all over for you."

Locking my door, I turn around to see Mira leaning against someone else's car; Ryan isn't to be seen. "I was trying to give you guys some alone time, I'm playing matchmaker tonight."

"You are the best!" She squeals, throwing her arms around my neck. "He's looking for you though. It was pretty awkward in the car, he had no clue what to say to me. We reached for the music volume at the same time, and our hands touched. He pulled away so fast."

"He just realized you are a hot woman, go talk to him. If it's still weird, go find Justin. I saw him earlier, and he looked hot in just his swim trunks." I wiggle my eyebrows up and down.

"Perv!" At least I got her to laugh.

I tell her where she can get changed and head to the bar, handing over my keys and ordering a Bahama mama. I like sweet drinks, don't judge.

I sip it slowly, looking around at the party. It really is small, I'm surprised I was even invited. Normally Justin invites every-one from school over. This is tame for him. Mostly there are a lot of hunky guys from the football team and a few girls spread here and there. I wander around and sit down on the edge of the pool with my feet in the water. No one is swimming yet, and I don't want to be the first one to jump in. Everyone is talking and drinking, just enjoying the evening. There's no rush tonight.

Screw it. I set my drink down and slide myself into the water and close my eyes in bliss. I love being in the water. I feel more comfortable with the looks I'm getting now, makes me feel like they are wondering why I'm in the pool and are not eyeing my body like I suspect some guys are. I take my drink and walk through the water to the deeper end where there is some bench seating in the water. Taking a seat, I sip my drink and look around.

Ryan is over with a few guys from the football team, talking and joking around. One of them must point me out because he turns around to stare at me with intense eyes. I avoid his gaze and take a huge gulp of my drink, almost choking myself. Please don't come over here. I risk a look underneath my lashes and see he's turned back around, talking to his friends again. A few of them point at me, so I assume I'm a part of whatever conversation they are having. Great.

Everyone seems to be in small groups like that, spread around the party. A few are by the woods, like Ryan's group, and others are at the bar or sitting on lounge chairs. I seem to be the only one sitting alone right now, besides Justin who is nursing what looks like a whiskey on a chair nearby. He seems perfectly con-tent with being alone, just like I am.

"Hey," Ryan says from behind me. I didn't even see him leave his friends and come over. Damn. He takes a seat beside me, leaving just his feet in the water instead of his whole body. "Enjoying the party? I saw you alone."

"Yeah, I am. I like being alone, you know that Ry," I say, picking up my drink and taking another sip. At this rate, I'm going to need another just to have something to do when he's talking to me.

"I know. I just felt bad with you sitting over here all alone. Where's Mira?"

"I assume touching up her makeup in the bathroom."

"Most likely," he says, taking a deep breath and looking at me. My eyes are wide, he's closer than I thought he was. Where the heck is Mira? I need backup here! I can't be alone with Ryan. "Wanna go out sometime? Like a real date?"

Fuck. What do I do now? I look around and seeing nothing that can save me, I grab my drink and take another huge gulp. This time, I do sputter and the drink splatters onto my chest.

"Damn, need some help?" Ryan asks.

"Uh no. I'll be right back," I say, hoisting myself up onto the concrete and out of the pool. I rush to the bathroom without looking back.

I walk into the kitchen and practically run to the bathroom. Of course, it's occupied. Remembering there are other bathrooms, I start to search the bottom floor. After opening another wrong door, this one leading to a music room, I turn around and slam into a hard chest.

"Woah. I don't mind you getting this close, but I wasn't expecting a sticky mess just yet." It's Ryan, with no shirt now. And he's flirting still. I look up, about to tell him no to his date and to stop it with the flirting, but when I look into his eyes, I can't seem to push him away.

My hands move from his arms to his bare chest and his arms remain wrapped around me, pulling me close. I've never been this close to him before. He smells of rain and trees. It's a pleasant scent and I start to feel a little dizzy, but I can't back away from him. My hands feel tingly where I'm touching his skin and his lips part. His eyes drop to my lips and mine follow, what am I doing?

His lips come closer, and before I know it, he's kissing me. I've never been kissed before. It's not as wet as I thought it would be. My mind can't think straight and suddenly I'm kissing him back. My whole body is buzzing, and I feel like I can do anything in the world. His lips are soft against mine and electric pulses flow from him to me. I can't break away, even though I know I don't like him. This is wrong, and yet I can't stop.

"What the fuck are you doing?" Ryan is pulled away from me, I look around confused and see Justin is holding Ryan back, Ann and Mira are standing behind him. Mira's eyes are filled with tears and I can see the betrayal on her face. She turns and runs down the hallway, and I hear a door slam somewhere in the house.

I try to go after her, but Ann puts her hand on my arm, and I freeze. My whole body feels like an ice cube now, I can't move a single part. What's going on? Ryan struggles in Justin's arms, trying to get to me, but Justin holds tight and looks at Ann.

"Take Ryan out of here. Now," Ann says, not letting go of my arm. Justin drags Ryan down the hall, Ryan's eyes stay locked with mine. A wild look is on his face, and he desperately tries to get back to me. They disappear down the hallway and I hear another door slam. Ann and I are alone now, and honestly, I'm scared.

"What are you?" She asks. I can't move my lips to respond, I can't even move my eyes to stare at her. My gaze is fixed down the hallway where Mira, Justin, and Ryan left. I'm not even blinking. She lets go of my arm and blood starts to flow through my body again, my muscles come to life and I turn to look at her, fear in my eyes. Ann's are filled with terror, staring straight at me. "Seriously, what are you?"

"What am I? What the fuck are you? How did you freeze me like that? I wasn't even breathing. What the fuck," I say, my brain trying to comprehend what's happening. I turn away from Ann, trying to run down the hallway, but before I can lift a foot I've frozen in place again.

"You aren't going anywhere." Against my will, my body turns and opens the music room door again and walks inside. I sit on an armchair and stare straight ahead as Ann moves in front of me. "I don't know what you are, but you are dangerous. I'm calling the council, maybe they will know what to do with you."

I struggle against whatever is holding me down and regain control of my body. I jump from the seat and stare her in the eyes. What is she talking about? I'm not dangerous, I was just kissing a boy. A boy I don't even like, but that's not the point.

"I don't know what you are talking about. Me and Ryan kissing is our business, not yours. What's your problem? Are you jealous? And how do you keep controlling my body like that?"

"So, you can fight my control. Interesting," she says, eyes curious but they turn steely again. Her brown eyes hold mine captive. "You weren't just kissing him Lyra and you know it. Get out of here. Go home, pack your shit and get off this island. We have a peaceful place here and you aren't welcome. You're lucky I'm letting you go, you should be thankful Ryan cares for you. You have until midnight to be out after that we won't let you leave. The pack will have you locked up until the council decides what to do with you."

"The council? Pack? What drugs are you on? Actually, what drugs am I on?" I ask, standing up and beginning to pace. She looks at my wild look, and suddenly I feel like my brain is on fire. "STOP!" I feel like I'm melting, my limbs become heavy and I drop to the ground, shaking.

"Hear me well Lyra. I don't care who your friends are. I will protect my family and this pack. I can kill you right now if I wanted to. I said to get the fuck off this island. Go home, get your shit, and leave. Now. I won't tell you again."

The pain goes away as soon as she stops talking. She's standing by the door with a smirk on her face. She has all the control here, and she knows it. I jump to my feet and sway a little on my way to the door. I use the wall as support as I walk down the hallway, Ann walks behind me. I pause when I reach the kitchen, trying to steady myself before I walk outside.

Everyone is tense now, only a few people look confused. Most of the guys are glaring at me now, no longer are their looks filled with curiosity and longing. They are dangerous now. Even Ryan is standing with them, arms crossed, his eyes no longer look desperate for me. Justin stands beside him, looking curious but not as hostile as the rest of them. He has my keys in his hand and he steps forward to hand them to me.

"What are you?" He whispers, Ryan and his friends tense up and I get the feeling they can hear every word.

I look around at all of them and know I have to get out of here, I'm not safe. I don't know what time it is, but I know I have a deadline. Looking at Justin, I whisper, "I don't know."

I grab my keys and walk away, not looking back at anyone. I didn't see Mira and wonder where she is. Does she hate me now? I can't think about her now though, I need to focus on getting my ass home and out of here. I walk through the tangle of cars and see Mira leaning against the hood of my SUV.

"How could you?" She asks, makeup running down her face and her forehead wrinkled. She's obviously been out here for a while, sobbing. Her words are still choked up.

"Mira, I can't explain right now. Some scary shit when down in there and I have to go home," I say, stepping towards my door and unlocking it.

"Of course, now isn't the time. You just kissed the guy I've been crushing on for years. I never thought you would do this to me. I trusted you when you said you didn't like him. I thought you were my best friend Lyra. You could have just told me you had feelings for him, and I would have let you have him."

"Mira! Didn't you hear me? Ann is some crazy mind-controlling alien, and she threatened me. I have to leave, now! She fucking tried to kill me. I'm not into Ryan, I told you that. I have to go, are you coming with?" I ask, opening my door and waiting for her.

"Is that supposed to make everything better? That you don't like Ryan? So, you hurt both of us, just for a kiss? What is wrong with you? You are an awful person and I never want to see you again."

I stare at her, tears dripping down her face again as she looks at me in hurt and anger. She must not have heard what I said about Ann being crazy. All she could focus on were her hurt feelings and I just don't have time for this right now. I wish she would just listen to me and get in the car, I wish I had more time to apologize and explain more, but I'm scared. At any second, they could come after me. I almost don't want to go home. I'm tempted to jump in my car and drive as far as I can, without looking back.

"I'm sorry Mira, I don't have time for this. I have to go. I know you're upset with me, and I get it, but my life is in danger. I'll call you when I can. I still love you and you are still my best friend." She scoffs at me and I know she won't believe me right now. Hopefully tomorrow she will realize that I'm telling the truth and will forgive me. For now, I have to get out of here.

I jump into my car and start it. Thankfully, no one parked behind me and I can easily back out to the road. I look forward again, my headlights are on Mira. She's standing where I left her, looking broken with her arms wrapped around herself. Justin is beside her now. Whatever he says, makes her cry, and she turns to him hugging him tightly. Good. Maybe something good will come out of all this.

My emotions are all over the place. I'm freaking out. I'm scared of what will happen, sad I'm having to leave my home and my friends, disappointed in myself that I've hurt people I care about. My breathing picks up and I have to stop the car, I'm hyperventilating. Tears stream down my face and big sobs whack through my body. I can't do this alone.

Suddenly, a sense of calmness fills me. I can do this and I'm not alone. I still have Miss Lynn and my dad. I still have a soulmate out there. Determined, I take deep breaths and try to focus on driving. I need to get to the one person I can trust on this island right now. Miss Lynn.

Chapter 6

Unknown

Looking at my computer, I feel my chest tighten and I'm assaulted with emotions, feelings that are not my own.

I find myself scared for my life and a great sense of sadness settles over me. What is going on?

I close my eyes, breathing in deeply, and try to focus on the feelings, separating my own and determining what's not mine. There. Scared, sad, angry, fearful and lonely. I've never felt emotions as deep as these before, sure I've felt them but nothing of this depth. These must be from her- from my soulmate.

I've seen her in dreams before, I know I have a mate out there, but I've never *felt* her before. I'm terrified of what she's going through at this moment and I wish I could take away all her hurt and pain.

I focus on her emotions and try to push calmness to her, I'm not sure if this will help her or not, but it's the best I can do from so far away. Her emotions abate a little, calmness and determination settle over her and I no longer feel her inside me.

Needing to do something, I bolt out of my seat and run outside. I need fresh air and to put my thoughts in order. A part of me wants to search for her right now, leave my life and put everything I have into finding her. Another part of me tells me to stay put. I have a feeling she's coming to me and if I was to leave now, I'll miss my chance of finding her.

Shifting, I rush through the trees. My heartbeat escalates and my muscles tense with restrained energy. It takes everything in me not to just run away, but I need to stay here. She will come for me, I know it. I just have to be patient.

Chapter 7

Lyra

It doesn't take me long to reach Miss Lynn's. Pulling into her driveway, I glance down at my clock and see it's just past ten. I have less than two hours to get out of here. Stepping out of my car, I feel a breeze against my still bare skin. Thank goodness I put my dress in the car, I doubt I would have thought about grabbing it on my way out. I grab my dress and my purse, looking around me carefully to make sure no one is hiding in the shadows. I feel so paranoid now and it wouldn't surprise me if someone was watching.

Miss Lynn is already waiting for me with the door wide open. "Come in, child."

"Oh, my God. I don't know what happened," I sob, running up the steps and into her embrace.

"Shh," she says soothingly, stroking my hair. "Just take a seat at the table and I'll fix us some hot cocoa." Even though I know time is running out, I obey and take a seat at her little round table. I wait patiently while she fixes us both a cup, she puts a dash of cinnamon in mine just how I like it. I grab a napkin and dab at my skin, but it's already sticky, and it's useless. Miss Lynn brings over our cups and hands me a wet washcloth to clean up. I give her a teary smile and clean up my chest before placing my dress over my suit. I take a sip of the warm drink and when I'm calm, I turn to look at Miss Lynn.

"What happened tonight?" She doesn't beat around the bush at least.

"I'm not even sure. I went to a party on the west side of the island tonight. Everything was fine until I spilled my drink on myself and went inside to clean up. My friend Ryan came in after me."

"Ryan James, right? His dad is the doctor?" Her eyes are filled with concern now.

"Yea, why?" I don't know why that would matter.

"Just curious. What happened next?"

"Well... this is awkward. He came up behind me and I didn't know. I turned around and as soon as our skin touched I felt weird, my fingers tingled and next thing I know he's kissing me. I couldn't even stop. I knew it was wrong, I don't like him like that and didn't want to lead him on," I pause, wondering again why I let him kiss me and why I kissed him back.

"And what was it like?" She asks curiously.

"Weird. I felt this surge of energy flow from him to me and I couldn't seem to get enough of that," I admit.

"And then?"

"God, it was awful. Mira, Ann, and Justin came in and broke us up. Mira really likes Ryan, and she ran out crying. I don't know if she will forgive me. Justin took Ryan outside and Ann did some freak shit. She put her hand on me and I was frozen. I couldn't even breathe!" My eyes start to fill with tears again, but I know I have to tell her the whole story. "She accused me of trying to hurt Ryan, said I was dangerous and controlled my body. I guess I fought it off somehow and when I tried to leave, she did something else. My head felt like it was on fire, like my brain was literally melting away. She told me to get off the island that I had until midnight and the pack will come after me and won't let me leave until some council decides what to do with me.

I have never seen Miss Lynn look scared before now. The whole conversation she looks thoughtful, encouraging and supportive. Now she looks terrified. She gets up and starts looking out her windows, "Oh dear. This is not good. I had hoped this wouldn't happen."

"That what wouldn't happen? What's going on? Please tell me. I'm so confused Lynn and my dad isn't here, I'm scared. You're the only person I knew I could come to."

"I can't tell you everything, it's not the time, but I can tell you some things. Sit down, we don't have much time," she says, ushering me back to my seat. "Short version is there are mystical creatures in the world. That boy Ryan? He's a wolf shifter, he's part of the Rowan pack that lives in the refuge." I can't help but laugh. This is too crazy! A mind controlling alien makes more sense to me than a werewolf. Miss Lynn doesn't laugh though; her face remains serious. If she isn't telling the truth, she believes it to be true at the least. "Ann would be Ann Nikos?" She asks. At my nod she continues, "She's a witch. Some wolf packs align themselves with witch covens. The pack protects them, and they protect the pack. She must have seen you as a threat. She will kill you if she has to. I'm surprised she let you walk out of there. Your friendship with Ryan must have saved you."

"What do I do? I didn't mean to be a threat. I don't even know what I did that was so bad!"

"You leave. You're special Lyra, different from anyone else in the world. Your father is a wolf shifter, he's been a lone wolf for a very long time now and came here for my help. He knew you would need guidance and without your mother here, I'm the best he could do."

"My dad is a shifter? But I've never seen him turn into a wolf, I would have noticed that!" I'm shouting and without realizing it, I'm standing from my seat and pacing the floor. This can't be right. Dad can't be a shifter and what did she mean about my mother? "So my mom was different too? And you are like her?"

"Yes," she says smiling. "Your mom and I are... were the same. I knew her mother, your grandmother, many years ago. When your mom and dad met, I helped them out. Their relationship was forbidden, and many people frowned upon it. Some even tried to stop them from being together. I can't get into the whole story right now. You need to go west, to a place called Sylva, North Carolina. There's another wolf pack there and they will help you until your dad gets there. You can't tell them the full details of what has happened. Just tell them your dad sent you there and you are to wait for him, they will keep you safe."

"And what exactly did happen? What am I? You said I'm different from everyone else, but you and my mom were the same. Am I not like her?"

"You are very much like her, and like me, but you are still different. A hybrid. I'm not sure exactly what your powers are and telling you what I am will only put you in danger. Your dad will explain everything when he comes for you," she says, getting up and reaching into the cabinet above the fridge. She pulls down a large canister and sets it on the table. "I know you have questions, but I can't answer them all right now. There isn't enough time and some answers might put you in danger. You have just over an hour now before you need to be out of here. Go home, pack some clothes, and go to Sylva. Go to the library there and ask for Jonathan Platt. He's the alpha of the BR pack,"

"BR?" I ask, curious.

"Blue Ridge Mountains pack. He's the head honcho. Your dad and him know each other, and he promised your dad he would help if need be. He doesn't know much about you and we need to keep it that way. He knows your dad ran away from his pack eighteen years ago, and that he has a daughter. Go there, ask for him and he will protect you with his pack if needed. I'll tell your dad what has happened, and he won't be far behind you."

"Can't I just stay in a hotel nearby?"

"No. The Rowan pack might let you go tonight but they will call the council. I'm sure they will send someone out to investigate and they will hunt you down. You trust no one and stop as little as possible. It's an eight-hour drive to get there, they live up in the mountains." She's packing food for me in a plastic bag as fast as she can.

"Is this where dad wanted to take me for my birthday next week?"

"Yes. The older you get, the stronger you become. You are almost eighteen now Lyra and will fully come into your powers, whatever they will be, in a few days. I could sense them growing inside you. That's why you've been eating less and feeling off. Your dad wanted to take you up there until you fully emerged. Jonathan owes your dad a life debt and your dad trusts him. I'm not sure if he's trustworthy or not. I'm not in the habit of trusting wolves. Take this," she hands me the canister, "this is filled with a powder. I won't bore you with the specifics, but it will help you from getting sick. I added this to the shake you had the other night that's why you've been feeling better and able to eat again. It will wear off every few days. It's flavorless so you can add it to anything you want. Make sure to add a spoonful."

"This entire time it's just been me coming into my powers?" I wonder out loud.

"Yes. A witch bound your powers many years ago, your Aunt Karen? She's a witch. One who doesn't report to the council. Her and your mother grew up together in Arizona." How had I never known? This entire time my Aunt Karen was a witch. "She's your godmother. She bound your powers so no one could find you, she has to occasionally replace the spell, but with you being eighteen soon that's not going to matter anymore. The time for binding your powers is over. Nothing can stop your powers from manifesting anymore. I can help you control them once we figure out exactly what they are."

"So, what happens after my birthday? I won't be allowed to come back here and see you." I'm panicking. Great.

"Honey, breathe," Lynn says softly. "Everything will be alright. I'm going to make my way to your Aunt Karen. It'll take me probably a week. By that time, you'll know what your powers are and be ready to learn. Until then, just be careful and try not to touch anyone. I'm not sure what the extent of your powers are... but you can do this. Go home, pack, and go to Sylva. Your dad will come for you and we will take it from there, okay?" I nod.

She walks me out to my car, placing the bag of food on my passenger seat. I set the canister down beside it and turn to hug her before I go. She plants a thin, cylinder into my hand. "Keep this close to you. It won't activate until you've come into your powers, but it will protect you. It was your mother's."

"What is it?" I ask, looking down at it. It's thin, almost like a pin, but it looks like it has nothing else on it. No designs or indentions.

"I can't tell you now. Just keep it close by. You will know how to use it when you need to."

"Thank you, Miss Lynn. I owe you one," I say, trying hard not to cry.

"Anything for you my dear. Now give me your cell phone." Curious, I hand it over. I already have her phone number programmed into it. She throws it against her house, and it smashes. I stare at her, wondering if she has finally gone crazy. "You won't be needing that. The council has the technology to track phones now. If you have time, print some directions off at home. Otherwise, follow signs for Raleigh and take Interstate 40-west. Head towards Asheville and look for Nantahala National Forest, Sylva. You'll find your way. Stop by an ATM sometime after you pass through the refuge, get as much money out as you can. Then don't use your debit card after that. They can track that as well. I love you little one. I know I've never told you that, but I loved your mother and I love you too. Please be safe and be careful who you trust."

I give her a big hug. "You be safe too, Miss Lynn. I love you too."

I climb into my car and with a final glance at Lynn, I back out of her driveway and make the short trip to my house. When I get there, I run inside throwing on the lights. Everything looks the same as it always has. The clock above the tv reads 11:02. Damn, I don't have long. I rush into my room and go straight into my closet. I pull out all the duffle bags and suitcases I own and throw them on the bed. I don't think I'll have enough time to fill them all. Thinking fast, I decide on my duffle bags. Smaller and easier to throw over my shoulder to run if I need to. I'm able to fill two bags with the majority of my clothes and the third I put my toiletries in, I doubt I'll have time to stop and grab any when I'm on the run. Checking the time, I see I still have thirty minutes before midnight. I take my three bags and leave them by the front door and sit in front of the little desktop computer we have in the living room. Waiting for it to boot up, I look around and wonder if I need to grab anything else. I don't know what all I'm going to need. I wanted an adventure but not of this type. Guess you should be careful what you wish for. I log onto the computer and quickly look up directions to Sylva and print them out. Grabbing them, I look around one last time.

I've lived in this house for four years now, the longest of any place yet. This is my home. The green, comfortable couch me and dad have sat on watching movies together, the kitchen island we have sat at many times. Our pictures adorn the walls. I grab two of them, one from many years ago where we are looking at each with love, I was probably 5, and a more recent one of us on his boat together from spring break. I don't know what all dad will grab when he comes back home and finds me gone. Probably not anything to be honest. He's going to freak and leave right away. I take the two from the wall, and the ones off the fridge, and throw them in with my shampoo and grab up the bags. I look at my house one last time with tears in my eyes before heading out to my car. I load up the bags in the back seat and hop into the front.

My dash clock reads 11:43. I'm making good on time. I get on the highway and drive as fast as I dare. Once I hit the refuge, I keep looking around expecting someone to jump out at me. I breathe a sigh of relief once I'm halfway through. Miss Lynn says they live in the forest and while I can't see anyone around, I do feel their eyes on me. They know I'm leaving.

Suddenly, someone runs into the road right in front of me. I slam on my breaks and swerve to the right, barely missing whoever it is. My door is opened, and Ryan ducks his head down to look at me. "It's just me, calm down. I can hear your heart racing," he smiles. Well, at least he doesn't hate me for whatever it was that I did. He's wearing a pair of sweatpants and nothing else.

"Ryan." I climb out of my and go to hug him, but he takes a step back and looks over my head, towards the woods and shakes his head. I turn around, expecting to see someone, but I see nothing but darkness.

"I wouldn't touch me. They don't trust you, Ly. Ann said you could have killed me earlier. What are you?" He asks me. Like I freaking know.

"I have no clue. One second, I was going to push you away and the next I couldn't seem to stop. I don't know what I am Ryan. I just know I have to get out of here. Ann threatened to kill me if I didn't leave before midnight."

"She won't touch you," he growls. "No one will. I won't allow it." Breathing deep, he tries to compose himself. "So, you were going to push me away?"

"That's what you chose to focus on? Yes, Ryan, I was. Mira is into you and honestly, I've never seen you in that way. You're hot, and you know it, but I wouldn't do that to Mira."

"I don't want to hurt her either, but this isn't about her. This is about you and me." He takes a step closer, we are almost touching, but I don't dare reach out for him. "How do you feel Lyra?"

"Before tonight, I would have said nothing but friends. But after that kiss... I don't know anymore. But it doesn't matter now. I'm leaving, going somewhere safe until my dad can find me. I can't come back here, Ryan."

"I'll protect you."

"You can't. Ann has already called the council," the voice is behind me. I turn around expecting to see another guy from the high school football team. Instead, I see Dr. James, Ryan's dad. He's shirtless, just like Ryan (what is it with wolf shifters and not wearing clothes!) "You have to go Lyra. I know you didn't mean to hurt Ryan. You've been a good friend to him for years now. But our hands are tied. The council already knows you are here, it won't be long before they come after you. Leave and don't come back."

"But dad–" Ryan's dad cuts him off, "No Ryan. There's no other way, at least right now. Let her go. Maybe you'll see her again."

I look at Ryan, his face is sad. His eyebrows are drawn together, and his lips are pinched. He knows his dad is right.

"It's okay Ryan. Maybe I will come back one day, once I figure out what I am and how to control whatever it is I do."

"Lyra... you almost sucked out my soul," Ryan reluctantly tells me. I can't wrap my mind around what he just said. His soul? I can't do that. There's no way. Thinking back to the kiss, I remember feeling that energy flow into me. The energy that came from the kiss, that must have been Ryan's soul. I gasp and tears spill from my eyes. Ryan tries to hug me, but I dodge him and walk away trying to process everything. I stare down the road and breathe in. I'm not safe here and Ryan isn't safe with me.

"I have to go. You aren't safe with me, not now. If I ever get my powers under control, I'll let you know where I am okay? I'll understand if you never want to see me again–" Ryan hugs me from behind. His bare skin touching my arms. I can feel it now, the energy beneath my fingertips. It takes everything in me not to pull it inside.

"Of course, I'll want to see you again. You're my best friend Ly. It doesn't matter to me if you don't love me as I love you, or if you are tempted to take my soul again. I love you and I'll be here in whatever capacity you want me as. Now go. I don't want them to find you."

I turn around in his arms and stare in his eyes. I don't know if I do have feelings for him or not; it could just be his soul that I want. I might never know for sure. What I do know, is Ryan is one of my best friends and I care about him.

"I can feel it now, your soul. It's beautiful Ryan, filled with goodness. Take care of Mira for me. Tell her I'm sorry I had to leave. I told her Ann was a mind-controlling alien or something like that so I'm not sure what she thinks went on. Just let her know I love her, please."

"A mind-controlling alien?" Ryan laughs. The more we stay in contact, the harder it is not to pull his soul from his body. My hands are starting to tingle, and Ryan is beginning to look funny, his eyes are glazing over. I quickly let go of him and take a step back. He shakes his head as if to clear it. "Was that it? I could feel it that time. It's like a wave of euphoria comes over me. I couldn't pull away if I wanted to."

"Sorry, I didn't mean to. I could feel it this time too," I say, looking down.

"It's okay. I know you wouldn't hurt me on purpose. I'll handle Mira, and any questions she has. Let me know you are safe please if you can. The council will be monitoring all contact, so don't tell me where you are and use a secure source of contact. I'll miss you, drive safe." His dad clears his throat from behind us. Well, that's awkward, he witnessed me almost suck his son's soul from his body. Again. I'm making a banging impression here. "I have to go. Get out of here. I'll try to hold the council off if I can. Wherever you are going, get there fast

I risk another hug then climb back into my car. By the time I turn it back on, Ryan and his dad are gone. I still feel eyes on me, the wolves are still watching. I put the car in gear and get the heck out of there. I have a long night of driving. Sylva, North Carolina here I come.

Chapter 8

Lyra

I can't wrap my mind around everything.

Finding out I'm not human, nor are the people around me... it's a lot to take in and I have so many questions still. For now, I have to wait until I see my dad, and that'll be a few days at the latest.

The clock reads 3:13 in the morning and I'm just outside of Raleigh, North Carolina. Miss Lynn said not to stop, but I can't drive for much longer. Seeing a sign for a Motel 6, I turn off the interstate and follow the signs. It looks deserted with only two cars in the lot, one I assume is a worker.

I park in front of the office and head inside. A young woman is behind the desk, her black hair is shaved on one side and cut short on the other. Her arms are filled with tattoos and her face has multiple piercings. She doesn't look up as I enter the room; her focus set completely on her cell phone. I walk up to the desk and clear my throat. When she still doesn't look up, I ask her for a single room.

"Credit card?" She asks without looking up at me, her fingers fly across her phone typing out something.

"Cash," I say dryly. That gets her attention. She looks up at me, sizing me up and finally, she nods, handing me a key from behind her.

"You aren't a runner, right?"

"Nope. Visiting family." Keeping it simple is best, right? She grabs a form and has me fill it out, I use a fake name and thank my lucky stars she doesn't ask for my driver's license.

"Mira, huh? Didn't take you for a Mira," she says, reading the form and raising an eyebrow at me. Thankfully, she doesn't comment further and takes my money. She hands me a receipt and goes back to looking down at her phone. "Your room is third on the left soon as you walk out. You can park your car out front and we don't serve breakfast. Checkout is ten."

Shaking my head at the clerk, I walk outside to move my car. She seemed friendly, not. I move my car and grab two duffle bags and my purse. Using the key, I open the door and switch on the light. It's actually not as bad as I thought it would be, with a queen bed, two nightstands on either side, and a small round table with two wooden chairs tucked underneath. I drop my bags on the green printed comforter and go to the bathroom. I've had to pee since before I left my house over three hours ago.

Washing my hands, I look at myself in the mirror. I look a mess. I'm still wearing my green halter dress, with the purple bikini underneath. My hair is still thrown up in a messy bun and my makeup is a bit runny, but altogether still there. I don't look like my whole life has changed in less than twenty-four hours. I scrub my face with water and a heavily scented soap that tickles my nose. Once I'm satisfied my face is clean, I turn off the light and flop onto the bed. I don't even bother changing my clothes or getting under the blanket. I'm exhausted and I need to be up in a few hours. I close my eyes and my thoughts drift to my soulmate before I'm gone to the world.

***

Light shines into my eyes, waking me. I peel them open and glare at the offending window letting all the light inside. The curtains are a dull brown, not my usual light purple and I sit up, looking around frantically. It takes me a moment to remember where I am and where I'm going. I jump out of the bed and look at the clock, almost ten. Dammit! I wanted to be up hours ago. I use the bathroom and brush my teeth before heading out. I drop my key off, this time it's a man behind the counter and he gives me a weird look at my rushed pace, and I throw my bags in my car before backing out of the parking lot.

I should have been gone hours ago, I can't believe I forgot to set an alarm. Stopping at a red light, I take a deep breath and close my eyes, allowing myself to think for a second. I need to stop by a bank then I can go. A growl fills my car and I glance down at my stomach. Bank and food. Starving myself isn't going to make it any easier to get away if I need to. The light turns green and I pull away, looking for a place to stop. I never realized how much I depended on my cell phone until now. I have no way of calling anyone and I can't look up anything. This sucks.

Seeing a little breakfast diner, I pull up and head inside. I can ask someone where the nearest bank or ATM is and get something to eat before I get back on the road.

The diner isn't very crowded; the breakfast rush has passed, and it's not quite time for lunch. I take a seat and flip through the menu, pursing my lips trying to decide what I want to eat. I'm starving but my stomach is a little upset too. Probably nerves. My eyes peruse the menu until a chirpy waitress, Joy, appears to take my order, thinking fast I choose blueberry pancakes with bacon.

"Nice choice," she says, walking away to give my order to the cooks. Her blonde hair is flowing down her back and her blue eyes optimistic. She seems like the type to find the beauty in everything.

I look around the diner, taking note of the people inside. There's an older couple at the bar top, sipping their coffees and talking quietly to each other. I want that, to grow old with someone and still be so in love. There's another couple sitting in a booth a few places down from me, they ignore each other and stare down at their phones. A young woman sits watching Joy with interested eyes. Hmm. My waitress stops and drops off juice to her and they smile at each other, hands lingering as they transfer the cup. That's sweet.

Looking out the window, I wonder about my soulmate. What will we be like together? Will we be sweet or fight passionately? I've never wondered what it would be like to meet him. I've just accepted he's it and we will work things out, but now I wonder if he will like me. If I will like him? Will we be enough for each other?

"Here ya go," I look up at Joy.

"Thanks. Do you know where I can find an ATM?" I ask. Her eyes look to the ceiling in thought.

"There's a bank about a mile away from here, they will have one. Turn right on the main road and it'll be on the left," she says, pointing out the window in the direction she's speaking of. I thank her again and dig into my breakfast. She goes off and sits with the single lady, good for her.

Finishing my breakfast, I drop a twenty on the table and stand up preparing to leave. Spotting a payphone in the back, I hesitate. I know I shouldn't, but I step over to the phone and dial my best friends number. It rings a few times before her voice rings through the receiver.

"Hello?"

"Mira, it's me," I say quickly, hoping she won't hang up. She's silent on the other end but doesn't immediately hang up on me at least. "I'm so sorry for everything that happened. I can't explain it all, everything is so crazy now. I had to leave the island and I don't know if I can ever come back."

"It's always about you isn't it?" She asks, hatefully. Damn, she is pissed. I expected her to still be upset, who wouldn't be after seeing their best friend kiss the guy you are in love with, but I had hoped she would have had some time to think things through.

"You know I wouldn't intentionally hurt you, Mira. I wish I had more time to explain, but I have to go. I just wanted you to know that I love you and I'm sorry for everything that happened. I hope to see you again someday. You have no idea how much your friendship meant to me," I say, tears filling my eyes.

"You hurt me so bad Lyra. I don't know if I can get over it. I love him. He's all I think about," she says, clearly crying as well. We are both silent for a few moments. "I don't know if I want to see you again."

My eyes close. So, this is what it's like to have friends. You finally open yourself up and you get hurt. I nod, even though I know she can't see me. "Okay. I... I hope things work out for you Mira."

"Thanks. You too," she says. The line goes dead, and it hangs in my hand for a second before I hang it up. I've lost so much in less than a day. Both of my friends, my home, my idea of who I am. I want my dad.

Walking out of the diner, I head to my car and down the road. Spotting the bank Joy had mentioned, I pull in and walk inside. I wait in line behind an older man who's talking about his cat to the teller. My foot taps impatiently and it takes everything in me to not yell. I take several deep breaths before he realizes someone is waiting for him to move and he finally steps aside with an apologetic smile on his face. I ignore his smile and stomp up to the teller.

"How can I help you?" She asks sweetly. She's an older lady, probably the same age as the man before me. I wonder if they were flirting for a second, before I whip out my debit card and driver's license, asking if I can make a withdrawal. She takes my cards and goes to the back. I wait at the counter and look around, no one else is here. When she returns, she smiles and says yes, they can. My luck hasn't run out just yet, this happens to be a sister bank to my own. I withdraw all my money and leave as fast as I can, tucking my debit card in my wallet to probably never be used again. The money is in an envelope, and I place that directly into my purse for safe keeping.

Finally, I can get back on the road. It's almost eleven now and I have just under five hours left of driving until I reach Sylva. Hopefully, they take me in with no questions asked, because honestly, I'm not sure how I'm going to answer them.

Chapter 9

Lyra

I've been driving for hours before I finally pass through Asheville, now I have less than an hour left to go. I'm starving but I can make it until I get to Sylva. I'll feel much safer there. The whole drive I've been paranoid, constantly looking over my shoulder. Turning up the radio, I listen to random music for the rest of the way.

Passing the welcome sign is a relief. It feels like years since I left home even though it was just last night. Now that I've arrived, I have to find the library. Following signs, I pull up below a steep hillside with a pretty fountain in front of me. There has to be hundreds of steps leading up to a tall two-story white building. It has four columns in front and a clock tower on top. It reads Jackson County Courthouse, huh. Is this the right place? I continue following the road around to behind the building. There, now it says Library complex. Guess they converted it.

Parking my car, I look at myself in the mirror. My skin is bare of any makeup and my hair is still up in its bun. I pull it down, undo the braids and run my fingers through my hair, trying to get out all the tangles. Oh, the woes of having curly hair. Satisfied with my reflection, I get out of the car and walk to the large double doors leading inside.

I walk inside and down a long hallway. There are stairs leading up to the upper levels and bookshelves along the side. In the middle of the room is a long receptionist desk with three cutouts. There is a teenager sitting at one, waiting to assist anyone and check them out. Her face is round with freckles spread along her cheeks, her hair a mousy brown and hanging in loose waves just past her shoulders. Her green eyes look up as I approach, and she smiles.

"Hi, how can I help you?" She asks with just a slight lisp.

"Hi, I'm supposed to ask for Jonathan Plott. Do you know where I can find him?" I ask.

"I'm sorry, I don't. The name sounds familiar though. Is he supposed to meet you here today?"

"No, not exactly. I was told to come here and ask for him, I assumed someone here would know who he is."

"Well, I don't know. I can ask one of the other– There! Hey, Lucas! Come over here for a sec," she says waving someone over who is behind me. "Don't just stand there looking stupid. I have a question." Turning to me she whispers, "He's totally checking you out." I turn around expecting to find some creepy old guy and instead find a young man a few years older than me walking forward. He has messy black hair and a light stubble surrounds his jawline and full mouth. His eyes are ice blue and are staring right at me. Coming closer, I can see just how tall he is, about 6'3, and he's built. He must work out every day to get muscled arms like that. I can't pull myself away from looking at him and miss him asking me a question.

"Miss? What is it that I can help you with?" His voice is gruff like he just woke up and rolled out of bed.... would explain that messy hair.

"It's Lyra," I whisper, then shake my head trying to clear it. Damn, he's distracting. "Sorry, it's been a long day for me. Do you know where I can find Jonathan Plott? I was told to come here and ask for him," I say. I can't stop fidgeting my hands. His eyes make me feel weird like he can read my thoughts and I can't hide anything from him. At my question, he looks me up and down, surprise clouding his features.

"Marcy, can you excuse us for a minute," he says to the girl behind the desk. He goes to grab my arm, but I flinch away not knowing what to expect. The last thing I want to do is lose control of myself and kill this hot guy. He doesn't comment on me flinching away, just nods his head towards a table and starts walking to it. I follow behind, eyes locked on his backside, and take a seat across from him. "Why do you need Jonathan Plott? Who are you?"

"My name is Lyra. I'm just a girl from Cedar Island. He's a friend of my dad's. I was told to come here and ask for him, I need his help. Do you know him?"

"Yeah, I know him, he's my dad. He's never mentioned a friend from Cedar Island though," he says, narrowing his eyes. He's staring at me hard, looking for something. Either he's checking me out or he doesn't trust me. Which is fine by me, I'm not here to find friends.

"If you are his son, then you are a... uh..." I hesitate. I don't want to go throwing around the word wolf to just anyone.

"A what?" He sits forward in his seat, waiting expectantly.

"A... you know?" He looks at me still waiting. Dang, he's going to make me say it. I look around making sure no one is near us then lean towards him and whisper, "a wolf?"

I'm not even sure he heard me at first, I said it so low that any normal person would ask me to repeat. But he's not normal. He's a wolf and if he's anything like the other wolves I encountered, he should have excellent hearing. He leans back in his seat, still studying me before nodding.

"The library closes at six. You can hang out here or come back. I can take you to him."

"I'll stay here... look for a book or something." He nods at me, a small smile on his lips, then he stands up and walks away. Man, what a view though. I didn't see what he was wearing earlier, and I didn't want to stare any harder than I already was, not that I didn't see him checking me out a few times. Now without him looking I can take my time. He's wearing dark blue jeans that fit him nicely with a light blue t-shirt that's tight around his arms and upper chest, then falls loosely around the rest of him. His white and gray sneakers barely make a sound as he walks on the wooden floor. He walks into a room and I can't see him any longer. I look around and see the girl behind the desk, whom I assume is named Marcy, looking at me trying to suppress a laugh. She must have caught me. Oops.

I walk around the shelves, checking out the different books. Occasionally I see Lucas putting away books or walking around. His eyes find me often but he doesn't come near me until it's almost six. By this point, I'm settled down on a comfy armchair with my feet tucked under me reading a book about wolf shifters. I'm so engrossed, I don't even notice Lucas standing in front of me.

"If you know anything about us, you know that book is mostly trash." Startled I look up to find him towering over me. I close the book, setting it down on the table beside me. At his pointed look, I pick it up with a huff and walk it over to where I found it. Guess that would annoy me as well if I worked at a library.

"I don't know much honestly. So no, I didn't know that book was trash." He lifts an eyebrow but doesn't say anything as we walk towards the back doors towards the parking lot. I feel his hand touch my lower back slowly guiding me. I almost jump away, but I manage to just walk a little faster hoping he doesn't notice. Marcy walks out ahead of us and holds the door open, she's eyeing us like we are the freshest gossip and she can't wait to dish to her friends. Great. Lucas turns around and locks the door, saying goodbye to Marcy who jumps into a waiting car.

"Where's your car?" I point to my Ford Escape parked a few spots down. I don't see any other cars in the parking lot. Seeing me look around he says, "I didn't drive today. I'll have to ride with you." Nodding, we walk to my car together and I unlock it. I settle in and quickly grab up the bag of food on the passenger seat so he can sit down. He eyes the food and turns around, seeing the three duffle bags taking up the entire back seat. He looks at me again before adjusting his seat and buckling up.

"So where to?" I ask, starting the car.

"Nowhere until you tell me why you are here," he says, crossing his arms and making his muscles pop out. Wowza.

"Look, I was told to talk to your dad specifically. Not you. I don't have to explain anything," I huff.

"You do if you want me to take you to him." He has a point.

"Fine. My dad is a wolf shifter, I guess. I didn't know until last night. I ran into some trouble and found out the truth. A friend of my dad's told me to come here until he can follow me. He should be here tomorrow night or Monday morning." Not technically a lie.

"Wait, you had no clue your dad was a wolf shifter? You should be a shifter too. You smell human to me." He breathes in, inhaling my scent. It's a little creepy but in a hot way.

"I am human." Ok, that's a lie. "Guess the wolf gene skipped me? I don't really know. All I know is I've been living a normal life until last night. My dad is away on a fishing trip and I needed to leave. Our neighbor, who knows about my dad thankfully, told me to come here and ask for protection until he gets here."

"What type of trouble did you get into?" He asks leaning back in the seat. He doesn't really look comfortable sitting in my little SUV, it's a good thing I don't drive a tiny car. Poor guy looks squished.

"I upset a witch. Her boyfriend flirted with me and she told me to leave town and to not come back." Only a half lie this time. I did upset a witch.

He stares at me for a long moment, assessing me to tell if I'm lying. Either he doesn't pick up on it or he chooses to ignore it for now. He starts to give me directions on how to get to his father's house and takes his phone out of his pocket texting someone. Maybe he has a girlfriend? My stomach growls loudly, and he looks up and over at me.

"Hungry?" He's laughing at me!

"Yeah. It's been a long drive."

"When did you leave home? And when's the last time you ate?"

"Around midnight. She told me to get out before then. I stopped around three this morning at a motel in Raleigh then ate breakfast. I made a stop for gas once but otherwise, I've kept driving," I admit quietly.

"You didn't eat lunch?" At my nod he continues, "Pull down here." I take a left and see a Mexican restaurant. He tells me to pull in and without question I do. I know I need to get to the Alpha but I'm so hungry. I grab my purse from behind me and step out of my car, surprised to find Lucas right there waiting for me. He's so close that I can smell him, he smells like the woods, fresh air, and water. There's another scent to him that I can't seem to place but I like it. I want to step closer and breathe in his scent, but I refrain. He reaches out to touch my cheek and I quickly step to the side and walk to the door. Talk about awkward.

It's bright and colorful inside the restaurant. The host is a friendly middle-aged man who seats us immediately. It's a small, two-person table pushed up against a window looking out at the woods. He hands us our menus and I open mine without looking at Lucas. I don't know why he keeps trying to touch me, but I need it to stop. I could barely control myself from touching Ryan, someone who has been my best friend for years and who I didn't find nearly as attractive as Lucas.

I settle on seafood nachos, then just stare at the menu. A waiter comes up for our drink order, this one a younger guy around Lucas's age. He flirts heavily with me and ignores Lucas, who has to clear his throat to get any attention. We are both ready to order our food, Lucas orders a fajita steak burrito and we both want cheese dip for our chips. The waiter tries to touch my hand as he grabs the menu, but I pull away fast not even bothering to hide it this time. He frowns and takes the menu walking away. Hopefully, he doesn't spit in my food now.

"So, it's not just me, you don't like any guy touching you?" Lucas says staring out the window. "Do you have a boyfriend back home then?" I see Ryan in my mind, we aren't dating now, right? We did kiss and I know he likes me but I'm still not sure about my feelings for him. We've been friends for so long now, I don't know if we could ever be anything more.

"No, I don't. And it's not just guys. I don't like touching anyone period." Before he can answer, the waiter comes back with our drink order, both Pepsi, and sets them down on the table. He places the cheese dip and chips directly in the middle then walks away. At least he can take a hint.

We eat the chips in silence, neither of us knowing exactly what to say. I know I don't come off as approachable, even before I was trying to avoid touching people so I don't suck out their souls. Now I must be awful. Our food arrives fast and we both dig in. The waiter drops off our bill about half way through and Lucas reaches for it.

"I can pay my half," I say reaching for my purse.

"What type of man would I be if I didn't pay for a beautiful lady's meal?" He smirks. I know he's partially teasing me, but I sense the truth beneath his words.

"The type of man who's not my date," I say, opening the envelope full of cash. I hide it inside my purse, so no one sees, and grab out a twenty. I throw it down and look up at Lucas. He's still smiling at me.

"I can appreciate that," he says putting down some cash as well. "When we do go on a date though, I'm paying." I choose to ignore his last comment and stand up from the table. I hide my smile as we walk out to the car.

"How far away are we now?" I ask buckling myself in the car. Lucas climbs in beside me and leans back, trying to stretch his legs in the little bit of leg room available in here.

"Not much longer. He lives on the outskirts of town, almost directly in the forest. It's a small, gated community. The entire pack lives inside. Easier to keep humans out and we can be ourselves."

Nodding, I continue, following his directions. I'll be happy to finally be there. Hopefully, my dad will show up tomorrow and I can get the answers to my questions. Then I want to sleep for a year. I have this foreboding feeling though like something is going to go very wrong.

Chapter 10

Lyra

The ride is mostly silent, the only words spoken are directions. I feel Lucas's eyes on me often, but I don't comment. We pull up to a tall, thick stone wall. There's a guardhouse at the gate, a man in a security uniform steps up to my window and bends down to look at me.

"You don't live here. I have to ask you to turn around," he says. Not mean or anything, but very matter of fact. Lucas leans over so the man can see him. He nods at the guard, who's eyes zero in on Lucas and flick to me once before nodding back. "Sorry about that Miss. We take security very highly here. Go on through."

I look at Lucas, eyebrow raised. He smiles sheepishly at me and nods ahead once the guard opens the gate. I drive through and see rows of houses. We are on a wide street that branches off on both sides. There are a few people walking about and they all stop and stare as we drive past. I glance at Lucas, but he doesn't offer an explanation.

"Wow. I didn't know you had so many pack members," I say, looking around.

"We have just under forty, mostly men. We have more houses than we have people right now. It's easier to build a larger community than to keep adding on as we grow. My dad's house is straight back on this main road."

This looks like a typical suburban area. I didn't expect this when he told me the pack lives all together in a community. I thought they would be in small houses, but most of these are rather large. I drive down to the last house on the street, it's by far the biggest of them all. It's made out of white stone and has a large front porch. Most of the windows are lit from within and I can see some curious faces looking out at us through curtains.

"I texted them earlier and warned dad we had a human visitor. We don't often allow humans here, usually we have to give a days' notice to everyone to make sure no one runs around in wolf form. Dad is probably wondering what's up." I park the car in the circle driveway, and we get out. Lucas walks around to my side and tries to touch my back to lead me inside. I try to act like I didn't notice and walk ahead of him. The door opens before we reach it, a man stands in the doorway with brown hair and the same blue eyes as Lucas. They have a similar facial structure and build, so I assume this is his father or an uncle. I would have said brother, but the gray at his temples suggests he's older than he looks.

"Lucas, I wasn't expecting you to bring someone over tonight. You hadn't mentioned having a new friend," he says, looking at me curiously. He glances at Lucas, who subtly nods his head. His tense muscles release and he smiles brightly at me. "Welcome to my home. I'm Jonathan Plott, please call me Jon. I'm Lucas's father. Who might you be?"

"Dad, this is Lyra. She has come here to see you," Lucas says. His dad looks at him confused, then turns back to me.

"Come this way, we can speak privately in my office," Jon says, leading me past a winding staircase, towards the back of the house. I see a large living room on my left that has a few people in it, all of which are looking our way. I wonder if there's any point in us going somewhere privately in a house full of wolves with good hearing. We reach a wooden door and Jon holds the door open for Lucas and me.

The office has bookshelves built into the walls on both sides, with two sofas on either side of the door angled diagonally. The whole back wall is an entire window with the desk sitting in front of it. Seeing nowhere else to sit, I take a seat on one of the couches. Lucas sits beside me, but not close enough to touch. Jon sits behind his desk and looks at me, waiting for me to speak.

"My dad is Felix Vander," I say. Recognition lights in Jon's eyes, good at least he knows who I'm talking about.

"I know Felix! It's been a while since we talked last, maybe four years ago? He told me he had a daughter entering high school and was moving close by."

"You aren't surprised I'm human?" I ask, eyeing Lucas.

"No, he told me his daughter didn't inherit the wolf gene. It's rare, but I've heard of it happening before. I was under the impression that you weren't aware of his wolf nature," he says, looking at me expectantly.

"I wasn't aware until last night. I had a run in with a witch at a party, her boyfriend flirted with me and she wasn't too happy. She freaked out on me, tried to kill me and told me I had until midnight to leave town before she came after me." Lucas looks furious now, his body tense beside me and his eyes wide. His fists are resting against his knees now and stares down at me, hard. I might have left out the part of almost dying before. Oops. "My dad is on one of his fishing trips, so I went to our neighbors.

90

When I explained what happened she came clean about my dad being a wolf. She took the threat seriously enough that she sent me here for protection, told me my dad would come after me when he gets home."

"How does your neighbor know about your dad?" I didn't consider this. Shit.

"I'm not sure. I was a little freaked out when I went to her house, I didn't think to ask, and she didn't have much time to explain, anyway. Just said I needed to go home and pack up, then get out of there. She told me to go to the library in Sylva and ask for you by name."

"She must be some type of mystical creature or a witch. We aren't allowed to reveal ourselves to humans unless we are related to them. Your dad must have told her about my pack in case of an emergency, like this. My family has run the library here for generations now. We like to keep someone from the pack there in case someone suspects something and goes there to research wolves. When will your dad be here?"

"I'm not sure. He's supposed to get home tomorrow morning from his fishing trip. If he leaves right when he gets home, he should be here late tomorrow night. At the latest, Monday morning. Miss Lynn, my neighbor, told me to ditch my cell phone and not to use anything that can be tracked to me. I emptied out my bank account this morning in Raleigh and have only used cash since."

"Good. Your neighbor is very smart. Witches can be vicious and aren't above using technology to find people these days. I would say you can call your dad from here, but I'm not sure if they are keeping track of his phone. If this witch was serious about hurting you, I wouldn't risk it. You can stay here, I'll have my wife set up a room for–"

"Actually dad," Lucas interrupts, "Lyra will be staying with me at my house. She needs 24/7 supervision until her dad gets here. I know you are very busy running the pack, and Lewis has Julie. I can watch over her and protect her."

I look over at Lucas, wondering if he's serious. The look in his eyes says he is. He wants to protect me. I'm not sure how I feel about being in a house alone with him, but it should only be for one night, maybe two. I can do this. Just because I can't touch him, doesn't mean I don't want to get to know him better. There's something about him that draws me in, makes me want to be near him even if we aren't talking. Back at the restaurant, it should have been awkward when I wouldn't let him touch me and it wasn't. Everything felt natural, except me pulling away.

"Are you sure that's okay? I know how you like your own space Lucas," Jon asks. He smiles lightly like he's making a joke. Lucas turns to me to make sure I'm okay with this. I smile and give him a nod, he nods to me and tells his dad yes. I'd like nothing more than to stay with Lucas, as long as he keeps his hands to himself. "Well, now that that's settled, why don't I introduce you to some of the pack."

We walk out of the office and head back to the living room we passed earlier. There are five people in the room, two males and three females. The guys hang in the back, but the women rush forward when we enter. Jon wraps his arms around one of them, I assume his wife and Lucas's mother. She has black hair, like Lucas, but hazel eyes, she is curvy like me and about the same height, 5'5. She smiles at Lucas and pats his cheek.

Beside her, is what most would call a bombshell. She has golden blonde hair and cornflower blue eyes. Her face is coated in makeup, eyes lined in black and lips painted a deep shade of red. She is lithe, with big boobs that could pop your eye out if you get too close. I wonder if she has had surgery. I instantly dislike her and don't like the way she eyes Lucas. She throws her arms around him in a tight hug that Lucas does not return.

"Nessa now isn't the time," he says, turning to his mom and smiling back at her. "Mom this is Lyra. Lyra this is my mom, Kim. This is Vanessa, the beta's daughter, and this is Julie, my brother's mate, and my sister-in-law. My brother, the inconsiderate doof that he is, is sitting on the couch over there. He's Lewis." Julie is a pretty girl with brown hair and brown eyes, she's super tiny but I have a feeling she's a firecracker. Lewis stands up when he's mentioned and stands beside Julie, he easily towers over her, and everyone else in the room. He has his mom's black hair and hazel eyes. If I thought Lucas was built before, I stand corrected. He has nothing on his brother. He's built like a freaking bear. I don't know how he doesn't squash Julie just by standing beside her. They do make a cute couple though.

"Everyone always forgets me," this is the last guy in the room. He's older, like Jon, and has blonde hair and dark eyes. So dark, they almost look black. "I'm Leo, the beta of this pack and Vanessa's father." Ah, they do look alike. Leo is lean like the rest of the wolves I've met, but not nearly as fit. He must not work out much.

"I didn't forget you, Leo, I was just saving the best for last," says Lucas. All night he's seemed so quiet and almost grouchy, but here with his family, he's happy and charismatic. Maybe I've been misreading the signals. Maybe he's not into me and just doesn't like me being here. He seems so relaxed around everyone but me.

"Guys, this is Lyra. Her dad is a lone wolf," Jon says as everyone glances at me and I see everyone, but Kim, take a subtle sniff towards me. Creepy. "She's not a wolf shifter herself. She's in some trouble with a witch and will be staying with us for the time being. Her dad will be here soon, hopefully, tomorrow, and we can figure out how to handle this situation. Witches can be nasty sometimes, so we want to handle it carefully. Treat Lyra with respect please."

"Oh, so you won't be staying long. That's good," the bombshell says to me, then turns back to Lucas. Yup, she has to be his girlfriend. "Why don't I come over to your place Lucas, I can make us dinner?"

Lucas looks uncomfortable. "Actually, Lyra will be staying with me. We are heading to my house now, we had dinner already and I'm sure she wants to sleep."

"Don't worry about me Lucas, you can spend some time with your girlfriend. I'm good here." My voice doesn't betray my feelings. I didn't realize I was so freaking jealous, man. I've never been this way before. I want to slap bombshell around the room, she looks happy as a clam at my words and starts to walk towards the door, grabbing Lucas's arm.

Everyone stills as a growl sounds in the room. I look around, trying to figure out which one made the noise, but everyone is looking at Lucas, who is staring at me. My eyes widen at the anger glaring from his. I take a step back, but Lucas just steps closer and grabs my hand in his.

"She's not my girlfriend and won't be coming home with me tonight, you are. Let's go." He flings Nessa's hand off him and tows me to the door. The whole room is silent as we leave, and it takes everything in me not to drain Lucas.

I knew it would be hard touching him and not pulling his life force inside me. I knew before I even laid a finger on him that his soul would be full of light and good. What I hadn't expected though, was to feel so many emotions coming from him. I can feel his anger and his love for his family. I can feel his lust for me, and man was there a lot of that. His soul is pure white energy, and his touch burns me almost to the point of pain. My hand begins to tingle, and I quickly pull my hand out of his grasp.

That tingle reminds me of what I can do to him with just a single touch. I can make him gaga over me and kill him. I can't do that to Lucas, I don't want to do that to anyone but especially not him.

"Sorry, forgot you don't like to be touched," he says, looking down at me. His eyes are softer now, the anger depleting from his eyes and his body relaxes. With a light smile, he climbs back into my SUV and I follow behind him. He points to a house two lots down from his parents, his is smaller with a light gray color siding and a wraparound porch. It takes us a few seconds to pull into the driveway behind a dark blue Ford F-150 and get out. Lucas helps me grab my duffle bags and we walk up the steps to the porch.

He opens the door for me, and we walk into an inviting living room combined with a kitchen, separated by an island with two stools seated at it. The living room has a fireplace with a flat screen tv mounted above it. There's only a three-seater gray couch facing the tv with a red painted coffee table in front of it. The kitchen is decorated in reds and grays. Everything looks top of the line appliances and not a single dirty dish is waiting to be cleaned. The stairs are right in front of you when you walk in and I see a hallway behind the stairs, back by the kitchen.

Lucas sets my duffle bags down at the bottom of the stairs and gives me a tour. The downstairs is pretty simple consisting of the living room and kitchen, and a door leading to the back yard. The little hallway behind the stairs leads to a half bathroom and a mudroom with a washer and dryer inside. Grabbing my bags again, we head upstairs and immediately turn right as there's a wall to my left and in front of me. There are two doors on the left and one on the right. Lucas shows me to the first door on the left, which happens to be a guest bedroom. It has a queen bed in it, one-nightstand and a tall dresser. There's a door to the right as soon as you walk in which leads to a bathroom.

I set my bags down on the bed and walk through the bathroom, seeing a door on the opposite side. Walking through, I find another guest room, this one looks like Lucas's office. It has a desktop computer sitting on a desk, a big comfy computer chair sitting in front of it. There are two bookshelves on either side of it and a couch on the other wall.

"Your office?" I ask him.

"Yeah, I'm an architect and I work from home. I work part time at the library because I love to read, it's calming there. You'll find me in here often enough. My bedroom is across the hall and I have my own bathroom, so I won't have to use this one connected to your room. It's all yours."

"You act like I'll be staying here for longer than one night," I say, looking at him.

"You never know, your dad isn't here yet and until you are safe from that witch you are staying here with me. I'll let your dad take my room when he gets here. I can sleep on the couch in my office."

"That's not necessary. We can move over to your dads or something."

"Nope. You are staying where I can see you," he says seriously.

"Why? Don't you want me gone so bombshell can come over here?" Stupid mouth. Why did I have to ask that? Lucas looks at me curiously.

"Bombshell?" Damn. I was hoping he would just ignore me.

"Nessa," I say quietly, hoping the ground will open up and swallow me whole. Or Ann will come bursting through the door and Avada me like in Harry Potter. Lucas bursts into laughter and my cheeks heat.

"You think Nessa is a bombshell? Hardly. She wears too much makeup and is too thin for my tastes. I like a woman with a little more meat on her bones," he says, eyes dropping to my curves in emphasis. So, I wasn't misreading anything. Good to know. "Plus, she's not really into me so much as she's into the power. She went after Lewis first before he found out Julie was his mate. Then she set her sights on me and I'm not interested."

"Oh." I know I'm blushing now. I don't think I have ever blushed before in my life.

"You seem awfully jealous for someone who doesn't like me touching her," he comments thoughtfully. Great. Now he knows I like him and wonders why I don't touch him. He takes a step towards me and I step back.

"I'm not jealous! It's been a long day and I'm just tired. I think I'll go to bed now. Hopefully, my dad will be here tomorrow, and we will be out of your hair in no time." I start going through my duffle bags, searching through for some night clothes.

"Is that what you wore to the party? No wonder someone's boyfriend hit on you." I look down, realizing I'm still wearing my green party dress and purple swimsuit on underneath. I look like a hoe hoe. Grabbing a thin shirt and some underwear, I march past Lucas and into the bathroom with my toiletries bag to get ready for bed. Hopefully, Lucas gets the hint and gets out.

I take a quick shower and find only one small towel in the linen closet. Fantastic. I use it on my hair and let my body dry off on its own before putting on my clothes, they cling to my damp skin. I quickly brush my teeth and hair, stepping out of the bathroom without checking if Lucas is still in the room.

Damn. Mistake. He's still here, laying on my bed and staring right at me. I wish I would have grabbed some sleep shorts now, but I never sleep with anything around my legs; it's too restricting. Now I wish I did though.

He looks me up and down, pausing on my slightly damp shirt then moving on to my legs. The shirt barely covers my underwear and my long legs are fully on display. I have never really cared about my curves before, sure I've dieted but I did it for other people. Never for myself. I find myself caring now though as Lucas stares at my thick thighs.

I decide to ignore him and start braiding my hair, forgetting- of course- that reaching my arms up made my shirt come up as well, revealing my not so sexy underwear. I don't like the feel of lingerie, just didn't do it for me. I much prefer comfortable, soft underwear that actually covers me. I'm not sure if I'm regretting that choice now or not. A part of me wishes I was in some sexy number on display for Lucas, another part of me wants to be covered as much as possible. Either way, Lucas doesn't seem to mind. He doesn't even glance down at them, instead, he focuses on my hands moving through my hair. I can't tell if I'm offended or even more turned on that he finds something as silly as braiding my hair attractive. Finished braiding it, I go back into the bathroom and grab a hair tie. My cheeks are flushed, and my braid looks half-assed. Oh well.

Walking back into my bedroom, I expect Lucas to still be sitting there waiting for me. I find my bed empty and my door closed.

Sighing, I turn off the light and climb into bed. This has to be the earliest I've gone to sleep in a long time. I'm so used to staying up late and swimming in the ocean. I'll have to get used to staying in the mountains now, maybe someone has a pool where I can swim in?

Closing my eyes, I can't help my thoughts going to Lucas. I don't know what it is about him, but he makes me crazy. I want to touch him all the time and talk. At the same time, I want to sit in silence with him, just enjoying his company. I want to ask questions about his architecture and what books he likes. But I can't do any of that. I can't even touch the guy. I slowly fall asleep, thoughts of Lucas swirling around my head.

Chapter 11

Lyra

My eyes pop open, sweaty clothes stick to my skin and I turn my eyes to the window by my bed. Darkness is still present. Throwing the covers off my sweaty body, I try to remember my dream but come up blank. I remember Lucas being in it, but that's about it. I swing my legs off the bed and head downstairs. There has to be a clock somewhere around here.

The hallway is dark when I leave my room. Lucas's door is firmly shut so I assume he's still asleep. My feet lightly pad down the stairs and I walk into the living room. Still no clock. Who doesn't have a bloody clock in their house? Walking through to the kitchen, I finally spot the time on the microwave, 4:43 am. Normal wake up time for me.

"What are you doing up so early?" I scream and swing around looking behind me. Lucas is standing there in some sleep shorts, it's too dark in the room to make out the color. There's enough light for me to see he's not wearing a shirt. Man is he ripped. His abs are tight, shoulders wide, and his body glistens with a faint sheen of sweat like mine. He laughs at my startled expression and flips on the light switch. "Didn't mean to scare you. I heard you get up. Was making sure you weren't trying to take off."

"Why would I leave? You guys are protecting me," I say, taking a seat at the little island. The granite countertops are white and gray speckled, they feel cold against my still hot skin.

"I don't know. Why else would you sneak downstairs at almost five in the morning?" He walks over to the coffeepot and starts it up. The smell makes me feel nauseous, I usually love coffee.

"I like to get up early. Back at home I would wake up and go for a swim in the ocean before getting ready for school."

"Wait," he freezes, "Are you still in high school?" His shoulders are tense, and he won't look at me. I decide to tease him just a little. I have to fight the smirk off my face.

"Well, yeah. I'm only sixteen." He gets even stiffer. I didn't think it was possible. I can't help laughing out loud. "Just kidding! Geez. My last day was Friday, graduation is supposed to be this Friday coming up, but I doubt I'll be there to get my diploma."

"Not even funny. Want a cup?" He asks, body relaxing and going to a cabinet. I shake my head no and he pulls out one mug. "So, you are eighteen then?"

"Nope. I'm seventeen still. Late birthday. Mine is this Tuesday. I'm curious though, what would you do if I was sixteen?"

"Let's not talk about it," he mumbles. "This Tuesday? We'll have to do something special." Nice, he's trying to change the subject. I decide to let it go and stop teasing.

"Maybe. My dad wanted to bring me up here, actually. I didn't know it at the time obviously, but he mentioned taking a trip up to the mountains for my birthday."

"So, no matter what we would have met eventually," he says nodding to himself.

"I guess so. I was always meant to come here. Destiny," I say. Lucas looks at me intently, like he's trying to read my thoughts again. I keep my face blank giving nothing away.

"You mentioned swimming in the ocean, I take it you like to swim?"

"Like to? No. I love to. It's where I feel most comfortable in the world. I'd go out every morning for an hour or two then go back out before bed." Lucas sits beside me but angles himself so he can look at me. It's weird being so close to him and not touching. It takes everything in me not to reach over and touch his arm. He must be having similar issues because his hand reaches toward me for a second then he clenches his fist resting it against his leg.

"You get up early every morning and go to bed late every night. That makes a lot of sense," he says looking down at his cup.

"Why does that make sense?"

"No reason." He shakes his head and continues, "Why don't you like being touched?"

"Can't a girl keep some secrets?" I ask coyly, my eyes locking with his. "Do you know of a pool around here or even a lake? I feel weird not swimming." Yup, I'm totally avoiding the question. Not like I can tell him the truth. At least not now.

"I know of a few," He says smiling. "There are a few houses in the community that have one. Not many wolves are interested in swimming, it's something we grow out of when we first shift. Something about running as a wolf takes precedence over swimming. My dad has a pool for all the kids to come over and swim if they'd like."

"That will work. Do you think you can take me over there now so I can swim? It's not too early, is it?" I ask, already standing up to head upstairs and change. He grabs my hand to stop me from running to my room. I look down at our hands and he quickly drops mine.

"You didn't let me finish. You're in luck, I happen to love swimming. I specifically chose this house for the pool in the back. I know I could go to my dads whenever I wanted but there's never any privacy over there. Between my parents and my brother and Julie, I'm always being pestered. Not to mention all the kids coming by to swim."

"Why didn't you say that in the first place! I'm going to go change." I run up the stairs and into my room. I completely forgot I was downstairs in my underwear again. I don't even want to know what Lucas thinks of me prancing around in practically nothing. I dig through my duffle bags looking for a swimsuit and lay a few of them out on the bed trying to decide which one I want to wear. There are a few one pieces that would cover me up nicely. Or did I want to wear a bikini that showed off more skin? Hmm. He's already seen me practically naked. I decide on a plum-colored bikini and I change before running out the door colliding with Lucas in the hallway. His arms immediately wrap around me and press me closer to him. Oh no. This can't be happening. I look up into his ice-blue eyes and find myself lost. My body is beginning to tingle all over and where our skin touches it burns. Shaking my head, I take a step back from him and smile.

"Are you coming to swim too?" I ask, noticing his swim trunks.

"Is that okay? It's not often I have someone to swim with besides little kids." His hand rubs the back of his neck in nervousness. For such a hot guy, he sure is shy around me.

"I don't mind. I sometimes would swim with Ryan back home but, usually, I was by myself," I say, walking to the stairs.

"Who's Ryan?" He asks, following me down the stairs.

"A friend of mine. He's a wolf, actually." What is up with my mouth just blurting things out?

"How do you know he's a wolf? I thought you didn't know about wolves until the other night?" He moves in front of me, staring me down. He knows I haven't told him the full truth about everything.

"I didn't. He was at the party I went to. The witch I pissed off? That's her boyfriend." Total lie. Gosh, I'm going to hell. "He kissed me, and she flipped out. She kept mentioning the pack and blah blah. So, when I went to my neighbor's house and told her everything, she told me he was a part of the wolf pack there. When I was leaving town, he stopped me from leaving. I assume him stopping me in the woods half naked confirms he was a wolf shifter."

"He kissed you without your permission?" He asks, looking pissed off.

"It's... complicated," I admit.

"How is it complicated? Did you want him to kiss you or not?" He asks loudly, his pupils dilating.

"Not really. At least I don't think so. Something weird happened, I can't explain it."

"Why don't you try?" Lucas still looks like he wants to punch a wall. His fists are tight, and his body shakes in anger. Normally, this would scare me but with Lucas, I'm just turned on. God, what is wrong with me?

"Can't we just go outside and swim now? Please. I don't want to talk about it," I say, walking to the back door. Lucas takes a deep breath and follows me outside.

I didn't have a chance to come out here yesterday when we got here. There is a tall wooden privacy fence on either side of the yard and the tall stone wall surrounding the community is at the back. Walking down the porch steps, I look at the mostly barren yard. There is nothing else out here but grass and the pool to the right. Without feeling the temperature, I just jump in.

The water is a bit on the cold side, but I barely notice. The ocean is usually cold too unless it's the middle of the day in the summer. I reach the surface and look around for Lucas. I don't see him anywhere. Turning around in the pool, I feel a light touch on the bottom of one of my feet. I can't help but giggle as I swim away. Lucas comes up laughing behind me.

"What was that for?" I ask.

"Testing if you are ticklish. Which you are." He's grinning.

We swim around for a while, occasionally splashing the other. I keep things light and playful, just enjoying this side of us. I have a feeling he doesn't get to be this way often and neither do I. Eventually we both just float and stare up at the sky which is just beginning to lighten.

"Do you see that star there?" I say pointing up at Vega, the brightest star in the Lyra constellation. He hums his yes. "If you look closely you can make out a harp, do you see it?"

"Yeah, I do. Why?"

"That's the Lyra constellation. My mom used to be into astronomy, I guess. And out of all the stars in the sky, Lyra was her favorite, and she named me after it."

"You've never mentioned your mom before, what happened to her?" He whispers.

"She died after giving birth to me. She had some complications in labor and died just after giving birth to my twin brother."

"You have a brother?"

"I did. He was stillborn. My dad doesn't talk about it much but said my mom didn't know. She thought he was born alive and her last words were his name, Phoenix. At least she died thinking we both were okay."

We both are silent, just watching as the stars slowly fade and the sky begins to brighten.

"Ready to go inside?" Lucas asks. I look at him and nod. Thankful that he didn't bring up my mom or brother again. Most people feel the need to talk to me about them and apologize for their passing. Lucas wasn't like that. He was just there for me, letting me grieve silently. I appreciate that.

We walk inside, both dripping wet, and head up to our rooms to change. I take a quick shower to rinse off, then get dressed for the day in a blue summer dress. It has thin straps, cinches around my waist and flows down to just about my knees. I don't bother wearing a bra with it, I rarely wear one anyway. I might have curves all along my body, but I wasn't too blessed in the boob department. I had enough to make guys interested when they saw me but not enough that I had to worry about wearing a bra every day. Perfect to me. I brush my hair out and braid it to one side, then slip on a pair of gray flip flops.

Walking down the stairs, I start to feel a little dizzy and I pause for a second, leaning against the wall beside me. My head feels fuzzy, and I take deep breaths. Feeling a bit better, I continue down. It probably happened because I need to eat. Lucas is in the kitchen making some breakfast when I enter the kitchen and take a seat at the island. Silently, I watch him as he puts bacon in the oven and makes some eggs and toast. Finishing up, he sets two plates down on the island and takes a seat beside me, again his chair is at an angle so he can see me better.

We eat in silence for the most part. Occasionally I'll look over at Lucas and watch him eat, sometimes he's already watching me. We hold eye contact for a few seconds before we both look back at our food. The silence is filled with tension, but it's not awkward. It just feels natural to me, sitting beside him eating breakfast. The only thing I would change is being able to touch him.

Finished, I push my plate away and fill a glass with water from the filter. Lucas is eyeing the rest of my plate and then pointedly looks at me.

"I'm just not hungry this morning," I say picking up on what he means with his eyes. I decide to change the subject. "What are we doing today? I'm not sure when my dad will be here."

"I figured we could just hang out here. Talk some. I'm sure you have some questions about wolves. You are taking this all very well," He comments.

"Yeah, I do. Like the whole mate thing. You guys have mentioned mates a few times but what is that? Like husband and wife?" I ask, walking over to the couch and sitting down. Lucas tenses up in his seat at the island, then relaxes and follows me to the couch. We both sit facing each other, leaning against the armrests. My feet are tucked under my butt and his stretch out almost touching me. His eyes are dark as he stares at me, figuring out what all he should tell. Why would he hold anything back in this conversation?

"Yeah, I guess you'd say like a spouse. We see it deeper though. We don't believe in divorce and if one of us dies, we don't get over it easily. Usually, the mate left behind will spend the rest of their life alone," his voice trails off, and his eyes flicker around the room. I wonder if someone he knows has lost a mate before?

"How do you know who your mate is?" I try changing the subject, wanting to wipe off the sad look on his face. Lucas looks at me for a second, then glances down at his lap. Eh, at least he's not sad anymore.

"It depends. Technically speaking, you can choose your mate, and most wolves do. It's said wolf shifters were created by the Greek God Apollo, who created us to protect humans and to be his messengers. He can see the future and supposedly he passed that on to us when we were made a long time ago. We can't see the future per se, but we can sense when someone could be our perfect match. We just know in our hearts that they are it for us. Their touch warms us and sometimes we even share dreams, emotions, thoughts, but it doesn't happen often and more likely than not, wolves choose their own mates." He shrugged his shoulder slightly.

"So, what would happen if a wolf chose someone as a mate and then their perfect match came walking through the door?" I ask, knowing I'm asking for personal reasons. I know I can't be with Lucas, but that doesn't mean I don't have feelings for him.

"Once we fully mate with someone, they become our mate. No one else matters to us. We wouldn't be able to tell if someone else was a better match or not. All we see is them and no one else will compare." His voice trails off, eyes locked on my face. This is getting a little too intimate for me.

"You haven't found your mate then?" I ask curiously. A part of me hopes he hasn't- even if we can't touch, I feel so possessive over him. He looks away from me and out the front window, silent for a second.

"She's not a part of my pack and not a human from this town," He says, looking at me sideways before his eyes drift back to the window. "Once we reach maturity, which is between sixteen and eighteen years old, we have our first shift and then we can find our mate. Most wolves wait until they are twenty-five and if they don't find theirs, they will choose a suitable match."

"And how old are you?" How have I never asked him his age before?

"Twenty-two, why?" He asks, eyes watching me. Four years older than me isn't too bad. I've heard of larger age-gaps than that.

"Just curious. You haven't chosen a mate yet?" I ask, hoping he says no.

"No. Nessa has mentioned we should mate if neither of us finds our soulmates, but for years now I've known I had someone out there. It's just this gut feeling." He glances out the front window again.

"Oh," I say, looking down at my lap. So, he does have a soul-mate, he just has to find her. "I get that. Sometimes I have these dreams, and I know the guy in them is meant for me."

"You do? Tell me about them?" He asks, sitting forward with interest. His eyes are bright now, no longer a dark blue.

"Not much to tell," I say, eyes locked on his. They flow over my face, searching for more details. "I've had them for a few years now and I have this gut feeling too that someone is out there for me, just waiting to find me or for me to find them. I never remember his face though and I'm never aware I'm dreaming, I never think to ask him his name or where he is."

"You should look into lucid dreaming, basically you become aware you are dreaming, and you can then control it. I've been practicing it for years."

"I've tried, it's never worked for me," I say, locking eyes with him. We sit in silence, staring at each other and I decide to change the subject. "So, your parents are mates?"

"They are now, but no my mom was not my dad's soulmate. They went to school together here in Sylva. My dad grew up loving her, but they never dated because she's human. When my dad first shifted, he thought for sure she would be his mate, but she wasn't. He pulled away after that and when he turned eighteen, he went looking around the states hoping to find his perfect match. It devastated my mom, she always thought he would ask her out and then he just disappeared. But he couldn't get my mom out of his head. He came back home a few years later looking for her. He still loved her, even after being apart for years and him looking for a mate. He gave up his search and decided to take her. He was only twenty. Everyone thought he was crazy for giving up so early. He didn't care though, he thought my mom was perfect for him and honestly, he was right. No one gets him like my mom does. They've been happy together ever since."

"That's sweet! They do seem so perfect together... So, how do you mate fully?" I ask, excited to know more. Lucas gives me a heated look like it should be obvious. Oh. It is obvious. I squeeze my legs together to stop the ache between my legs. I shouldn't have even asked that.

"First you have to start the mate bond. You kiss them with the intent of them being your mate and if it's two wolves, then they both have to have the same intent. After that, the bond will pull you closer and lower your inhibitions... until you fully mate." His eyes are dark again, voice gruff. His nostrils flare and I squeeze my legs tighter. His eyes drop down to them, and his eyes get even darker than before. I go back over what he said and decide to focus on the inhibitions part. If it forces you to have sex, that's kind of disgusting.

"Basically, it makes you have sex?" I ask horrified, my hands coming up around my mouth. That sounds awful! To be forced into having sex. My face must show my horror because Lucas laughs, the lusty atmosphere disappears for now.

"No. It lowers your inhibitions, not throw them out the window. Like if someone is super shy and normally doesn't make the first move, the mate bond will allow them to do what they want without worry. You have to want to have sex for it to push you to have sex. After you seal the mate bond, you won't be able to see other people. It's impossible for mates to cheat on each other." That makes more sense to me. I relax again and play with the end of my hair, watching Lucas watch me.

"And your brother and Julie?"

"They are true mates," he says, smiling fondly. "They hated each other growing up. My brother always made fun of her for being so tiny and Julie hated that. Julie is older than him by a week. They both shifted within a month of each other, it didn't take them long to figure out they were mates. My brother described it as being hit in the head with a fat brick. They've been together ever since."

"Aw, that's so sweet. What does it feel like? Finding your mate?" I ask, curious. I would love to have a mate.

"When you look at them, you just know they are meant for you. You find yourself beyond sexually attracted to them. You'll want to be with them all the time, rather you are talking or just sitting together. It doesn't matter as long as you are with them. When you touch them, you'll never want to let go, and their touch will warm you. Their smell will appeal to you as well," he says, voice excited. The entire time Lucas is talking, he's looking into my eyes with a smile on his face. For a second, he scoots closer to me and I think he's going to touch me again but instead, he closes himself off again and stands up. "Of course, that's how my brother explains it. Want to watch tv?" I nod and he turns the tv onto some crime show I've watched before.

I know he is trying to change the subject, and I let him. Talking about mates makes me want one myself. It must be hard for him knowing he has a mate out there and he just hasn't found her yet.

We sit together and watch tv, sometimes we talk about the show or make fun of the characters. I guess who the killer is almost every episode and Lucas is impressed. That's right, I could be a crime scene investigator.

During commercial breaks, we talk about our lives. I tell him about my life growing up, moving a lot and Aunt Karen. He tells me about his brother being the next alpha, and because of that his dad and Lewis were very close growing up. Lucas is closer to his mom. He moved out when he was eighteen because he couldn't stand living with his parents, his brother and Julie anymore. Julie moved in when they found out they were mates, I find this a little weird considering they were both sixteen but I guess when you know someone is your soulmate why wait. Lewis lives with his dad still to learn the alpha ropes. Lucas likes to live on his own and prefers to see his family only once a week during Sunday night dinner, which is tonight.

"Do you have sandwich meat? I can make myself a sandwich for dinner if I get hungry," I say. I stand up and go into the kitchen to check out what's in the fridge.

"What? Why? You are coming with me!" Lucas says following behind me closely.

I turn around and place my hands on my hips, eyeing him up. Does he really want me to go with him to a family dinner? Lucas crosses his arms and his muscles bulge out from his shirt.

"Are you sure? It's a family function, and I'm not family." My voice is quiet. Lucas's arms fall to his sides and he smiles at me. His dimples even poke in on both sides. He's so hot. Calm down Lyra, you are acting like a dog in heat.

"Of course, I'm sure. Mom came over while you were in the shower upstairs. She was cool with it when I asked her. Plus, I want you there," He says, stepping closer to me.

How am I supposed to keep away from him when he says such sweet things?

"Okay, I'll come. What should I wear?"

"What you are wearing now is fine. We don't dress up. I'm not changing." I look him over, he's wearing jeans and a black shirt. He looks me over from head to toe and looks back into my eyes. "You look beautiful. You could be wearing a brown sack and you would be perfect."

I know I'm blushing now. It's not just his words, it's the way he looks at me. I believe him when he says I'm perfect.

"Thanks. Though I wouldn't be caught dead in a brown sack, I don't look good in brown." We both laugh and go back into the living room to relax before dinner.

***

We decide to walk over to his parents' house, there's no point in driving when Lucas lives two houses down. Our hands occasionally brush against each other as we walk close together. I want to just reach out for his hand and hold it, but I can't risk it.

Lucas opens the door without knocking this time and we walk to the right, away from the living room, and into the kitchen which is one big room open to the dining room. It's black with red accents and everyone seems to be in here.

"You are here!" Lucas's mom, Kim, says giving Lucas a hug. She goes to hug me as well, but Lucas clears his throat. She looks at him in surprise then recognition lights her eyes, she turns to me and smiles instead. "Thank you for coming, Lyra."

"It's no problem, thank you for inviting me," I say smiling back at her. Could Lucas get any more perfect? He must have told her I don't like being touched and she respects that. It means so much to me that he made sure I would feel comfortable.

"Oh, I didn't invite you. I mean I would have but Lucas asked me if it was alright soon as I came over earlier. He wasn't taking no for an answer either," She says patting his cheek. Lucas ducks his head and I can just see a light blush coating his cheeks. Score! At least I'm not the only one who blushes between the two of us. "Now come on in. Dinner is just about ready."

Lucas lightly touches my arm and I feel a hot tingle almost instantly, and not from my power this time. I look at him and he nods his head over to Lewis and Julie, who are both standing near the dining room table talking quietly. I nod and we both walk over to join them, taking a seat beside each other. They both look up when we come over and smile, Julie sits across from me and Lewis across from Lucas.

"Hi, I know we didn't get the chance to really talk yesterday. I'm Julie," She says smiling at me. She reaches her hand out across the table for me to shake. I look at it for a second not sure if the same thing will happen to her as it has for the guys. I decide to risk it and shake her hand back. After a second, I feel the tingle in my hand and I release her, setting my hands in my lap. At least now I know it goes off for guys and girls. Lucas looks at me and drops his eyes to my hands but doesn't comment. Julie looks between the two of us curiously.

"She doesn't like to be touched, Julie. She's being polite by not telling you," Lucas says. Julie looks at me apologetically.

"It's okay, you didn't know," I say feeling awkward with the three of them looking at me.

"Hey, I can respect that. I don't like random people touching me either. Only Jules." This is the first time I've heard Lewis talk. His voice is just like him, very manly and bear-like.

"Thanks," I say wringing my hands together. Lucas starts asking them how the week has gone and different things about the pack. I appreciate him trying to take the focus off of me and try to follow along with the conversation though I have nothing to add to it. Soon enough, Kim and Jon walk over with plates of food in their hands placing them on the table.

"Can I help bring anything out?" I ask, standing from my chair. Lucas grabs my hand. I look down at him and our eyes lock. The rest of the room fades away and it's just the two of us. My hand feels hot from his touch and my heart beats faster. When I start to feel that familiar, bad tingle I pull my hand out from his and look around. Everyone is staring at us. I forgot they could hear my heart racing, this is embarrassing. I sit back down and fiddle with my hands in my lap, refusing to meet anyone's gaze.

"Sweet mom, I love chuck roast," Lewis says. He starts pulling off some meat and placing it on his plate. Everyone else turns to the food as well and ignores me. Except for Lucas. He glances over, and mouths *are you okay?* I smile and nod, grabbing food like everyone else.

The rest of the meal is spent chowing down and everyone talks. Their family dinner is lively, and I love that. It's what I've always wanted. I love my dad and we talk during dinner as well, but we usually eat together while watching tv and it's just the two of us. I imagine this is how our dinners would be if mom and Phoenix were still alive. All of us sitting together eating and talking. Laughter would fill the room. I get lost in my thoughts and it's not until Lucas touches my hand again that I realize I've just been sitting there staring down at my plate. No one else has seemed to notice, they are busy with each other. Lucas has a way of knowing when I'm inside my own head and needing help to get out. I look at him and for the first time I turn my hand over so it's holding his and I squeeze it. It's just for a second, not long enough to cause any harm, but it's enough to let him know I'm fine.

Dinner is delicious. Pot roast, mashed potatoes, green beans, and carrots. I could eat this every day. I manage to finish my whole plate since I skipped lunch today. I thank Kim for dinner before we head back home.

We don't talk much for the rest of the night. Lucas had some work to do in his office and I was pretty tired. I went out for a swim by myself and then went upstairs to get ready for bed. This time I wear a tank top and sleep shorts. I'm not making the same mistake of wearing nothing but a shirt and undies around Lucas again. Deciding to say goodnight, I walk over to his office door and knock.

"Come in Lyra." I open the door. The only light in the room is coming from the computer. Lucas doesn't even look up. I come up behind him and look over his shoulder. He's working on some type of sketch. "It's a new building in Charlotte. Well, not new. Technically, it's old but I'm making it look like new."

"I don't know exactly what I'm looking at, but it looks nice," I say looking at the lines.

"This is the outer wall. These designs here will be different office spaces and a break room goes here. This will be the front lobby with windows bringing in natural light," he says, pointing out different parts to me. I can see what he's envisioning, and it looks great. Done pointing out everything, he starts to draw a few more lines and I walk around the room, stopping at the bookshelf and checking out the titles in the dim light. The light flips on and I blink until my eyes adjust. Lucas comes over and leans against the shelf.

"See anything you like?" I look at him. I sure do see something I like. Pretty sure he doesn't mean what I'm thinking though. He smirks at me. Okay yeah, he did mean it like that. I shake my head and turn back to the books.

"They are mostly books on architecture. Not my favorite genre," I say with a smile.

"That's because you're looking at the wrong shelf. You'll want that one over there." He points to the other shelf. I go over there and take a look. Young adult fiction and books on Greek mythology.

"Do you really believe Apollo created the wolves?"

"There are a few other beliefs going around about us, but yeah that is the prominent one. I'm not sure what to believe. Whoever created us doesn't bother with us anymore."

I hum and grab a book about mythology.

"I didn't take you for a mythology girl," Lucas says with a soft smile.

"I'm normally not but I don't know much about wolves," I say. Or even about myself. Maybe there will be something in here that points to what my mother was.

"So far, that's the most accurate book I've found about wolves and other mystical creatures. Some I'm sure are real, others I'm not so sure of."

We stand in silence for a second, looking at each other. I feel that tension between us again and I want to reach out and touch him. His hair is falling gently over his forehead and his eyes smolder into mine. Being this close, I can see how sharp his jawline is underneath his stubble. I want to run my fingers over it and before I realize it, I'm doing it. My fingertips lightly prickle with the feel of his beard, not quite touching his skin.

Lucas closes his eyes and leans into my hand, breathing in deep. My fingers trace their way along his jaw and then drift up his cheek. He turns his head and kisses my hand, causing a zing of heat to flow into me. I have never wanted a man more before in my entire life. I want him more than I need to breathe. Just as he reaches to grab me, I snap out of it.

"Goodnight! I'll see you tomorrow," I practically yell, running out of the room and towards my bedroom. I lock the door just in case he decides to follow me. That could have gone too far. I can't risk his life like that. I need to put some distance between us but I'm not sure if I can.

Laying the book on my nightstand, I turn off the light and climb into bed. I hear Lucas's door shut across the hall, guess he is going to bed too. I wonder what he thinks about me constantly pulling away. Does he think I don't want him, or does he suspect there's something more to it? Rolling over I try to get my thoughts off Lucas and focus on other things. Like my dad not being here yet.

He should have been here by tonight. His fishing trip could have gone over, but I doubt it. Not with my birthday being this close. If he's not here by tomorrow, I don't know what I'm going to do. I'm not sure what's going to happen on my birthday Tuesday, but I want him here just in case. If Lynn is right, I'll come into my full powers.

Whatever those are.

Chapter 12

Lyra

I wake up early on Monday morning, just before five, and change into my purple bikini again. Reaching the living room, I see Lucas is sitting on the couch already dressed in his swim trunks. Without a word, he stands up and walks out the back door and I follow.

We swim in silence, neither of us wanting to mention last night and just how close we came to crossing the line between friends and more. I'm pretty sure the line has already been crossed though. With all the little touches and the heated looks; there is no way we are just friends anymore.

"What are we?" I ask. I can't believe I said that out loud. It's like I have no filter.

"What do you want us to be?" Lucas swims over to me so he can look into my face. His hair is wet and sticking to his face. He looks even better all wet. I search his blue eyes, not sure what to say.

"I don't know," I finally admit. "I have issues with being touched and I'm not sure if we can get past those issues."

"I know there is more to it than you are letting on. You've let me touch you before Lyra. It can't be that you don't like being touched, I see it in your eyes when I touch you. You like it. Your heart beats faster, your pupils dilate. You want me. So, what's the issue?" He sounds frustrated. His eyebrows are drawn together, and he tries to reach out to me. I swim backwards, away from him.

"I can't tell you," I whisper, trying not to cry. I want so badly to touch him, to kiss him, to be with him. It physically hurts me not to be close.

"Why not?" He asks, starting to yell. "What's so bad about us getting closer? You're into me and I'm into you. There's nothing more to think about."

"Lucas..." I whisper, he swims closer and I stay where I am, leaning against the pool edge. I look down into the clear water, thinking through my options. Lucas reaches his hand out and touches my chin, tilting it up so he can look into my eyes. My chin burns and heat spreads out into my whole face. I want to feel his touch on the rest of my body, starting with my lips. I need to kiss him. But I can't. "I'm sorry, I can't right now."

Turning around, I pull myself out of the pool and walk inside; leaving Lucas alone. I sprint through the house and up the stairs, slamming my bedroom door shut and jumping into the shower. The water feels cool against my heated skin, I let it fall around me, not bothering to wash my body just yet. Just letting myself relax. I strip out of my bikini and hang it over the shower rod, closing my eyes. My tears are covered by the water brushing my face. I almost kissed him, and it would have been all over. Even if I did manage to pull myself away, which I'm not sure I'll be able to, he will have to know something is up. Then I'll have to tell him everything and he might hate me after that.

Giving up on relaxing, I wash my hair and body and step out.

Dammit, no towel. I keep forgetting to ask Lucas for some and I'm certainly not going to ask him right now after we almost kissed. Walking into my bedroom I find a baggy sweatshirt of mine and wrap my hair inside it. I wipe down my body with another shirt then slip on a green shirt and loose white capris. I don't plan on going anywhere today until my dad gets here. Then I'm having him explain what I am and getting out of here.

At least that's my plan. I'm not sure I'll be able to leave Lucas. I know right now I have no control over myself and I'm dangerous to him, and others here, but I don't think I can leave him. He's too important to me now and I'm in too deep to let him go. Which is stupid, not only can I kill him, but his mate can appear at any time and then what? I'll just be tossed aside for the real love of his life. I'm not naïve enough to think he will choose me as a mate. Lucas deserves his perfect match, and that's not me.

Sitting down on my bed, I pick up the Greek mythology book and flip through the pages. There's a lot on different Gods and Goddess, I pass those up and go straight to mythological creatures. There are wolves, vampires, fairies, nymphs, sirens. The list goes on and on. I read a bit on wolves, it's pretty much what Lucas told me. They can transform whenever they like, they are not bound to the full moon. They have mates and they mate for life, occasionally after losing a mate they are able to move on and mate again; it doesn't happen often.

I read through the vampire section and find out there are different types of vampires. There are bloodsucking ones, energy ones, and ones called Empusae which are half woman, half snake and they literally eat people and suck their blood. Yikes.

Apparently, nymphs are the real deal and there are different types of them as well, some dwell in the water, others the trees and mountains. It's pretty cool to find out these are real. Some even have the powers of healing and seeing the future. Harpies look pretty cool as well. They are depicted as beautiful, fair women who have blue tattoos around their bodies. They are the living embodiment of wind and justice warriors. Harpies often find evildoers, particularly men who murder their children and deliver them to the Erinyes, the furies in the underworld, where they are then tortured for eternity. Sounds lovely.

Shutting the book, I lay down and sigh. The book was a nice distraction, but it got boring fast. I just have too much on my mind between Lucas, my dad still not being here, whatever it is I am, my birthday tomorrow. It's just too much. A tear slips down my cheek and I quickly wipe it away. I don't know why I'm crying, that's not going to help anything. Leaning back against my pillows, I shut my eyes thinking I might take a nap even though I'm not tired. There's a knock at my door.

"Lyra, can I come in?" Lucas says. I decide to not answer and pretend to be asleep. "I know you are awake, you can't fool a wolf. We won't talk about it... I promise."

"Fine." I don't bother sitting up, I know it's rude but I'm not the one who wants to talk. He is.

"I know you have a lot going on so why don't we get out of here later? I have some work to do first then maybe we can get lunch, hang around town, what do you think?" I look over at him. He's still wearing his swim trunks and no shirt; his arms are crossed over his chest and he looks delicious. Why can't I keep my mind out of the gutter around him?

"Like a date?" I ask. I know I shouldn't but I'm definitely teasing him. He smiles and leans against the door jamb.

"Exactly like that. If I promise not to touch you, will you promise to drop the hot and cold act? I never know if we are supposed to be flirting or avoiding each other." I think about it and decide what's the harm? We can have one day where we pretend to be a couple. We'll come back here, my dad will be waiting, and I'll get the answers I need. Maybe I'll get Lucas out of my system and we can both move on. Okay, yeah, that's a lie. I'll never be able to just move on that easily.

"We have a deal. No touching, flirting allowed. Yes, it's a date," I say smiling. Lucas grins and walks to the door.

"Sweet. I'll be back to pick you up at this door at noon," he says, almost closing the door behind him before he opens it back up and looks at me. "And I agree to not touch you, but if you touch me all bets are off."

He gives me a heated look, one full of promises I know he can keep, and shuts the door. Damn, I'm so screwed. Or I wish I was being screwed. Gah, I'm awful.

Wait, I don't have a clock in here to know when to be ready.

"Lucas!" I yell out, knowing he can hear me. I probably could whisper his name and he'd be in here. I hear his door open and he opens mine, popping his head in.

"Yes, my lady?" He asks, smiling sweetly.

"Your lady requires a clock. Who doesn't have little clocks on the nightstand in guest rooms?"

"Who doesn't have a cell phone to check the time themselves?" he teases.

"Someone who's on the run," I taunt back.

"Valid point. Hold on." he walks out and walks back in a few seconds later carrying an alarm clock. And he's in nothing but a towel. He plugs it into the wall and sits it on the side of my bed beside me setting the time.

"Um, not that I mind all the much. But why are you in a towel?" I ask staring at the planes of his back. Gosh, he's fit.

"I was just about to jump into the shower when you called my name. Would you have rathered I came in here naked? I can do that next time if you'd like."

The correct time set, he twists his body, so he's facing me now. He's so tempting being this close in nothing but a towel. My hands itch to yank it off and pull him on top of me.

"Lucas…" I whisper, eyeing his plump lips.

"Right, I'm out. I made a promise and I'm sticking to it. If I stay here any longer, that's going out the window," he says, standing up and walking out the door. "Be ready at noon baby."

He shuts the door as I stare dumbly at it. Baby? I kinda like it actually. We are in so much shit. If he only knew exactly who he was playing with.

***

Sliding my hands down my body, I look into the mirror one last time. I'm wearing a silver, flowy tunic tank top that has flower designs stitched throughout and black leggings that cut off just under my knee. My hair is hanging freely around my face and down my back; I'm letting my natural curl run free, and my makeup is simple. Just a smidgen of eyeliner and a deep purple-tinted lip gloss. I know this is a date, but I don't want to be someone else, I want Lucas to like me for me.

Right as I walk out of the bathroom, there's a knock on the door.

Grabbing my purse, I open the door to see Lucas leaning against the wall across from me. He cleans up good that's for sure. He's wearing his usual dark blue jeans and a sage green button up short-sleeve shirt, the top two buttons undone. His hair is combed back and to the side, so it's out of his face for once, and he trimmed his beard just a little so it's more of a stubble again. All in all, I still want him.

"You look amazing. You know how to tempt a guy from breaking his promise," He says looking me up and down. "You ready to go?"

"Yes." I go to walk out but he puts a hand up so I can't pass without touching him, I give him a look and he just smiles nodding down at my feet. My bare feet. Oops. I sheepishly walk back into my room and put on my gray flip flops. "Now you look ready."

I know he's teasing me but I'm not rising to the bait this time. I lead the way downstairs and walk outside. I forgot my car is behind his truck, guess I'm driving.

"You wanna move your car and park on the street? I want to drive," Lucas says, pleading with his eyes.

"Does my driving suck that bad?" I ask laughing, walking towards my car.

"No, but your car sucks. For an SUV it's tiny. I'd rather not hit my head whenever we go over a bump." I laugh at the pained expression on his face and move my car.

Walking back to his truck, I'm not sure how I'm going to get in it. It's a monster and I think he's had it lifted. I eye it like I would eye a horse, trying to make a plan of action. Lucas sees my expression and comes to stand beside me, holding his hands out.

"This won't count. I'm just helping you into the truck." I cautiously nod my agreement and he wraps his hands around my waist and sets me down in the truck. I'm no skinny stick either. God, everything he does makes me want to jump his bones. He shuts the door and runs around the truck, jumping inside and starting the engine. I quickly buckle before he backs out.

The drive is silent. The whole time I'm holding onto my seat for dear life. I can't believe I asked him if he thought my driving was scary. Man was that a joke! He has to be the worst driver in the world. He's speeding down the road by at least 20 over the limit.

"Can you slow down? You are going to get us killed," I say, hanging onto the oh shit bar when we take a turn.

"I'm a werewolf baby, I heal fast," He says, turning to look at me. He looks amused, he's gonna be amused when I kick him in his smug face.

"Not all of us have super healing, slow down please." Well. I could have it. I don't really know.

Thankfully he slows down as we get closer to town. He pulls into a restaurant and finds a spot right up front. He comes around again to help me down, and I accept his help this time; I know if I attempt to get down on my own, I'm going to fall flat on my face.

We walk inside the well-lit diner and are immediately seated by a pretty waitress who seems to know Lucas.

"How's it been? I haven't seen you around here for a while, how are your folks?" She asks, twirling her stupid blonde hair. Her name tag reads Kaley. Well, Kaley, I hate you.

"My parents are great. I just haven't found the time to come down here for a while, been busy," Lucas says, smiling at her. Yup, I hate her. It's official. She hands us our menus and asks what I want to drink, I guess she already knows what Lucas wants because she doesn't ask him. I order a Pepsi and glare at her retreating form.

"Damn. If looks could kill, she would be dead ten times over." I look at Lucas and he looks back at me startled. "Your eyes look different." I look down at my menu and blink a few times trying to calm myself. Miss Lynn's eyes did that freaky thing too. That's the last thing I need, freaking out my date. Lucas doesn't bother picking up his menu, he just continues to stare at me. I ignore him and pick out a cheeseburger with French fries.

"Why did you pick this place?" I ask. The waitress shows back up before he can answer and sets our drinks down. After she takes our orders, she tries to start up a conversation with Lucas and I glare at her again. This time she sees my stare and quickly walks away.

"Glad to know I'm not the only one who is possessive," Lucas jokes, smiling at me, he looks between my eyes for a second then shakes his head. "This is where my mom used to work before my dad came back here and swept her off her feet. This is where he decided she was his mate. We come here as a family every once in a while, thought it would be nice to take you here. Plus, Sylva doesn't have too many options on restaurants."

"I am not possessive!" I say loudly. I look around and cover my mouth, I can't believe I said that so loud. Geez, Lyra. Lucas looks amused. "Fine. Maybe a little. We are obviously on a date and she keeps giving you gaga eyes."

"I'm not interested in her, I'm here with you. I can't say much, if a guy was flirting with you, I'd probably punch him in the face." His eyes go dark, almost a black, I have never seen them do that before. I'm so used to seeing his eyes an ice blue. I guess all mystical creatures have eye changes. I reach out about to touch his hand to calm him, then think better of it and pull mine back and grab my soda instead. Sipping from the side, I watch Lucas over the edge of my cup. He's slowly trying to calm himself down, I can't believe he got so worked up over thinking about a guy flirting with me. I would hate to see how he would react if that actually happened.

"Sorry. You mean a lot to me Lyra. I can't stand the idea of another guy near you." His breathing has leveled out, and his fist relaxes on the table.

"I know what you mean Lucas. I about clawed Kaley's eyes out and thinking back she was probably just trying to be friendly," I say, setting down my drink.

"She's a year younger than me, we went to school together but didn't really hang out. She's never hit on me before. You have nothing to worry about, promise." He smiles so big his dimples show again. I love when he smiles, makes me forget all of my problems.

We talk for a few more minutes before our plates are sat down and Kaley quickly runs away again. She got the hint. I was so worked up earlier I didn't even hear what Lucas ordered, I look over at his plate and see a cheeseburger just like mine, the top bun is left off so you can add the toppings. He adds ketchup, mayo, lettuce, and tomato. Just how I take mine. I smile and dig into my burger. I look for the ranch to dip my fries in and remember I forgot to order it. Lucas has a large cup on his plate. I eye it and then smile sweetly at Lucas. He narrows his eyes, wondering what I'm up to. I sneak my hand across fast and grab it, he reaches down at the last second and wraps his hand around mine before I can swipe the ranch.

When our hands connect, the world fades away. It's just the two of us in our own little world. My hand is hot and tingly. I can feel his lust through our touch. I know given the chance he would throw me over this table and have his way with me. I also feel his love. I didn't expect that. I know he likes me sure, but love? That is surprising. What's even more surprising is I feel the same way, or at least I will soon. I'm falling in love with him and I can't seem to stop myself.

Lucas lets go of my hand right before I feel his soul start to come into me. I let go of his ranch and put my hands in my lap and stare down at them. I didn't let go of him myself. I almost hurt him. If he hadn't let go of my hand, this date would be totally over.

"Lyra, what's wrong?" Lucas asks me gently. I look up at him, the ranch has been moved between our plates so we can share. He's so perfect for me.

"I'll make you a deal," I say. "If we can just relax the rest of this date and enjoy ourselves, I'll tell you the truth when we get back to your place."

Lucas searches my eyes and nods, agreeing to my terms. I can't keep the truth from him any longer. It's too dangerous for him to not know and I care more about his safety than my own now. I just hope he won't hate me after I tell him.

We eat our food with light conversation for the rest of our meal. We don't go into anything too in depth, we stick with stories of our childhoods and our likes and dislikes. We have similar tastes in food, movies, and books. Lucas insists on paying for our meal and I let him this time since this is an actual date.

"Here are the keys," Lucas says handing them to me. "I'll wait in line to pay and then I have to go to the bathroom. I'll be out in a minute."

I nod and take the keys from his hand, our fingers brushing lightly. I walk out to his truck and beep the unlock button before I can make it there, I feel a gust of wind and suddenly I'm flying through the air.

My hair whips around my face and I can't see anything, I can feel the wind taking me somewhere and it bites against my skin. Something has the back of my shirt, causing a rip and I almost drop. I'm not in the air for long before I'm suddenly falling down to earth again. My back hits the ground and I hear a crunch. That's not good. A face leans over me, inspecting my body. Her blonde hair is stick straight and lightly touches my face. It's so light, I have to squint to see her eyes. They are a light blue and her face is pale except for the light blue designs swirling around it. Tattoos.

"I am Aella. By order of the council I have come to arrest you," she says. Her voice sounds like music and flows over me.

"Arrest," I wheeze out, "I didn't do anything wrong." I try to sit up through the pain in my back and succeed. Aella is now squatting in front of me. It's not just her face covered in blue tattoos, but her entire body. She's wearing a blue, flowy Grecian style dress that hits above her knees.

"I don't know the specifics of what you have done, I'm just doing my job. The council demands your presence and I will take you."

"And if I refuse?" I say, glaring into her eyes. I'm gearing up for a fight, I won't be taken easily.

"You are wanted alive or dead. It matters not to me."

I swing my fist at her face, and she recoils back. Her body transforms in front of my eyes. Instead of the beautiful woman, there is now a half bird, half-human creature. Her body has sprouted blue feathers almost everywhere, her face remains that of a human, but I can see the beginning of feathers peeking out above her neckline. Her arms remain human, but her fingernails elongate like claws. Her legs are entirely bird like but thick like a humans would be.

Remembering the little cylinder Miss Lynn gave me, I reach into my purse and pull it out. I know she said it shouldn't work until my birthday but a day away might be enough. I grasp it in my hand like a weapon and will it to do something, anything. It remains a thin, cylinder. Damn. Holding it in my hand still, I stand up and run. She screeches loudly behind me and I hear her take off into the air.

She dropped me right on the edge of the forests, perfect. I take to the trees hoping they will cover me from above and make it harder for her to get me. I race through and finally stop, leaning against a tree and trying to quiet my breathing. My back aches. The forest sounds quiet, not a single animal is around me. I look up into the leaves but see nothing. Maybe I lost her?

I hear a sound to my left and my head whips over. Pain erupts from my left arm and I scream. Her claws are sunk deep into my bicep.

"You shouldn't run from me Lyra. I will find you," She says, her claws sliding out of my arm as she faces me. "There is nowhere for you to hide and your wolf won't get here in time. Come with me quietly and I'll spare your life."

My body reacts without thinking. My left leg swipes out and knocks her legs out from under her, she falls flat on the ground and looks up at me surprised. I bring my right hand down onto her stomach, the cylinder clenched in my grasp activates and becomes a long, black sword. It stabs her right through.

Her mouth opens and her eyes widen in shock. I twist the blade inside before I crumble down onto my knees. Suddenly I can't breathe anymore, it's like the air has been sucked right out of my lungs. My hands reach up, releasing my sword, and I grasp my throat as I look around wildly.

Aella is bleeding profusely from her wound but has a wicked smile on her face. Whatever is happening to me, she is doing.

Black spots dance around my vision and I fall backwards. The last thing I see is the trees above me, gently swaying in the wind.

Chapter 13

Lucas

I hand Lyra the keys and step in line, waiting to pay our bill. Turning around, I watch her walk out the door. Damn, she is fine. I can't stop myself from checking out her ass in those black leggings and traveling upward to her silver tank top. She looks amazing from behind but even better from the front. The silver top really brings out her eyes and makes them sparkle. I love that she didn't put on a lot of makeup, she doesn't need it and I'd rather see her real face. She walks just out of view and I turn around facing the front again.

The date had been great, and she seemed to really enjoy herself when she let go of whatever was holding her back. Hopefully, she will tell me today and we can work through whatever it is. We are mates and I'm not giving up on her.

Finally, I step up and pay our bill. I leave a hefty tip for Kaley; I know she deserves it after the looks Lyra gave her and decide not to go to the bathroom now. With the way I drive, I'll be home in no time. I feel antsy and scared leaving Lyra alone.

Walking out of the restaurant, I head towards my truck and stop in my tracks. A harpy is taking off in the air with Lyra in her clutches.

Without thinking, I shift into my wolf form and take off after them. The harpy has an advantage though and can fly over obstacles; I have to run around them. Breathing in her scent, I follow her through smell instead of sight.

I run through the woods tracking them, trying to be quiet; I don't want her knowing I'm on her so fast. While running, I send my pack a message, *"Need help in the east woods. A harpy is attacking Lyra."* I send it out and hear a few replies from the wolves on patrol. They will get my dad and brother. I doubt I will need them but just in case I want them here. After a few minutes of running, I find their scent in the trees. Maybe Lyra has gotten away and found shelter. I rush through the clearing and follow their scent.

From a distance, I can see the harpy on the ground and Lyra is above her with a glowing black sword, she plunges it into the harpy's stomach. Even knowing Lyra is in danger, I can't help but find her strength hot. Running forward, I'm almost to them when Lyra grasps her throat with her hands and falls to her knees. I push my legs to run faster but it's not fast enough, she collapses on the ground before I can reach her.

The harpy is trying to sit up now and I latch onto one of her legs with my teeth, sinking them through her flesh. Her blood tastes disgusting, but I hang on and shake my head tearing her muscle apart and grinding my teeth into her bone. She shrieks and tries to claw at me with her hands, but I dodge out of the way at the last second. I know her claws are dangerous, and I can't risk being put down by those when I need to protect Lyra.

I jump on top of Lyra, shielding her with my body, and face the harpy down. Her leg and stomach are both bleeding profusely, and I know she can't put up a fight against me. I hear more wolves coming in the distance too. She is no match for us, and she knows it.

"She's dangerous, wolf. You don't know who you are protecting," She says, backing away. I growl at her. I don't care what Lyra is, she is mine. I snap my teeth together and let her know if she comes closer, I'll tear into her. Harpies are immortal but they can feel pain just like the rest of us and have their limits.

"Don't worry, I'm done. I won't be the only one the council sends. They will get to her and you can't fight them all." With her words ringing in my ears, she takes off on the wind just as my pack bursts through the trees. The danger gone, I turn to Lyra and check on her.

She's breathing, but it's shallow. Her arm is torn to shreds and her blood is black, poisoned. I shift to my human form and tentatively pick her up, not caring about my nakedness.

"I'm taking her directly to my dad's house, search the woods. Make sure the harpy is gone and nothing else is lurking around here. I need someone to get my truck from Lulu's diner as well and drive it to my house," I say to the pack, my eyes trained on the unconscious girl in my arms. I know they will follow my orders, I might not be next in line to be alpha, but I am to be listened to.

Lyra barely weighs anything in my arms as I carry her through the woods as fast as I can. I can't lose her now that I've found her. She means so much to me already and I can't imagine living the rest of my life without her. She's my mate, even if we haven't fully mated yet. It's too late for me to choose someone else. Lyra is it for me and if I lose her... I'll die too.

Chapter 14

Lyra

My whole body aches and my mouth is parched, my tongue sticks to the roof of my mouth. Eyes feel too heavy to lift. I think back to what I last remember. I was on a date with Lucas; we had a great time… What happened after that? I try thinking harder and remember going out to the truck alone and… who the hell was that? I remember the half bird, half human woman who took me. We fought in the forest and I stabbed her in the stomach with that cylinder thingy I got from Miss Lynn. Then I remember her sucking the air out of my lungs and suffocating me. My eyes spring open.

Where am I? I'm in a bedroom of some sort, but I haven't been here before. I try to lift my head up and look around, but it hurts too much. I groan.

"Lyra?" I know that voice, that's Lucas.

"Lucas…" I whisper. He rushes into my line of vision. His eyes are bloodshot, and his hair is more of a mess than usual; it sticks up at all angles. "What happened to you? You look awful."

"I look… Are you serious right now? You were attacked by a freaking Harpy! And I look awful? She tore open your bicep and ripped your muscles to shreds. Then knocked you unconscious.

If I hadn't shown up when I did, she would have killed you or taken you far away. Gosh, I could have lost you." His eyes are filled with tears.

I find the strength to sit up in bed and I grab Lucas into a hug with my good arm. I know it's risky, but he needs me right now and I need him too. He holds me so tight that it hurts my back a little, but I say nothing. We slowly pull apart and look into each other's eyes. I know it's wrong, but I can't stop myself, I lean forward and press my lips to his.

My world explodes. Our lips move in sync and mine feel so hot. Heat races up and down my spine, my right-hand tangles in his hair and I pull him closer. I can't get enough of him. I don't even notice when the kiss changes, becoming something different. I don't even feel the tingle spreading from my lips and down into my body; the one that means I'm taking his soul into me. His hands are in my hair, trailing down the nape of my neck, and I can't think straight. I'm so full of energy now that I forget the pain in my body. All I need is more of Lucas... and his soul. I rip myself away and push him off. What was I doing?

Lucas looks at me with lust, his eyes are completely dazed and unfocused. He takes a step toward me, wanting to continue where we left off. His body moves like a predator, and I'm his prey.

"Lucas, no. We can't," I say, trying to scoot further up the bed.

"I need more," He says, walking towards me again. I try to kick at his body, but he doesn't stop.

"Help!" I yell at the top of my lungs. Hopefully, someone is nearby. Lucas isn't thinking straight. His hands grasp my ankle and he pulls me farther down the bed, his warm body settles over mine. Squeezing my eyes shut and my fists together, I try to put as much space between us as possible.

The door burst open, Lewis and Jon rush inside. Seeing me terrified on the bed and Lucas on top of me, they grab onto him and tug him off. His mom and Julie run in right after them and come towards me trying to calm me.

"Don't hurt him, it's not his fault," I sob. How could I let this happen?

"Hunny, it's not your fault. You aren't ready yet for the mate bond and that's okay. He rushed things," Kim says soothingly, glaring at Lucas.

"Mate bond? What are you talking about?" I ask. This is all so confusing. I'm not Lucas's mate. Lucas struggles against his dad and brother, eyes still locked on mine. Slowly he stops struggling as much and clarity comes into his eyes again.

"What happened?" His dad asks. Lucas just shakes his head, refusing to look at anyone now. His gaze on the floor.

"It's me. I'm what happened." I can't stop crying. I almost killed Lucas.

"I couldn't control myself Lyra. It's not your fault," Lucas says, not understanding. He blames himself for having no control. Why is no one listening to me?

"Are you not hearing me? It's my freaking fault!" I scream. "This has happened before."

Everyone turns to look at me now. Finally, they are listening. I tuck my legs underneath me and wrap my good arm around my body, needing to support myself.

"What's happened before?" Kim says, reaching out to touch me. I shy away from her. I don't need to do this to someone else.

"Don't touch me. That's how it happens." My eyes are tearing up again. I look at Lucas and he looks so confused. Lewis and Jon have released him from their hold but are sticking close just in case.

"Explain," Lewis says gruffly.

"It started the night of the party," I say as I lick my lips. It's time I told them everything. "Before that, I thought I was normal. I spilled a drink on myself and went inside to clean it up, my friend Ryan followed me."

"The boyfriend of the witch who threatened you?" Lucas asks.

"He wasn't her boyfriend," I whisper, closing my eyes. "He was just my friend. One second he's flirting with me and I'm about to tell him off and the next he was kissing me. I wasn't into him at all, but I felt this energy flow through me and I wanted more of that."

"Energy, what type of energy?" Julie speaks up for the first time, I look over at her and she looks confused.

"I didn't know what it was then. It made me feel incredible. Like I could do anything. Ann, her brother Justin and my friend Mira came inside then. They broke us apart and Mira ran away, she really liked Ryan. Ann looked furious and Justin grabbed Ryan and took him outside. Ryan was the same way as Lucas, almost uncontrollable. Ann then threatened me, told me I was dangerous and that I almost killed Ryan."

"How could you have almost killed him?" Lucas says.

"I didn't know. I didn't understand what was going on. Ann told me she was calling the council and if it wasn't for Ryan, she wouldn't be letting me get a head start."

"The council?" Lucas's dad looks intrigued and takes a step closer to me. "Not many people believe in the council anymore. They are a bunch of different mystical creatures who claim to work for the Gods. Why would she call them on you? You are human."

"I'm not," I whisper, looking down at the bedspread. "I ran away after Ann almost killed me and gave me her warning. I went to my neighbor's house, Miss Lynn's. I didn't know where else to go and I trusted her. She told me about the mystical world and told me I was different, special. That I took more after my mom than my dad, a hybrid."

"There is no such thing as hybrids. When two different species mate, the child will be one thing or the other. Species don't intermix and make hybrids." Jon seems so sure of himself, confident in his answer like he's reading it from a textbook. I hate to burst his bubble.

"Well, apparently they do. Whatever my mom was, I am too, but it's different with me. I'm not fully like her. My powers will be different from hers."

"What was your mom?" asks Lucas.

"I don't know. Lynn wouldn't tell me. Whatever she was, Lynn is. She admitted that much and said it was dangerous for me to know any more. Told me to come here and not tell the whole truth. She didn't trust you guys, but my dad did. He wanted to bring me up here for my eighteenth birthday to let my powers come, whatever they will be. He trusted you enough to protect us during that time. I hated lying to you all, especially you Lucas, but I didn't know if I could trust you at first. I thought my dad would be here soon after me and he would explain everything."

"So, she didn't tell you why the council was coming after you?" Jon says.

"No, she didn't. Ryan did. When I was leaving town, he stopped me and told me what happened. I…. I almost took his soul," I whisper, a tear falling from my eye.

"His soul?" Lucas says. I nod, looking down again and wiping my face. I can't face them. Now that they know the truth.

"I've never heard of anything being able to take someone's soul before. That's new," Jon says. "How does it happen?"

"When I touch someone. It doesn't happen right away, but the longer I touch someone the more I feel it. It's like a tingle that starts where our skin is touching. I can feel their soul, who they are as a person and then it will just flow into me. If I break off contact fast enough, nothing happens but if we touch for too long and then separate, the person acts a little crazy afterwards. Whatever I'm doing, they feel a rush of euphoria and want more of it as well. It's hard for me to pull away too. Each time has gotten worse for me. Eventually, someone is going to touch me and I'm going to kill them without meaning to."

"Does it just work on wolves? How often has this happened?" Jon asks. Hmm, I've never thought of that.

"Only the one time with Ryan and then with Lucas."

"So, it could just be wolves or just males. We should test it out, see exactly what limitations you have," Jon says, looking over at

Kim. She nods at him and comes closer to me and I shrink back.

"No way! I'm not intentionally going to try to hurt someone," I say, tucking my arm against me. No way in hell am I doing this.

"Lyra, it's okay," Kim says, smiling at me. Her eyes crinkles and a dimple pops out on one cheek. So that's where Lucas got his dimples. "We are in a room full of wolves, all of which can easily pull me away from you. It'll be fine."

I look around the room and everyone looks back. They seem a little apprehensive, but overall not scared that I'm going to kill Kim. Hesitant, I reach out my good hand and lay it on Kim's arm. Immediately I feel at home and I want to laugh. Her soul is motherly and energetic, it makes me want to curl up on a couch and snuggle with her while she reads me a story. Amazingly, Kim isn't scared at all. All I feel from her is complete trust and love. My hand begins to tingle, and I look up at Jon, nodding my head letting him know I feel it. Her soul starts to flow into me and I rip my hand away from her, putting some distance between us as Jon comes up behind her and lifts her away.

"It works on females and on humans. Good to know," Jon says, placing his wife down beside him. She leans against him in a daze and her eyes dreamily watch me.

I curl my legs up so my head rests on my knees and I sob. No one says a word. They know I'm dangerous now and will kick me out. I'll be all alone.

"Lyra," Lucas says. I don't look up. I can't see his face when he tells me to go. I feel a weight shift on the bed and then someone sits down beside me. I feel a touch on my arm, and I jerk upward. "No. We can touch a little. Just tell me when it's too much. Don't pull away from me now. Please."

I let Lucas touch me for a few more seconds, allowing his touch to soothe me. A burning sensation rushes through my body, not unpleasant and not anything to be alarmed at; it's unlike the tingle I feel when I'm taking someone's soul. This touch feels like warmth and home, of everything I want in life.

"Okay, now." He lets go but remains seated beside me.

"We'll figure this out Lyra, I promise." His eyes are pleading with me. I don't understand why he won't just give up on me.

"Why? Why put this much effort into me, Lucas? I could have killed you when we kissed earlier. I need to leave," I say, trying to get off the bed but I can't. My left arm doesn't move and moving my legs makes my back ache even more. I untuck them from under me and stretch them out; they feel sluggish and heavy now that I can actually focus on them.

"Lyra... I didn't tell you this before because I wanted you to get to know me first. You are my mate." I look at Lucas, trying to tell if he is serious. He is. Well, this makes so much more sense. "And you aren't going anywhere, except to see a Nymph to be healed."

"What?" I ask.

"Harpies are dangerous, their claws are poisoned. You need to be healed by a water nymph," Jon says, coming up behind Lucas and laying his hand on his shoulder. "We will get you to one and protect you from the council Lyra. You are Lucas's mate and are now family. We will have to figure out what you are somehow. Your dad isn't here and if that witch did call the council, there's a good chance they might have him. Lucas, wrap her up in the blanket carefully and carry her downstairs. Try not to touch her skin." Lucas nods and tucks the blanket around me before lifting me in his arms. He's careful not to touch me. Everyone files out of the room before us and Lucas stops before we reach the doorway, leaving us alone.

"Can I try something?" I nod and he leans down slowly, allowing me to pull back if I want to. I stay perfectly still as he gently presses his lips to mine. My mouth heats and I want more, but he pulls back fast. The kiss is short and sweet, not long enough for me to start pulling out his soul. He smiles at me, his face relaxing. "I know this is all new for you, it is for me too. We'll make it work. I'm not giving up on you."

"Okay." I say, snuggling into his shirt. It smells like him and I breathe in deeply. He walks down the stairs, following everyone out the door.

"We'll have to head to Tuckasegee River, it's the closest water source that I know has nymphs for sure. Lewis, you drive your truck. Lucas can lay in the back with Lyra. I'll drive behind you and make sure that Harpy doesn't come back."

Everyone agrees and Kim grabs some blankets to make the bed of the truck comfortable for me. She is so sweet. Lucas continues holding me until the truck is ready for us, then lays me down gently before climbing in with me. Despite all the extra cushioning back here, I already know this ride is going to suck.

***

I was right. The ride there did suck, but at least Lucas held onto me the whole time, while I was wrapped in a blanket obviously. It took longer than I expected, I thought the river was in the next town over, but we had to go to a spot that's unpopulated. In today's day and age, that's hard to get to. By the time we park the truck, I'm starting to sweat, and it has nothing to do with the blanket surrounding me. I can feel the poison working its way through my arm now and slowly moving throughout my body. I try not to let it show but Lucas knows something is wrong.

"We need to hurry," he says to his brother as he climbs down the tailgate and pulls me farther down. I can no longer move my legs at all to help. He easily picks me up and we start the long walk through the woods. I have no clue where we are going but I trust them to get us where we need to be.

Lucas's parents lead the way, Lucas walks in the middle and his brother and Julie bring up the rear. It's nice knowing so many people have my back.

I still can't believe I'm Lucas's mate. The thought never even crossed my mind. I mean, I knew we had a connection, and we were obviously very attracted to each other, I just didn't expect this. I sigh in contentment. Even if I do die today, I'll die knowing I found my soulmate. Now that I know it's true, so many things make sense now. All the dreams I've had most of my life suddenly come back to me. Lucas was in them all. It had always been him. We were destined to be together from the beginning. The thought fills me with joy.

"What are you smiling about?" Lucas whispers near my ear. I don't know why he bothers trying to keep quiet, everyone can hear us anyway.

"Did you have dreams of me before we met?" I ask.

"Actually yes," he says, looking down at me while stepping over a fallen log. Damn, he has good coordination. "I told you, sometimes wolves can see their mates in dreams, that's why some will search for a long time. They've seen their mates in dreams and it makes it harder for them to move on. It's not common and usually only happens when both mates are wolves. Did you have dreams of me? I know I saw you, but I wasn't sure if they went through to you or not."

"I did, but I never remembered your face when I woke up. Knowing we are mates now, I can look back on them and see your face clearly. It's always been you. My best friend thought I was weird when I told her I had dreams of my soulmate." Lucas laughs at me.

"Yeah, that's enough for them to think you are crazy. It's a big deal for wolves when we have those dreams. It means our connection is extremely deep. That's why it feels like we've already known each other for so long, technically we've been meeting for years. Our souls know each other on a whole different level."

"Okay, now you sound like a hopeless romantic." We both laugh, causing my arm to hurt. Lucas notices my flinch and walks faster. "How long does it take the poison to work?"

"Long. Harpies are meant to take criminals, mainly murderers, to the underworld where they will suffer for eternity. They don't want the pain over fast, the poison is just the beginning." Lucas hesitates to finish.

"Tell me. I need to know." I say, watching the trees go by fast. Wolves are fast walkers.

"You don't need to know because you're getting healed. But I'll tell you, anyway. The poison works its way through the victim's body, slowly paralyzing them. Then they will feel like a bird is pecking at every inch of their skin, its excruciating. They will start to hallucinate various things if they have any love ones it's usually visions of their death and torture. Finally, they arrive in hell and pretty much spend eternity like that and some. Basically, don't murder people," he says with a small laugh.

"How can you joke about that? It sounds awful," I say, my body giving a little shiver imagining it.

"I know I won't be going there, that's how. Now relax. You need your rest, trust me. Healing you won't be a walk in the park." I was afraid of that. I figured taking a walk through the woods and asking a nymph to heal me sounded too easy.

The rest of the walk is made in silence. The poison is into my chest now and I can no longer feel my left arm at all; I'm not even sure it's still there.

Finally, we come upon the river. It's moving at a fast pace and I can't keep track of it. I look around, wondering how exactly we are going to find the nymphs.

"We come in peace. Let us see," Jon says from the front. It's quiet for a second, then I hear giggling. The water no longer sounds like crashing waves, it now sounds like soft music, flowing through the forest. I see them now, the nymphs. Five naked women are dancing around the water. All of them are beautiful but there's something about them that sets me off.

"Won't you come join us?" The closest one asks. Her hair is so black you can see a blue sheen to it, her skin as pale as snow. "Come," She says, crooking her finger. There's a seductive tone to her voice that almost makes me want to follow her. Almost being the keyword.

"We won't be seduced by you. We need your help. She has been poisoned by a harpy," Jon says, moving his arm behind him to indicate me.

"What a pity. You look delicious. I'd love a night with you," says the nymph, looking at Lucas. I want to tell her off, but no words come out of my mouth; my body is in too much pain to speak anymore. "I am Shaya and lucky for you, I'm the healer. Bring her to me, set her injury in the water."

Lucas steps forward and gently unravels the blanket before setting me down at the bank. My left arm is laying in the water, but I feel nothing. I look down at it, the water rushes past it but I don't even feel the coolness I expect. Lucas sits down beside me and moves some hair out of my eyes. He rests his palm against my cheek and kisses me once, not lingering. He's careful not to touch me for too long but stays beside me while the nymph glides over.

"Mates. How sweet. Are you sure you wish to stay here wolf? She has to undergo a test and it will be hard for you to watch," she says, laying her hands upon my arm, under the water. I hope I don't hurt her, there's no way to know when I can't feel anything.

"I'll stay with her," Lucas confirms with a nod, not moving from his spot.

"Then I'll begin," Shaya says, moving her hands up and down my arm. "You are different from any creature I have seen before. You have darkness in you. You might fail the test."

"What is the test? I thought you could heal me?" I whisper, my voice too weak.

"The poison cannot be healed. Once it's inside someone, they must go through it. I simply speed it up to the end where it decides if you are deserving of relief, or more pain. Most who undergo this are sentenced to a life of suffering. If you are truly evil, there will be no helping you."

"Lyra isn't evil," Lucas says defensively.

"Calm yourself wolf. I did not say she was. It is not up to me to decide, the poison does. There is no way of stopping it. If I leave her be, she will suffer for a few days before the test is upon her. Or I can speed it up now. The choice is yours."

"Do it," I plead. This is a good way to know if I'm evil. If I am, then I'll suffer forever but Lucas will be safe from me. And if I'm not, then I'll know for sure I can control myself one day and not hurt him. Shaya looks at me and smiles.

"You are a brave one, I'll give you that. You are not scared of dying. I wish you well," she says before she places a hand on my forehead and the world goes dark.

I'm floating. I see nothing and hear nothing. I no longer exist. There's no Lucas. My dad is gone. It's just me. And who am I anyway? I am no one.

Pain surrounds me and I scream. So much pain. It feels like my skin is peeling off. I need it to end. There has to be a way to stop this. I feel myself convulse. I can't take this anymore.

There's a way.

Where did that voice come from?

I am you. You know how to end it Lyra. You need energy to survive this. You need to feed.

Anything. I'll do anything for this pain to stop. Please tell me what to do.

Blood pours from my mouth. So much blood. My body convulses again. A man appears in front of me, his black hair and ice-blue eyes draw me in. He looks familiar to me and his name whispers through my head, *Lucas.*

"Lyra do it. You need my soul. Take it and this will all stop. Please baby. I need you to live," Lucas says. He comes closer to me and puts his neck to my mouth.

I have no clue what he's asking me to do. I can't focus on anything else but the pain.

You know what to do Lyra. Feed on him. Take his blood and his soul. Save yourself. You will be free.

That's it? I just bite him, and the pain goes away? I lean forward, my teeth naturally elongating. I can do this.

Wait. This is *Lucas*. He's the love of my life. If I do this, I'll be killing him. His soul will be gone. I... no. I won't do it.

I press my lips together and refuse to go near him. I bite my tongue and blood fills my mouth.

Lucas disappears and in his place is an older woman, I barely recognize her as Miss Lynn.

"Take me Lyra. It's ok. You need to live, and this is the only way. I've lived a full and happy life. I'm ready to die. Please."

This isn't Lucas. Lynn is in her eighties. She can die any day now or I can kill her and save myself. My mouth opens and I go to bite her but stop myself. What am I doing? This is Lynn! What does it matter if she's going to die soon? No one's life is worth my own.

The pain intensifies and I'm tempted to bite down, but I hold myself back. I won't be a killer. I can die now, I can suffer through this, but no one will die for me. I bring my right arm up and I sink my teeth into it. I will bite myself before I kill anyone.

The pain is gone.

I'm looking up at the sky, the clouds move slowly, no place for them to be. The sound of running water rushes past my ears. My body hurts even more now than before but the poison is gone now.

"She passed," Shaya whispers, astonished.

"Thank God." Lucas. He's here. I try to turn my head to look at him, but I can't. I try to speak but my tongue is hurt, I must have really bitten my tongue. I groan instead.

"It will take you some time to heal. You had multiple seizures, biting your tongue and your arm. The water is healing you now, just relax." Shaya is right. I feel the water washing away my pain. I'm now floating in it. "I have never seen someone pass the test before. I am impressed."

"What? No one has passed? I thought you had helped people from this before," Jon says. He sounds far away.

"Yes, I have. People have been brought to me before and I helped them to the test. But no one has ever passed, at least not that I've seen. Lyra is strong indeed. The test makes you put your life above others you care about. If you choose to save yourself, you fail. If you choose to save the life of your loved ones, you pass. I imagine she saw you, Lucas. She put your life above her own. You are lucky to have a woman like her," she says, looking down at me now and gently touches my face. I feel that familiar tingle where she touches me, and she pulls her hand away fast. "You are different indeed. You might have been created by darkness but that does not have to define you, Lyra. Keep fighting it. Rest now. You need your sleep."

She's right. My eyelids are so heavy. My body feels better now but I'm exhausted. I'll take a little nap. Just a small one. Then I'll ask her what she means about me fighting the darkness. Maybe she knows what I am. First, I'll close my eyes.

Chapter 15

Lyra

I wake up so warm. Too warm. My skin feels like it's burning. Maybe I imagined going to the nymphs and being healed. I could have imagined it all and still be poisoned in the bed or I could have failed the test and be suffering for eternity. I can barely peel my eyes open to look at my surroundings. I'm back in my bedroom at Lucas's, tucked in bed. I try to move my arms to push the covers off, but they are so heavy. Giving up, I look out the window trying to tell what time it is. It's dark outside, so either late night or early morning.

"Lucas," I barely whisper. My mouth is parched. Hearing nothing, I try to wet my mouth and clear my throat. "Lucas." Well, that's not much louder. If he's sleeping, he might not be able to hear me calling out.

I have to do this myself. I focus all my effort onto my right arm and shove off the heavy blanket. I try to sit up and fall back down on the bed. Damn. How am I going to get out of this situation? Deciding my best bet is to make as much noise as possible I start banging my fist on the bed since that is the only part of my body I can move at the moment.

Still, I hear nothing in the house. Lucas must be out cold or not here. That would suck if I put all this effort into making a noise to wake him up and he's not even here. I wiggle my toes then my feet. They feel heavy as well. I need to get out from under the blanket before I burn up. Knowing this is going to hurt, I roll off the bed and onto the floor with a thump. Ouch. I hear rapid footsteps and a door is thrown open in the house, I assume Lucas's door. My door bursts open a second later and Lucas rushes in. Naked. How I manage to notice that when I feel like I'm on fire, I will never know.

"What's going on? Are you okay?" He says, falling down to the floor beside me and touches my arm. I can't even feel the normal tingles right now or the heat that usually accompanies his touch. I'm so hot. "You have a fever! When did you wake up?"

I wet my lips, trying to focus on his voice. It's so hard to focus, the room is spinning and I'm so tired.

"Water..." I finally breathe out. Lucas jumps up and runs out of the room. I hear him go into his room first before heading downstairs. I can hear him talking all the way from up here.

"I need you guys here. Lyra has a fever." He pauses and I hear a cabinet door open and shut, then the sound of water filling a glass. "Yea bring Julie. She might be of help." There's another pause and I can hear Lucas walking through the downstairs now. "No mom you don't have to come. Okay fine. Bring everyone, I don't care. Just get here now."

It's silent now, he must have hung up the phone. He walks up the stairs and into my room. Sitting down on the floor, he leans over and puts a straw to my lips. The water feels amazing going down my throat. He pulls it away and rests the back of his hand against my forehead briefly. *At least he's wearing pants now*, I think randomly.

"You are burning up. What happened baby?" He asks.

"I don't know. I woke up so hot. I could barely move anything, it took all my effort just to roll out of bed." My voice is barely a whisper. It's a good thing wolves have excellent hearing.

"Why did you roll out?" He asks as I hear talking outside. I twist my head towards the door expecting to see them come in, but they don't. Why are they standing outside the door talking? "Lyra, can you hear all that?"

"Yes," I answer, nodding my head. Can't he hear them too? A minute later his family walks into the room, all in various states of dress. Normally, this room is actually pretty big, but with everyone in here at once, the room is small. It suffocates me now and I can barely breathe.

"She's going to shift," Lucas says, looking up at his family. They all look at him, astonished. "Lyra take deep breaths and I'll get you outside."

He picks me up in his arms, I try to protest him touching me but no words escape my mouth. What if I start to hurt him? But my body doesn't even try to pull his soul. It's too hot and I want him to stop touching me. I try to wiggle out of his arms, but he holds me tightly.

"Are you sure?" His dad asks, following behind us.

"Yes. Her fever is too high, and her senses have increased. She heard you guys talking outside before you even came in." He looks between his family and then his eyes lower to me, giving me his full focus. "Lyra, I know it's uncomfortable, me touching you. Just try to hold on a few more seconds," he says. We've reached the back door now, and he walks across the yard. My eyes close for a minute, trying to breathe in the fresh air. He eventually sets me down on grass and stands a few feet away, giving me space. The earth below me is firm, and the air is cool against my skin, but it doesn't cool me down; I just seem to get hotter. I try to move my arms to rip off my clothes, but I can't move them.

"Don't worry about them Lyra. Focus on your arms and legs, just let them relax as much as you can. The more you fight the shift, the heavier and tighter everything will feel," Lucas says. Easier said than done. I try to calm my body and just relax. I open my eyes and look up at the stars, focusing on them. Nothing happens for a while. Then the pain starts in my limbs, they start spasming. I cry out and arch my back.

"That's it. Focus on your wolf. See her in your mind and become her. It will make the transition easier," Jon says. He sounds close but when I open my eyes, he's leaning against a tree with the rest of the family just behind him. Kim isn't with them, she must have stayed back at the house. My mind wonders how he's against a tree, but Lucas's back yard doesn't have any. I shake the thoughts away and roll my eyes closed, trying to visualize my wolf.

I don't see it at first, then it's like my mind expands. I'm no longer just Lyra- I'm so much more. I see a variety of animals in my mind's eye. There's a bear, a squirrel, a black snake and more. Almost any animal I can think of pops up. Finally, a see a beautiful red wolf, the same color as my hair. She has gray eyes just like me and her tongues licks out. I smile; this is my wolf. In my mind, I reach out to her and touch her nose. The wetness against my palm calms me, even as my body gets hotter.

I almost consider opening my eyes to check if I'm on fire, but I can't open them. My muscles spasm and I roll onto my stomach letting my body shift. My limbs shrink and contract, bones break and reform. My face burns and I feel it changing shape beneath my skin, ripping it as it expands out and new skin grows in its place. Teeth aching and elongating. I have never felt such pain before in my life. Then it stops just as suddenly as it began.

I'm on all fours and my hair bristles, I'm not alone. Jumping around I growl at the man closest to me without thought and he stands his ground, speaking to me. I can't focus on the words though. I prowl closer and he squats down, making himself eye level with me. The others call him back, but he ignores them, focusing on me. He's brave, I could kill him in less than three seconds if I wanted but I stop and look into his eyes. They are ice blue and something about them prickles at the back of my mind. He's important to me.

I stop growling and cock my head, assessing him. Trying to place his importance.

Lucas.

This is Lucas I'm looking at. I shake my head and I remember I'm not just a wolf. I'm a human girl who loves this man. I sit back on my rump and wait for him to come closer. He slowly moves down onto his hands and knees and crawls forward. When he's close enough, I lick his face from bottom to top.

"Thanks," He says sarcastically. Good, I can't be the only sarcastic one in our relationship. "Your wolf is beautiful, Lyra. Just like you." He reaches out slowly and pets the side of my neck affectionately. I lean into his touch, happy I don't have to worry about sucking out his soul for once. It feels so nice to just be with him without worry.

"Can I shift and let our wolves bond now?" My tail thumps happily and I hope he takes it as a yes. He backs up slowly and I can hear his bones crack as he shifts. His shift seems much faster than mine was. His body manipulates itself and black fur spreads over his skin. His ice-blue eyes remain the same. He's a magnificent all black wolf, just a bit taller than me in our wolf forms. He comes closer to me and nuzzles into my neck. As soon as we touch, I feel something pressing into my mind. I whine but he keeps nuzzling me and I relax allowing whatever is happening, to happen.

"Lyra can you hear me?" It's Lucas's voice inside my head. I'm not sure how to answer him exactly so I reach out to him and try to push my thoughts to him.

"Yes..." I think, waiting to see if it worked. I can feel his smile through our link.

"You did well for your first time. Usually, it takes a while for a wolf to get used to others being near it. Our wolf takes over during that first shift and it's hard to fight our instincts. I knew you wouldn't hurt me." He takes his time sniffing all around me and then I sniff him. I'm not exactly sure why we do it, but it feels right.

"Why are we sniffing each other?" I ask, amused.

"We are getting used to each other's scent. We are mates Lyra, rather we are human or wolf," he says, laughing. He takes off running through the woods and I follow him.

"How did we get out here?"

"There's a pass-through in the wall. We had a witch do it long ago so anyone from our pack could pass through. It makes patrolling the woods easier and provides an escape if needed," he says, running past trees. I easily catch up to him and pass by him. *"You are fast, faster than anyone else in the pack."*

I feel his pride through our bond, and I laugh in my head. A half howl, half cough sounds from my mouth; guess that's my wolf version of a laugh. I keep going, coming upon a small clearing with a creek running through it. I take a break and lap up some water, still thirsty from earlier. Lucas joins me and then we lay down side-by-side, just looking at the water flowing.

"Why can't I hear anyone else?" I ask, turning my head to face his and laying it down on my paws. It's hard getting used to a heavier head like this.

"You aren't a part of the pack. The only reason you can hear me is because we are mates. You'll hear everyone else once we fully mate," he says, turning his head towards me as well. He gets up and comes closer, laying his head across my body.

"So, I join the pack automatically once we mate?" I ask, curious.

"Yes. But we can choose to go wherever. If you want to move to another pack, I'll follow. Then we will swear allegiance to that alpha and join their pack and lose our connection to this one."

"Why would I want to go to another pack? This is your family." I say, eyeing him. Why would he leave his family for me?

"Well, I'm just letting you know the offer is there. It's not uncommon for families to split. Being a part of another pack doesn't mean we hate our family. It just means we can live somewhere else and still be with a group. There are other Blue Ridge Mountain packs, not just ours. It's too large for just one to cover."

That makes a lot of sense. I was wondering how they covered the whole thing. I don't want to leave his pack though, this is where he was raised and where he belongs. I don't have a pack of my own to follow.

"We will stay here. There is still so much we don't know about me. My only wish is we were closer to the ocean. I'm going to miss that," I say. Then I think about my dad who has been a lone wolf for years.

What about him? *"Can my dad join us as well?"*

"I don't see why not. My father offered him a place when he passed through a few years ago, but he said no. Probably because of you." He licks my ear. *"It's so nice to just be able to touch you like this. I wish it was the same when we are human. I've never been a people person and never thought I would be into affection, but I want to touch you all the time Lyra."*

"I want that too, not you licking my ear in human form though- just to be clear- but us being able to touch when we want. What are we going to do? My dad isn't here, and I can't go back to Cedar Island."

"You don't know, you might like me licking your ear," he teases. He might be right, I have little experience with my sexuality. I might like it. *"What about your Aunt Karen?"* He asks. Why didn't I think of her!

"She should know. Lynn told me she bound my powers for me when I was younger."

"Well, where can we find her?" He asks, his body tensing.

"She's in Georgia, I think. I don't have her number on me, or we could just call her. Lynn destroyed my phone. We would have to travel there and look for her. I know she's a midwife," I say.

"We'll find her. A road trip with you will be nice, just the two of us."

"It would be even nicer if we could touch," I say wistfully.

"Very true. We just have to be careful and you tell me when you start feeling it. I'm not going to shy away from touching you anymore Lyra. I can't. We will be careful and keep it to a minimum." He stands up and we decide to head back to his house. I let him lead the way as I'm not used to the woods. Eventually, I'll be able to tell

the smells apart and do it on my own. But for now, everything is too overwhelming.

I smell something delicious and stop. Lucas turns around and looks at me curiously.

"What is that smell?" I ask him, breathing in deep. He comes closer to me and sniffs as well.

"Rabbit. Are you hungry? I wasn't going to have you hunt tonight. It can be hard wrapping your head around hunting and eating live animals."

"Yes. I'm starving," I say, letting my instincts take over. I prowl over to a bush without making a sound and leap into it, catching the terrified rabbit in my teeth. It dies instantly and my teeth rip through its flesh easily. I don't even think about it as I quickly eat it and lick my snout. Remembering Lucas, I look around for him and find him chowing down on something a few feet away.

"Done?" He whispers into my mind.

"Yes. That was easier than I thought it would be." He finishes his meal and comes over to me. He licks around my snout, I must have missed some blood. He has a little left as well and when he's finished cleaning me, I clean him too.

"Does this classify as a date? Walk through the woods, a meal together and then kissing?" He sounds amused again and I grin wolfishly.

"Totally counts. Let's do it again as humans next time," I say laughing at him. He leads the way back to his house. We arrive at the community wall and Lucas shifts right in front of me. His family is gone but there are clothes sitting by a tree. He quickly pulls

on a pair of pants but not before I see his nicely shaped butt. Man, I wish he would have turned around. I couldn't focus earlier when he came into my room naked.

"Shifting back is usually pretty easy. Just focus on your human form and it should come naturally. This time it might hurt but after this first shift, you won't feel the pain anymore," he says, bending down and grabbing clothing.

Nodding at him, I close my eyes and try to expand my mind like I did before. I can still see other animals, but I think of my human face. My body starts bending awkwardly and changing shape. My fur recedes and in its place is smooth skin. On my hands and knees, I breathe deeply and finally open my eyes again. Lucas is in front of me, eyes closed and holding a robe. I take it with shaky hands and wrap it around my body.

"That was fun," I say. It feels weird to talk again. I try to reach out to Lucas through my mind again, but I can't find him. "So, we can only communicate through our minds while we are wolves?"

"Yes. All wolves are like that. Though I have heard of mates who can do it when fully mated. Since we dreamed of each other before we met, there's a good chance we will be able to," he says. "I also felt your emotions before, a few days ago. You were scared, sad... lonely. I tried pushing calming feelings to you, but I don't know if that worked."

I stand up, tying the robe securely. I reach out and touch his cheek and he leans into me and opens his eyes. We stare at each other and I lean forward, kissing him. Lucas wraps his arms around me and pulls me closer, dipping his tongue into my mouth. I thought he would taste like meat and whatever else he just ate, but he doesn't. He tastes like water, sweet against my tongue. I break the kiss before we can get taken away with it and step back. The tingles were just beginning to get overwhelming.

"I felt that calmness. I didn't know where it came from then. Thank you. I needed to feel that at that moment," I say, smiling at him.

"I'm glad I could help. That wasn't so bad," he says smiling at me. "I'll have to hold your hand when we walk back through the wall though. Are you ready or do you need a minute?"

Feeling the tingling die down a little, I nod my head. We walk to the wall and he grabs my hand, heat envelopes me and I smile, knowing this is the mate bond. We walk right through it. That is so cool! We are in his backyard and his family is waiting for us, all of them smiling happily.

"Thanks for coming out here and helping. I didn't know what was happening at first," Lucas says.

"No problem. The first shift is very overwhelming. But she could have attacked you, Lucas. You should have been farther away from her," his dad chastises him. I look down at the ground, refusing to look at anyone. He's right, I did come close to attacking him at first.

"I knew she wouldn't hurt me, she's my mate dad," Lucas says, squeezing my hand. The normal heat flows between us now when we touch. I savor that until I feel the tingle creeping up my arm and know I can't hold his hand much longer without risk. I squeeze his hand and then let it go.

"I've heard of wolves attacking their own mothers when they first shift. They aren't in the right state of mind Lucas. That was a big risk you took," Jon says.

"Too late now. It's over dad, so drop it," he says, leading us all back into his house. I glance at the clock and see it's just after one in the morning.

"When did I wake you up?" I ask Lucas, taking a seat at the island. I'm exhausted. His family crowds around the kitchen, all wearing night clothes or robes, and Lucas walks over to me.

"Just after midnight. Happy Birthday by the way," he says, leaning down and kissing me lightly in front of everyone. No one comments, but we do get some weird looks from them. He takes a seat beside me and looks at his parents. "Well, we know one of her powers now at least. Her birthday must have unlocked her shifting ability."

"Did it also change her sucking out your soul or are you just risking your life every time you touch her?" His dad asks. Damn, he is grumpy in the morning. Lucas and him glare at each other and I set my hand down on his arm.

"It's okay. He's right Lucas. We are risking it every time we touch," I say.

"No, it's not okay. He acts like this is easy for us. He knows once the bond starts it pushes us together. We can't not touch," he growls out.

"I know it's not easy. I know, I have felt it before you know. I just want you to be careful. I'm sorry Lyra. I know you wouldn't hurt him intentionally. I can see you care for him already," Jon says, sighing. Kim leans against him and he relaxes. I know he is just worried for Lucas, I am too. Who would want their child mated to someone who can kill them within minutes?

"We are being careful. She tells me when it's too much on her and we back off," he says, looking at me and smiling. "We can make this work."

"Yeah until you're pushed into fully mating. We all know the mate bond is hard to resist," his dad says, his voice concerned.

"I know dad. We will be careful, I promise. You guys should go back home now, we are all tired and can talk tomorrow," Lucas says, standing up and hugging parents. He claps his brother on the shoulder and briefly touches Julie on the arm. I have to push down my jealousy of him touching her. I know she's mated to his brother, but it doesn't change my feelings. The last one to walk out of the kitchen is his mom, Kim. She comes over to me and slowly places her hand on mine.

"Is this okay?" She asks and I nod. "Good. Happy birthday Lyra. I know my husband seems mean, but he's just concerned and comes off hard. He does like you, don't worry. Get some sleep."

She smiles at me and squeezes my hand, then follows everyone else out the door. At last, Lucas and I are alone again.

"She likes you," he says, coming over to me.

"Seems like it. I don't know how, I would be pissed if my son was dating me," I say with a laugh. Lucas's eyes darken.

"Let's not mention us having a son. I can't let my mind go there right now," he says deeply. I want to reach out and touch him, but I know right now we both wouldn't be able to stop. Instead, I get up from my chair and head up the stairs to my room. Lucas following closely behind me. We stop at my door and he closes his eyes briefly, breathing in and out. Under control again he opens his eyes and reaches out touching my face.

"Goodnight baby," he says, resting his hand on my cheek. I smile and turn my head, kissing his palm.

"Goodnight," I say walking into my room and shutting the door. I hear him stand there for a few more seconds before walking into his room and closing his door. We both wish we could sleep together tonight, holding each other close. But we can't.

I slip out of my robe and into a tank top and underwear, my clothes having been destroyed when I shifted earlier. Standing in my room, I wonder how we are going to get through this.

Chapter 16

Lyra

I manage to sleep for a few hours before I wake up; the sun isn't even out yet. Rolling over, I look at the clock and groan. Couldn't I sleep in on my birthday? I usually love waking up early every morning to swim, but after the night I had, I'm exhausted. It's just before five and I doubt Lucas is going to wake up with me today. Sighing, I get out of bed and go into the bathroom. Fantastic, I would have my period on my birthday. I wonder if wolves can smell it? I take a whiff and yup, I can, so they should be able to as well. Talk about awkward. I grab a tampon out of my bag and make a mental note to get some more today.

I pick out a royal blue bikini and quickly change, heading out the door and down the stairs. The house is empty and quiet, using my newfound hearing I can hear Lucas breathing deeply upstairs. I walk out the back door and dive into the pool. The water feels different since I shifted, almost overwhelming. I get why most wolves don't like swimming once they shift. Your senses are just so heightened. I still like it though, maybe I'm like Lucas and can handle it while others can't or maybe it's because I've been swimming my whole life. Who knows, but I love the feel of the water against my skin.

I swim for about an hour then head back inside, not bothering to change or dry off. I go straight for the fridge and pick out some bacon and ingredients to make pancakes. I used to make my dad breakfast all the time at home and Lucas has been cooking for me since I got here, it's time I return the favor. Cooking has always come easily to me.

Finished with everything, I head upstairs to wake up Lucas. I hesitate at his door for a second before going in. He hasn't shown me his room yet and for some reason, it almost feels like an invasion of privacy, but we are mates. Hopefully one day soon we will share a room.

His room is dark when I enter, the sun just barely has risen, and you can see it shining through his window. He sleeps with the curtains pulled aside so he can see outside, the same as me. The room is way larger than my own, as it should be considering I sleep in a guest room, it's large enough to fit a massive king size bed in it, two-night stands and a tall dresser with a built-in mirror. There's still plenty of space to walk around too, nothing is cramped. There are two doors on the left, to the bathroom and the closest I assume.

Lucas sleeps in the middle of the bed on his back, hugging a pillow to himself. I smile, imagining sleeping beside him one day and him hugging me to him like that. I can't wait to figure all this stuff out and for us to finally be together like we should be. His blanket looks dark, but I imagine it has more color when in the light, and it's settled low on his hips. And I'm pretty sure he's sleeping naked. I try not to glance down at his barely covered penis, but I really can't help myself. Oh wow. Yup okay, I looked. I bring my gaze up to his face; he's sleeping soundly still, and his face is perfectly relaxed. He's going to need to trim his beard soon, it's no longer a stubble. I don't mind it though; he pulls off stubble well and I have a feeling he will pull off a full beard too. I've never been particularly attracted to guys who have beards before, but on Lucas, I'll find anything attractive. Or nothing.

Nothing on him works too.

Geez, I'm turning into a horn ball. I shake my head and sit down on the side of his bed. I reach my hand out and rest it against his cheek and slowly move it down. I rest it above his heart, and I can feel it beating against my hand. Feeling the now familiar warmth, but not the bad tingle, I stand up and pull back the covers. Settling under them, I snuggle up against him and throw my leg over his. His arm lets go of the pillow and tugs me on top of him instead. Yup, very naked. Maybe I shouldn't have gotten in the bed with him.

His head goes into my hair and he rolls over on his side now, facing me. His eyes are still closed as he breathes in my hair and makes his way down to my neck. He nuzzles there for a second and then kisses it. Oh, God. This was a very bad idea. I feel his tongue run against my neck and he places another open mouth kiss. I moan and move my face to kiss him. He lifts me more on top of him so I'm straddling him now. His cock presses into my bikini bottoms. It's thrilling knowing just a small piece of fabric is separating us. My hands are in his hair, tugging lightly as we continue to make out. I gasp as his hands cup my butt in both his palms. I could die happy right now. Feeling the bad tingle starting to spread into my hands, I roll off of him, making sure there is space between our bodies. Both of us are breathing heavy and Lucas looks at me confused.

"Was that you the whole time?" He asks gruffly.

"Were you expecting anyone else?" I ask, half teasing and half suspicious.

"No. I was dreaming about you. I'm not sure when my dream became real," he says smiling over at me. "What made you decide to join me?"

"I made breakfast, and I wanted to wake you up. Thought this might be a good surprise." I roll so I'm facing him again and he rolls as well. We scoot closer so we are almost touching but not quite. Our breath mingles together we are so close. "I want this with you. I want to wake you up like that every day, the only difference is I want to wake up in bed with you first."

"I want that too. Though I want to wake you up sometimes too," he says smiling at me, he lifts his hand slowly enough I could move away if needed, but I'm good for the moment. He rests it against my cheek and brings me forward, kissing me lightly this time. "Good morning baby."

"Good morning," I giggle. I never giggle. What is wrong with me? I'm falling in love so fast and we barely know each other. With anyone else, I would be creeped out, but Lucas is my soulmate. The one person meant for me in this world. We stare at each other, his hand still on my cheek, and I hate to pull away, but I know it's time. I roll out of the bed and walk to the door. "Get dressed. I can't handle it if you walk down to breakfast wearing nothing."

I close the door and lean against it for a second, listening to him getting up and dressing. I walk into my room and pull off my suit. Digging through a duffle bag, I pull out a pair of jean shorts, underwear, and a pink t-shirt. I walk downstairs and plate some food up for us. Just as I set the plates down, Lucas walks in wearing a pair of sweatpants and nothing else. I eye his chest and he catches me staring. He winks and kisses my cheek then sits down at his spot at the island.

"So, I have one more stipulation to waking up," he says with a mischievous smile. "You have to be naked too next time." My cheeks flood with blood and he takes a bite of bacon watching my reaction.

"If I do that, we won't stop next time," I say sadly. Taking a few bites of bacon. My stomach clinches, and I push my plate away.

"That would be the point," he says still grinning at me. I shake my head and get a glass of orange juice, I can't seem to finish my plate today.

"That's not a good idea. I had to drag myself away from you up there before I hurt you. I can't risk that Lucas. You mean too much to me," I say, reaching my hand out to rest on his.

"Have you noticed you can touch me longer and longer each time?" He asks. Huh?

"What do you mean?" I ask.

"Each time we touch is longer Lyra. Maybe you haven't noticed, but I have. We were kissing for almost five minutes up there before we pulled apart. Yesterday it was less than that."

I think back and he might be right. Touching him before, it only took a minute or two before it was too much. I didn't realize we were kissing for so long upstairs.

"I didn't notice, actually. I lost track of time up there," I say. Lucas looks at me and smiles sexily. How am I going to resist him much longer? "We need a game plan. I was thinking, maybe I can look up my Aunt Karen online. I know she lives in Athens, Georgia and is a midwife. She has to have something listed to contact her somewhere."

"That's a good idea. After breakfast we can go upstairs and look it up," he says, stuffing his face even faster. He looks at my plate and back at me. "Are you not finishing?"

"I'm just not very hungry. I was hungry earlier, but this just isn't doing it for me," I say. I wish it was doing it for me, I love bacon.

"Could this be another power of yours or something? You barely ate yesterday as well and normally after shifting we are starving," he asks. He has a point, is this linked to my powers? Remembering the canister Miss Lynn gave me, I jump out of my seat and rush over to the bag sitting on his counter.

"How could I be so stupid! Miss Lynn told me I would need to have this every few days. It's been almost five days." I reach into the bag and pull out the canister. I place it on the counter and pull out a spoon from the draw.

"What is it?" Lucas asks, coming over and inspecting it. He lifts the top off and smells it. "It doesn't smell like anything. It must have some spell on it, there's nothing that doesn't have a single scent to it."

"I'm not sure. I started getting sick last week; couldn't eat, and I had some dizzy spells. Miss Lynn brought me over a shake, and it made me feel better. When I went to her after the party, she packed this up and told me she had put it in my shake. I'm supposed to have a spoonful in something I eat every few days. Otherwise, I won't be able to eat."

Mixing a spoonful into my orange juice, I take a sip. Tastes like normal orange juice to me. Lucas takes the glass from me and sniffs it, then takes a small sip.

"I don't taste it in here. Why didn't you mention this earlier? You could have gotten really sick Lyra and I wouldn't have known what to do for you. Is there anything else you can think of you should tell me?" He asks. Sipping my drink, I try to think back.

"She said she would need to guide me once I come into my powers, she's supposed to go to my Aunt Karen's by the end of this week," I say.

"Anything else? I mean anything Lyra- even if it's something small it might be important."

"Well... there is something else, but it's probably nothing. When I was shifting and trying to focus on my wolf, I saw different animals," I say quietly. For some reason, this feels weird to talk about. Lucas stills.

"Are you sure?" He asks.

"Yes. There were a lot. I eventually found my wolf and focused on her like you said."

"Lyra, I don't think you are just a wolf shifter. We don't have access to other animals like that. You can probably shift into them as well," he says, going back to his breakfast.

"Is that a bad thing?" I ask.

"No. Just different. I have never heard of anyone being able to shift into multiple animals like that. There are a few different shifter species out there, like a bear or a fox. I've heard of a few witches being able to change form before but that's illusion magic, not shifting."

"So, what do we do?" I wonder, finishing my glass of juice.

"The plan stays the same. You try finishing your breakfast now and we'll go search for your Aunt Karen after. We will figure this out."

I sit back down and start to eat, he's right I am hungry again. We finish in silence, both too caught up in our thoughts to talk. Lucas loads up the dishwasher for us and we walk upstairs. He pulls out a folding chair from the closest in his office and sets it up for himself, allowing me to take the main chair.

"The password is saltwater123." At my stare, he looks sheepish. "Told you I've always had a thing for the water."

I shake my head and type it in, waiting for it to load up. Finally, it loads, and I click on Google chrome typing in 'Karen Johnson, Athens, Georgia, midwife.' A few searches come up and I click on the first one. Nope, she's white. Not Karen. I back up and try the second link.

"This is her," I say, looking through her website. It has a picture of her and her family up and has contact info. Lucas hands me his cell phone and I dial the number. It rings a few times before going to voicemail.

"Hey Aunt Karen, it's me: Lyra. I need you to call me back at 828-716-3399," I say, copying what Lucas says. "This is very important."

I hang up and ask Lucas for a piece of paper and a pen. He reaches into a drawer and hands them to me. I write down her number and the address for her business. Then I try searching for her home address or phone number, neither are listed online. Damn.

"Guess we will wait for her to call me back," I say, standing up. "What should we do now?"

"Hmm there are a few things I can think of," he says, standing up as well. He stalks towards me and I back up into a wall. He kisses me hard on the mouth. I will never get tired of this. He pulls away too fast for my liking though. "But probably not a good idea to do what I'm thinking."

"Is your mind always in the gutter or is this something new?" I tease.

"Very new. I'm not used to be controlled by my hormones like this," he says seriously.

"Have you ever had a girlfriend then?" I ask.

"Not really. Nessa tried hard, but I wasn't interested. I went on a date with her once just to get her to shut up, hoping she would see we weren't a good match but that did not deter her."

"Does that mean, um... you know?" I ask him. He smiles at me like he knows exactly what I'm asking but motions for me to go on. Ugh, fine. "Are you a virgin?"

"Is that so surprising? I've had dreams of you for years now. I was determined to find you, and I was planning on traveling in the next year to look for you but something kept me here. I must have known on some level you would come to me," he says, reaching out for my hand. "I wanted no one else even back then. It's always been you Lyra."

I lean forward and kiss him once, pulling away and walking downstairs.

"Just so it's clear- I'm a virgin too. I wasn't interested in other boys growing up. I knew I had a soulmate somewhere," I say, looking over my shoulder at him.

We sit together on the couch and he turns on the tv, letting me pick the show this time. I choose Jane the Virgin on Netflix and settle against him, making sure our skin isn't touching.

"Really? We talk about virginity and you pick this show?" He asks, laughing.

"Yes! Have you seen it?" I ask and he shakes his head no. "It's a pretty good show, actually."

"Can we have a date today?" I look over at him- that was kinda out of nowhere.

"Are you sure we should be leaving the community? The last time we left I got kidnapped by that harpy. Hey! We haven't even talked about any of that," I exclaim.

"Haven't had the time. You were kidnapped, poisoned, then going through your first shift. A lot has happened in a short time frame."

"What happened then?" I ask, leaning my head against his covered chest. While I hate him wearing clothes, at least I can touch him through the material.

"I decided not to go to the bathroom at the restaurant. I walked outside right as she was flying off with you. Luckily no one was in the parking lot and I shifted right there and ran after her. Harpies have no scent to them, as they are like the wind, but I could smell you. I tracked both of you through the woods and alerted my pack. They, in turn, told my family what was going on. I found you guys right as you stabbed her. What was that thing?"

"Miss Lynn gave it to me, said it would protect me when I needed it. I carried it around just in case. Where is it?" I ask.

"I have it. It's made of dark energy whatever it is, you activated it and it became a dark sword of some sort. I'll give it back to you today... anyway, I saw you pull it out and then she did something that made you stop breathing. I came up right as you knocked out. I bit into her leg and she took off. Harpies are immortal but can still be injured badly. I brought you to my parents where we waited for you to wake up. Then we took you to the nymphs. I'm not sure what you remember of it, but they sped the poisoning process up and you had to go through some type of mental test to see if you were worthy of passing. Do you remember it at all?"

"Yes," I say, ducking my head. Of course, he would ask me about that.

"Tell me," he demands. I look up at him and nod.

"I was in this black void and in so much pain. I could feel my body convulsing. It was worse than shifting. Then a voice in my head said I knew how to end it. You appeared in front of me and told me to take your soul. That you were okay dying for me to live. I... I almost did it too. It was so weird, instead of touching you I was going to bite you. When I refused, you changed into Lynn. The voice told me Lynn was old, and it was okay to kill her. She would die soon anyway, and I could live the rest of my life. I almost bit her too, it was almost out of my control so instead, I bit my arm. That was it."

"You really chose to die instead of me?" He asks, lifting my chin up so he could look into my eyes.

"Of course, I did. I will always choose your life over my own. I don't want to hurt anyone Lucas, much less you. You mean everything to me," I whisper, tears filling my eyes. Lucas leans forward and kisses me softly.

"I'm falling in love with you Lyra," he says.

"I'm falling in love with you too." We both know we are probably past the 'falling' part, but neither of us admits it.

***

We decide to go on a grocery store date. Lucas gives me back the small cylinder and I keep it in my purse. Neither of us bothers changing, we head right to his car.

"Can I drive?" I beg.

"Why?" Lucas asks.

"Because you drive like a lunatic!" I say. Lucas laughs and actually hands me his keys. "Seriously?" My eyes widen, staring down at the keys and then back up at him.

"Yeah, I trust you. Probably a better driver than me." I squeal and hug him tightly. He helps me into the truck, and I start it up as he walks around to the passenger side. I adjust the mirrors and the seat before backing out of the driveway. Lucas gives me directions to the nearest grocery store, and it only takes us ten minutes to get there.

We hold hands as we walk inside but have to separate when Lucas grabs a cart.

"So, what all do we need?" I ask.

"That depends, what do you feel like cooking tonight? I figured instead of going out on a date we can stay in and cook together if that's alright?" He's so cute when he's nervous.

"That sounds perfect to me," I say, leaning over the cart and kissing him. "What about steak and potatoes?"

"I'm down. I have a grill out back I can fire up."

We pick out steaks and grab some other things we will need for the week. I learn Lucas like ham and bologna on his sandwiches with Duke's mayo. Good to know I'm not the only one who only uses dukes. We are about to check out when I remember I need to grab tampons.

"I forgot something, I'll be right back," I say about to run off. Lucas grabs my hand.

"No way you are leaving my sight again. I'm coming with." I shrug, not really caring. We head down the feminine hygiene aisle and I grab a box of tampons. Lucas doesn't even blink when I grab them and just walks down the aisle grabbing a box of condoms. I raise an eyebrow at him, and he just smiles sweetly. Alright, I'll let that pass. We head back to the checkout lane and load our stuff up. I insist on paying but Lucas argues with me over it until I agree to half. He shakes his head and sighs.

Finally making it back to the truck, we load everything into the cab. Lucas has to help me up again and I check the time. It's lunchtime, maybe we can stop somewhere?

"Can we stop and grab lunch?" I ask. He looks at me like I'm crazy.

"I barely wanted to come here and now you want to go some-where else? Nope. Not happening," he says, turning to the front like that's the end of the conversation. That's cool, it is the end. I drive off and remember spotting a McDonald's on the way here. I turn into it and Lucas glares at me. "Really, Lyra?"

"Oh, I'm sorry, do you feel like telling me something else to do?" I ask sweetly. I pull up at the drive-through. "Now do you want something or not?" He looks at me for a few more seconds, then smiles at me and rolls his eyes.

"Yeah get me a number two with a coke."

I order our food and pull around, this time I am paying. Lucas reaches in his back pocket but seeing the look on my face he stops. He needs to know I'm a woman who makes her own decisions. I will respect what he says but at the end of the day, I'm my own person. I pay for the food and we drive home. I'm practically drooling from the smell of our food.

We get back and I park the truck. Lucas helps me out and then holds me to him.

"I love how you defy me. I didn't think I would like that, but damn is it sexy," he says, kissing my neck. He pulls away and goes inside. I quickly follow behind him, almost in a trance. He knows how to make me forget myself. Lucas stops suddenly in the doorway and I ram into his back with and oomph.

"Get out," he growls. I look over his shoulder and see bombshell standing at the bottom of the stairs, leaning against the railing in what I assume she thinks is a seductive pose. Really, she looks like a meth'ed up frog with her green eye makeup. Now that I know I'm Lucas's mate, I can see past her makeup to the ugly person beneath.

"But Lucas! I just want to spend some time with you." She pouts at him, then sees me over his shoulder. "Hiya Lia, can you go over to his parents' house and spend the day? It's time for us adults to spend time together."

Oh no she didn't. I push Lucas out of the way and grab a hold of bombshells arm and throw her out the door. Lucas looks on in shock.

"Yes, it is time for the adults to play, I've been waiting all day to get Lucas home alone. And if you forgot my real name, stick around outside and wait for him to moan it. Have fun!" I say, slamming the door in her surprised face. I turn around and Lucas is staring right at me.

"Damn. That was even hotter," he says coming up to me and pushing me up against the door. His hands are under my butt and he picks me up, kissing me. I grab at his shoulders and literally rip his shirt in two trying to touch him. Our bodies are pressed so closely together, I don't know where he ends, and I begin. There's a knock at the door.

"Ignore it," Lucas says, trailing his tongue up my throat.

"Let's not ignore it. Dad will be coming over in a few minutes if I'm not back." A voice says behind the door. Lucas stiffens and sets me down on my feet. I wobble a little, trying to control my breathing. I make sure I'm presentable before he opens the door. Lewis is standing there with his hand in front of his eyes. "Please tell me you are decent. My eyes would bleed if I saw your naked ass."

"Funny. I've seen your naked ass plenty of times," Lucas says. "We are decent. Come in." Lewis opens his eyes and then glares at Lucas.

"I thought you said you were decent! Your shirt is ripped in half." Oops.

"That would be my fault. Sorry," I mutter.

"I'll survive. Julie will have to pour bleach in my eyes later," Lewis says with a laugh. I didn't realize he was so funny!

"Why did you interrupt us exactly?" Lucas asks, agitated.

"Vanessa just came over crying saying Lyra attacked her." I can't help but laugh and Lewis looks at me. "Did you?"

"Yup. I threw bombshell out on her ass for hitting on Lucas," I say, getting comfy on the couch beside Lucas.

"Man, I missed it!" Lewis says sadly, pouting. I guess everyone hates her.

"You should have seen it! Nessa was hitting on me and asked Lyra to leave so we could spend alone time together. Lyra threw her out and told her we had been dying for some alone time all day," Lucas says laughing, putting his arm around my shoulder. "She called Lyra Lia, so Lyra told her to stick around and I would be moaning her name in a few minutes."

"Damn! I can't believe I missed that. I bet her face was priceless!" We all laugh, and Lewis gets a serious look on his face. "Dad also wants to know what the plan is. The pack has been asking about Lyra and you all day. They saw the two of you leave together and know Lyra is living here now."

"We called her godmother today, we think she will know something. We are waiting on a call back from her and go from there. Tell the pack she's my mate, I don't care if they know. We are still getting to know each other and waiting to solidify the bond," Lucas says, and I nod in agreement with him.

"And what happens if she doesn't call you back? What will you do then?"

"We will go to Georgia and find her. We aren't giving up. And if we can't find her, we will figure it out," Lucas says. I feel the tingle rising up to meet his arm around me and I shrug it off me. He looks at me hurt for a second then his face relaxes, remembering and nodding his head.

"When will you guys leave?" Lewis asks.

"Thursday morning. That will give her the rest of today and all of tomorrow to contact us," Lucas says looking at me, I nod in agreement.

"Need me and Julie to come with? We don't mind."

"Nah we will be fine. We are figuring it out."

"Alright. Just let me know if you change your mind. Let dad know before you guys leave," Lewis says, standing up and walking to the door.

"Wait, you wanna help us bring in groceries before you leave? We have a shit ton in the truck," Lucas asks, following him out. I stand up to help when Lewis agrees.

The three of us bring in all the groceries and we exchange goodbyes with Lewis. Lucas and I put everything away together and then chow down on our fast food. When we finish, we marinate the steaks together and have everything ready for later tonight. I'm looking forward to cooking with him

We spend the rest of the day talking, watching tv and then cooking. Dinner is fantastic and we have a lot of fun. We can't help but touch each other often, careful to keep the contact short but meaningful. We both go to sleep after a late swim, with the promise of a run tomorrow morning as wolves. I can get used to this. The only thing I would change is curling up in his arms at night and falling asleep beside him. Not yet, but soon.

Chapter 17

Lucas

I wake up first Wednesday morning, which is a feat considering Lyra is always up so early to swim. She must be exhausted after the last few days. Taking a quick shower, I dress for warm weather in shorts and a t-shirt. I take the stairs quietly, being careful of Lyra's newfound wolf hearing and head into the kitchen to write a note in case she wakes up before I get back.

I start up my truck and head out of the community to get coffee and donuts for everyone. Our little community is quiet in the predawn light, no one is out and about yet and the place almost looks like a ghost town. I'm so used to the hustle and bustle of everyday life here, kids always playing outside, young couples going for a walk alone, parents mowing the lawn in the summer or shoveling snow in the winter. I wave to the guard on duty, Rob, as I pass through the gate leading out of the community.

The drive to The Coffee Shop in downtown Sylva goes fast, I don't get to come up here often- usually only on special occasions. They have the best coffee in town, and pies. Their pies are phenomenal, and I can eat a whole one myself.

Pulling into the parking lot just before six, I sit back and wait for the store to open. I bet if I tried the door, they would let me in but I'm in no rush today.

Finding my mate has relaxed me a lot. Usually, I never find time in my schedule to get coffee, and when I do, I'm always in a rush to get back home to my work. Already, I've turned down two new projects and now I just have the one in Charlotte to finish up before I take a break from working. I have plenty of money saved away, I've always been frugal when it comes to my money matters. My house is paid for; my truck payment, food, and utilities are about it.

A few months off work will do me good, give me some time to spend with Lyra. After all these years of imagining her, I finally have her and still, we have a wall between us. I'm confident we will figure things out, we have to. I'm not willing to spend the rest of my life without her, even if I have to risk my life every day to be with her. It's all worth it.

The store sign flips from closed to open, and I get out of my truck, heading toward the door. I greet the kind cashier behind the counter and order coffees for my family, just the way they like it, and two cups of hot chocolate. Not often do I let myself indulge in the sweet treat, but Lyra mentioned that she loves to sit down at night with a cup of hot cocoa before bed. Looking at the dessert display, I pick out a few different pies and pay. The waitress gives me a big smile before I leave, thanking me for stopping in. Growing up, I always thought about traveling-leaving this little town and moving to a bigger city. Honestly, I'm glad I never left here. Small Town life, is the best life, and nothing beats hometown cooking.

Next, I swing by Dunkin Donuts for two dozen variety. My family likes different ones on different days, and the topic of donuts hasn't come up between Lyra and me just yet. I make sure to pick out a few sweet ones, knowing she has a wicked sweet tooth, and head home. Passing the Verizon store, I think quickly and pull into the lot. Lyra had to destroy her cellphone before coming here and I don't like the fact that she has nothing to communicate with people if anything happens.

Walking into the phone store, I pick out a simple Samsung active- something that will hold up against Lyra's clumsiness- and add her to my account. I figure she will be added eventually, at least this way she has a phone before we leave for Georgia and she can contact her friends back home if she wants too. The council already knows she's here, might as well keep in contact with her friends and call her dad. I know she's more concerned that he isn't here then she lets on. I hear her at night, talking in her sleep sometimes, and she mentions him a lot. I try not to think about her mentioning her friend Ryan while she's dreaming, he's often spoken of and that agitates me more than I'll admit to her. I have to remind myself, she's my mate, not his. She's in my house, and one day will be in my bed.

Finally, I head home. A simple trip turned into almost two hours. Pulling into the community, I start to see signs of life everywhere. A few people are walking their dogs and I pass by Miss Neland, who works at the library most days while her daughter is in school. I park in my driveway and tote everything in except the cellphone, I'll save that as a surprise for tomorrow when we leave. I just want one more day without her being distracted by her friends.

Opening the front door, I listen for Lyra and hear her splashing around in the backyard. I grin, setting everything down on the counter, except the pies, I put them in the fridge, and walk outside. The sun is bright, lighting up the yard and bouncing off Lyra's light red hair. She hasn't noticed me yet, she's facing the wall opposite me and seems to be enthralled with watching a bird the sits on the tall structure. I try to keep my footsteps light as I walk toward her. I'm almost to the pool when she turns around and splashes me, soaking my clothes and making my hair fall into my eyes. Blowing out my cheeks, I push my hair back and mock glare at her as she giggles happily at me.

"I have amazing hearing now, remember? I heard you pull up in the driveway," she says, her lips spread into a huge smile. Her gray eyes are light and sparkle with happiness. I do that. I make her happy without even trying, and that fills me with pleasure. "What did you bring back? Your note was pretty vague."

"First," I say, helping her out of the pool and pulling her into my arms- not caring my clothes are getting soaked in the process. "I want a proper good morning kiss." My lips seal to hers and my hands tangle in her dripping hair. I love the feel of her warm body pressed against mine, causing shock waves of tingles and heat to flood me. I pull away reluctantly and step away from her, she's too tempting. Her eyes are unfocused, and she touches her lips with a fingertip. "I brought coffee, hot chocolate, and desserts for breakfast. Go get dressed so we can head to my parent's house."

"I wanted to take a shower, why don't you head over and I'll be right behind you. I don't want everyone's coffee to get cold." I consider her words and decide that'll be fine. I can watch from the window as she walks over, and the community is locked up tight. That harpy won't be trying again any time soon, and she knows better than to try anything on our territory like that.

"Fine, but don't take too long. I'll miss you," I say, bending down and kissing her again. We get lost in each other for a few minutes before she pulls away and runs inside the house. I shake my head, a smile lighting up my face and run in after her, racing up the stairs and into my room to change my shirt before heading to my parents. I can hear her in the shower, singing a pop song I've heard on the radio. Her voice is pretty good, just like I imagined it would be. I stop at her bedroom door and listen for a few seconds, lost in her lyrical words. I pull myself away and head downstairs, knowing she is right about the cold coffee. That shit sucks.

I grab everything and walk out the door, I don't see many people about yet. Kids are already off to school for their last week, those who have work, have left, everyone else is still sleeping or relaxing in their homes. Walking inside my parents home, I hear everyone in the kitchen talking amongst themselves. Perfect, the kitchen has a view of my house so I can watch Lyra walk over.

"I just don't know if it's a good idea," I hear my dad say as I walk into the room. Everyone turns to me... guess they are discussing me and Lyra. I know my dad isn't the most supportive person when it comes to my relationship with my mate. He will get over it. It's my life and my decision.

"What isn't a good idea?" I ask, taking a seat with the best view of my house and placing everything in the center of the table for them to figure out. No one says a word. My mom glares at dad, Julie is looking around the room not allowing her gaze to land on anyone, and Lewis stares between me and dad as the two of us stare down. "If it's about Lyra, drop it. I'm an adult."

Sensing the tension, Lewis decides to crack a joke, "Where is your little mate? I thought you had her on a short leash." I turn my glare to him, though it's not as heated as the one I sent my dad. I know Lewis is trying to break the ice, but I'm not backing down.

"She's taking a shower and will walk over soon," I say, turning back to my dad. "And she doesn't need to hear how you don't approve of her, she's already aware and it stresses her out."

"I'm just worried Lucas," dad says, his face softening. He looks older now than a week ago, I know this is taking a lot out of him, but she is what I want in my life. "I don't want you getting hurt. We don't know what she is or what she is capable of. I just want you to be careful, that's all, and going to Georgia alone together isn't a good idea."

"Maybe not, but it's my choice. She's my mate. I'm not leaving her and we don't need a chaperone every second of every day. We spend every night together under the same roof and touch constantly. I have it handled dad, you need to respect that."

We stare each other down and movement outside the window catches my attention. I look away, spotting Lyra in a cute, light purple dress walking down the sidewalk. Her arms swing and I can see her smile from here.

"Please dad, don't upset her. She's going through enough right now. You don't have to agree with my decisions, but you have to respect them and our relationship," I say, not turning to face him, My eyes are trained on her, making sure she isn't in any danger. I'm half tempted to walk outside and meet her.

"Okay," dad sighs, and I glance at him for a second before turning my eyes back to my mate. "I'll respect it. Just promise me you'll be careful."

"Promise," I say, standing up and meeting Lyra at the front door. I open it just as she is about to knock and her smile widens when she sees me. Her heartbeat picks up and her pupils dilate. It's nice having the constant reassurance that she's attracted me. I pull her in my arms and kiss her quickly before dragging her into the kitchen where everyone else is seated.

Thankfully, the tension is lifted from the room. Everyone is digging through the donuts and passing out coffees. When we enter they all smile and greet Lyra, though my dad is a little less enthusiastic than everyone else. I shoot him a look, and he forces a bigger smile on his face. I can tell it's forced but Lyra doesn't seem to notice. I can feel her overwhelming happiness, it floods my body and I look over at her, wondering if she knows she's projecting her emotions to me. She doesn't act any different, and I assume she has no clue.

I pick out a chocolate cake donut and take my seat again. Lyra sits beside me and takes a bite of my food, smiling happily.

"Is there a reason you took a bite of mine and didn't get your own?" I tease her and her cheeks flood with blood.

"I prefer eating yours," she says, voice tinged with innuendo. I raise my eyebrow and feed her a bite. No one comments as I continue to feed her and taking sips of my hot cocoa, but I see the looks my mom and Julie are sharing. I know, I'm a hopeless romantic. I've imagined how it would be to have my mate for years, I've imagined this exact moment in my head. Reality blows my imagination out of the water. She beats everything I could have possibly dreamed up.

***

After breakfast, we take a walk around the neighborhood. I've been wanting to show Lyra around, meet some members of the pack. It's almost ten now, more people are walking around and we run into a few of them. I introduce Lyra to Jack and Jason, two of my friends from high school and we run into an older couple, the Gregson's, who embrace Lyra like their own child. They all tell me how lucky I am to have found her, but really she found me.

While walking back home, we run into Aurora, a beautiful girl with brown hair and green eyes. I would find her very attractive if it wasn't for Lyra. And the fact that she's mated to Bryden, a guy I went to school with.

"Hey, Lucas, who's this?" She asks, coming in for a hug and turning her curious eyes to Lyra. I feel my mate bristle, sensing a threat, and I wrap my arm around her waist and smile at down at her.

"This is Lyra, my mate," I say, still staring into her eyes. Lyra slowly relaxes in my arms and smiles at Aurora.

"Hi," she says. "It's nice to meet you."

"Oh, the pleasure is all mine! I'm Aurora, I'm mated to Bryden, one of Lucas's friends."

I feel Lyra relax some more, and the two of them engage in a short conversation that I mostly tune out. My thoughts too wrapped in the beautiful woman beside me, I don't even think she realizes how long we've been touching now and I'm not going to mention it.

"My parents were mates, my mom is human and had me before she met my dad. He legally adopted me, but I'm not a wolf shifter. I never felt a part of the pack until I mated with Bryden, but still, I don't feel like I belong. If you ever wanna hang out, call me. I'm in need of a good friend!"

I catch the end of their conversation and hand Lyra my phone so she can add Aurora's number. The two of them seem to have really hit it off and I want to encourage a friendship between them. I want Lyra to be happy here, and I'm not naïve enough to think I'm all she needs in the world.

We head back home with nothing really planned except a run as our wolves. I go to the fridge and grab out the different pies I bought and place them on the island table. Lyra eyes them without comment as I dig through the fridge, pulling out apple juice she picked out yesterday and mixing her a drink with the powder she needs. She sits on her barstool, watching me with interest until I set the drink in front of her and a plate for pie. I choose a cherry slice for myself and sit beside her.

"You didn't have to make my drink for me," she says softly, eyes locked on the glass.

"I know. I wanted to." Hmm, cherry pie is so good, especially homemade like this.

Lyra doesn't say anything, just drinks her class and chooses a key lime pie. I smirk, I had a feeling that would be what she chose. I'm interested to know if she likes it, she told me before that Florida had the best key lime pies and she's been addicted to them ever since she lived there years ago. Her moan rings through the room and my fork halts in front of my face as I swing around to stare at her.

Her eyes are closed, mouth slowly chewing and her face is screwed up in bliss. I feel my pants get a bit tighter just looking at her and have to adjust myself discreetly. She opens her eyes and drops them to my pants with a smile. "Sorry." She's not sorry. Liar. I think she teases me on purpose. Shoving the rest of my pie in my mouth, I clean my plate and wait patiently for her to finish her slice as well. Of course, she puts on a show the whole time- moaning and groaning through every bite- she even winked at one point. I'm a dead man.

Washing her plate and setting it on the rack to dry, we head outside into the sunshine for a run. The best thing about my wolf form right now is being able to touch her whenever I want. I take her hand as we walk through the wall and strip off my shirt once we are through. She stops and stares and I wink at her, paybacks a bitch.

"Why don't you try a different form today? See if anything comes through," I suggest, stripping down out of my pants facing away from her. I may be a tease, but I don't think she's ready for the whole picture just yet. I hear her intake of breath and I peak around my shoulder. She's leaning against a tree, eyes locked on my ass, and I flex it once. Her eyes fly to mine and I grin.

"Uh.... Yeah, sure. You need to shift first through. I can't focus," she breathes. One second I'm a man, next I'm a wolf. I stalk over to her, and sit on my rump, watching her intently. "Are you just going to stare as I get undressed?" I bring my paw up and lay it over one of my eyes and her laugh bounces off the trees. Knowing I'm also not ready to see her fully, I turn away from her, eyes intent on the forest. It's not quiet today, I hear the birds chirping and animals about. A little family of chipmunks scurries nearby, making noises as they communicate with each other.

Hearing nothing behind me, I cautiously turn my head and see nothing. My whole body jumps around, searching the area for her. She couldn't have disappeared without me hearing it. Her clothes are folded next to a tree, she can't be far. What the hell did she shift into? I'm so focused on what's at eye level, that a touch against my paw startles me. I look down and see an all black snake curling around me. I bring my snout down closer and it licks its little tongue out at me and winks. The inside of its mouth is pitch black; I'm not sure what type of snake is like that. I don't think any that are native to North Carolina. Sensing Lyra's presence, I open my mind to her. *"Lyra, can you hear me?"*

"Yes." Her voice sounds different as a snake, just a hint of aggression that I usually don't hear in her tone.

She slithers away and before my eyes, it becomes bigger, shifting first into the tanned skin of a woman, and then into the red wolf

I saw yesterday. In the light, I can make out greater details. Her markings are more intricate, mostly red but with hints of white throughout her fur. I come closer and lick her face, feeling her contentment.

"Why a snake?" I wonder through our bond.

"It just felt the easiest. I could have shifted into something else but it was much harder. I tried a bear first." She sounds disgruntled, and I laugh. A freaking bear?

"Maybe the larger the animal, the harder it is to shift?"

"Nope tried a chipmunk next. I just couldn't focus on the animal form so I flowed to my snake. It could be that it's easier to shift into something without bones unless it's my wolf form which is more dominant from my dad. I must admit, it's freaking badass being a black mamba."

"Is that what it was? I have never seen a snake like that." Honestly, what is a black mamba? I don't want her to know, but I have no idea.

"Yes. They are native to Africa and very poisonous," she says excitedly. Well, at least she seems excited about it. I think it would be weird looking up at the world from so far down. I huff out a breath, laying my head against her and then taking off as fast as I can into the woods. I know she's fast, I'll need the head start.

She catches up in no time and flies past me. *"Don't get too far ahead,"* I push into her mind. Her only answer is a laugh and I shake my head. She's so full of life, and she's all mine.

I have to push my muscles to the max just to keep up with her, without meaning to we both run right to the clearing we came to yesterday. The little creek rushes past, and we lay down beside it like yesterday, her head resting on her paws and mine over the top of her body. We lay there in silence, neither of us pushing thoughts around, our emotions flowing freely like this. I can feel her contentment, her growing feelings for me, how calm being out here makes her feel. I don't even bother masking my love for her, we both know I'm in love with her already and I know she returns my feelings, though we haven't said the words. It's a little soon to admit love, even though our souls have known each other for much longer than we even realize.

We rest like this for a long time, not wanting to move just yet. In human form, we couldn't touch for this long. Knowing it's nearly lunchtime, we head back home and shift at the wall. Being the great boyfriend that I am, I drag my clothes behind a tree and shift back. I hear her bones crack this time, and wince. Those first few shifts can be painful. "Dressed?"

"Not yet, still breathing through the pain," she mumbles.

"Do you need my help?" I ask, ready to turn around.

"No, just give me a moment." I hear her taking in a deep breath, and releasing it, then the sound of movement. I wait until I no longer hear her clothes moving to round the tree. She's sitting down, leaning against the trunk with her eyes closed, but at least she's dressed now.

"Rough shift?" I ask. Her eyes open, assessing me and nodding.

"Yes. The snake was easier. I felt liquid, then shifting into a wolf was awful. Having to regrow all the bones and expanding everything. That took a lot out of me even before we ran a few miles. I'm exhausted now." I walk over to her and hoist her into my arms. She doesn't even protest, just snuggles into my shirt as I walk her through the wall and into the house.

"I'll make us some sandwiches and you sit here. Pick out a show or movie for us to watch," I say, placing her down on the couch and covering her with a blanket so we can snuggle after. Handing her the remote, I walk into the kitchen and get everything out on the island so I can watch her. I add some chips to both of our plates and bring them over to her. "Harry Potter again?"

"Of course," she says, looking at me like I'm the crazy one in our relationship. "It's the second one this time." Yes, the second one makes all the difference. This is probably my least favorite of the franchise. She sees my face and looks at me curiously. "What's wrong with it?"

"The second one rubs me wrong. I like the idea of Hermione and Draco getting together, you know a bad guy with a good girl? I blame this one for the author not putting them together, he's just too mean to her. Though there are clues that he actually helped her."

"Oh my God," she whispers, eyes wide. What did I say? "You ship them? You are even more perfect than before!" Her arms circle my neck and she kisses my cheek with a loud smack. If I had known she would find this attractive, I would have told her sooner. "They totally should be together, I can't tell you how many fanfictions I've read about them."

"So, you like the bad boys then?" I ask, teasing her.

"Yes, but I much prefer dark hair," she says, eyeing my face. Knowing this is going into dangerous territory, I take a huge bite of my food and she laughs at me. We finish up our lunch, both watching the movie intently. This might be my least favorite, but I still love it.

Once we are both finished, and the movie credits are rolling,

Lyra gets up to wash our dishes. I watch her from the couch as she hums, cleaning them by hand instead of putting them in the dishwasher. I can imagine her now, in a larger kitchen, washing dishes as our kids run around and play. She'll be the same as now, focused on cleaning, humming a random tune, eyes occasionally looking out the window. I get up and walk behind her, wrapping my arms around her waist as she leans back into me. This is the life I want. The two of us, together, doing mundane things like watching Harry Potter and cooking dinner. I can't imagine a fuller life than this.

Chapter 18

Lyra

Aunt Karen never called us back. We did get a call from someone else in her midwifery practice who told us she was on vacation for the week. The lady refused to give me my Aunt's home phone number or address, said Karen didn't have any siblings so there was no way I was her niece. I tried explaining she just helped raise me, but she didn't believe me. We could call again next week when she is back, but I don't want to wait. We decide to go ahead with our plan and make our way down there. By the time we get there, it'll be Thursday around lunchtime. If we show up at her practice, we can make sure someone calls her and tells us we are there.

Thursday morning, Lucas's truck is all loaded up. We aren't sure how long we will be gone but just in case we packed a lot. Looking around my room one last time, I grab my purse and head downstairs. Lucas's family wants to get breakfast with us before we hit the road. We are meeting at the same diner we went to for our first date. I'm a little nervous being there again, but with Lucas and his entire family there I know I will be safe.

"All set?" Lucas asks, coming out of the office. He's wearing casual jeans and a black shirt. I'm noticing he favors black often, not that I'll complain because he looks hot in black. It really sets off his blue eyes. Plus, as he pointed out yesterday, I like bad boys.

"Yes. Are you sure you can do work on the road? I feel bad pulling you away from the library and your clients," I ask, looking down at his laptop bag hanging off his shoulder.

"It's fine Lyra. The whole reason I'm an architect is to do work from home or wherever I am. I only have one client at the moment and dad has plenty of people to cover shifts at the library," he says reassuringly, placing his hand on the small of my back. Lucas touches me as often as he can now. Each time I still feel an overwhelming warmth and a zing of pleasure. After a while, I will start to feel goosebumps up and down my arm. That's when I know it's time to let go and give me some time to cool down. He's right though, it's getting longer and longer before that happens. We've had quite a few make-out sessions and usually, we can go eight or nine minutes before it's too much on me. Even though it's becoming longer, it's also becoming harder to pull away. The need to pull his soul into me is strong, and it takes everything in me not to do it. I haven't told Lucas yet about that part. He's so happy we can touch for longer periods of time, how am I supposed to wipe the smile off his face and tell him it's becoming harder on me?

I lead the way downstairs and we do one more check of the house before we leave. We load up in his truck and Lucas backs out of the driveway. People are just beginning to come out of their homes, kids to go to school and parents to work. We get a few curious glances and some waves. Everyone knows I'm Lucas's mate now. Lucas took me for a walk yesterday and a few people stopped to congratulate him for finding me. He just smiled at them and told them he didn't find me, I found him. Everyone was very polite to me and I even found someone I might like; her name is Aurora, and she's a stay at home wife. Her mom is a human and had Aurora before she met her mate here. Aurora was raised as a part of the pack, but still feels a bit left out even though she's mated to someone here. It will be nice to have a friend, someone who wasn't completely raised here. We can bond over being different and we really hit it off, it helps that she wasn't eyeing up my man like he was a piece of candy. We made some plans to go see a movie once we get back from Georgia, a double date where I can meet her mate, Bryden.

"I have a surprise for you by the way," Lucas says, staring at the road still, he reaches into the console and pulls out a plastic bag. Handing it to me he says, "Here. You need this."

I take the bag from him and then stare at him, he just smiles at me and gestures to the bag, so I open it. Inside is a rectangular box and shows a picture of a phone.

"Seriously!? You bought me a phone!" I exclaim, opening up the box and pulling it out. It's a Samsung galaxy active. "What does the active part mean?"

"Uh... nothing," he says with a twinkle in his eyes. Uh, huh.

"Tell me! I don't think I've heard of an active phone before and I've had a lot."

"Yeah, I know you've had a lot," he says sheepishly. "An active phone is reinforced, it has like a case built around it. There's also another case inside the bag." I look back into it and he's right, there's a pretty deep purple case.

"Are you trying to tell me something?" I ask, teasing him. I know exactly why he got me all this. I may or may not have broken multiple phones before. Like three a year on average.

"Just that I want this phone to last. You need to be able to call me in case anything goes wrong. Plus, Aurora gave you her number and I don't mind you using my phone, but you really should have your own."

"Relax. I know, I was teasing you. Thank you," I laugh. I lean over and kiss his cheek, breathing in his scent before sitting back in my seat. I spend the rest of the ride setting up my phone and putting on the new case. It really is thoughtful of him to get me an active phone knowing I have a bad track record with phones. We pull into the diner and Lucas helps me down.

"Wait," I say, staying in his arms and getting closer. I turn on the camera on my phone and put it in selfie mode. Handing the phone to him, I say, "Here. I need a background."

Lucas just smiles at me and takes the phone. We lean in close and he snaps a few pictures of us before handing it back to me. Walking inside, I go through the pictures and pick out my favorite. Lucas had tickled me, and I was smiling brightly at the camera while he looked down at me with a smile on his face. I can see this look in his eyes, one I think looks like love, but we haven't used that word... yet. I slide it into my purse and follow behind Lucas.

His family is here already, and we quickly slide into the booth to join them, I make sure there's enough space between us so we aren't touching. I see the waitress we had last time, Kaley standing on the other side of the restaurant. Gosh, I really hope she's not our waitress today.

"Finally, you guys are here! I thought maybe you fell in a ditch or something," Lucas's mom, Kim, says smiling at us. I haven't spent a lot of time with Lucas's family, but Kim is the most loving out of them all. His dad was nice until he found out what I can do. He has vowed to protect me and wants Lucas happy, but he worries I will hurt him. I get it but that doesn't mean it doesn't hurt me a little when he doesn't smile at me.

"Or a bed. That was my guess," says Lewis. Of course. Lucas's brother is the most accepting of us and is a jokester. Already he feels like a brother to me and his mate, Julie, might be quiet but she's like a sister as well. She turns and stares at Lewis after his comment, not saying a word or anything but her stare is enough to make him jumpy. "Sorry, hun! I was just kidding. We all know they can't do that yet."

"Gee. Thanks, Lewis. I needed to be reminded of that," Lucas's says sarcastically. He throws an arm over the back of the booth, careful not to have our skin touch. I can feel his warmth through my top and it fills me with happiness. I've taken to wearing t-shirts more than tanks, that way Lucas can touch me through my shirt as much as he likes. John looks at Lucas's arm but doesn't comment on it.

"Are you sure you don't need Lewis and Julie to go with you? You might need chaperones," he says looking at Lucas now.

"Yes, dad. We will be fine. Lyra won't hurt me. We can touch for longer periods of time now, almost ten minutes," he says, smiling down at me. I smile back and reach my hand up to his on my shoulder. I squeeze it before lowering my hand back to my lap. His family watches our interactions in fascination.

"And is it still hard not to pull his soul out?" His dad asks, looking at me now. I fidget in my seat under his stare. Lucas glances over at me seriously.

"Is it still hard Lyra? You don't mention anything," he says. I avoid his stare and instead look across the room. Kaley is staring at us too. Great.

"Yeah it's still hard," I say finally.

"Is it getting easier?" Lucas asks. I know I can't lie to him, so I shake my head.

"It's getting harder. I didn't want to tell you, you were so happy with the progress we've made that I didn't want to burst your bubble." Lucas looks at me and nods. He doesn't remove his arm from my shoulders but is now tense; I can feel his arm harden through my shirt.

"You should have told me Lyra. If this is going to work, we have to be honest with each other," he says looking down at the table. I nod. A waitress comes up then and asks for our orders. Thankfully it's not Kaley, I can't handle her seeing me and Lucas so tense around each other. We both order chocolate milk with eggs over easy, toast, bacon and two pancakes. His family orders and then looks at us as the waitress walks away.

"Damn. You guys are alike," Lewis says. He knows just when he needs to make jokes and break up the tension between everyone. We laugh and make small talk for the rest of breakfast. No one is in a rush today, the trip to Athens is less than three hours away. This time when we stand up to pay the bill, I stay with Lucas. No way in hell am I leaving his side. His parents try to insist they pay for everyone, but the boys insist they can pay for their own. I try to argue with Lucas, but he refuses to let me pay for my food. I'll just slip money in his wallet later.

"Hey, guys." Oh great. Kaley is over here now. My favorite person.

"Hey Kaley, how are you doing?" Lucas says, trying to be friendly. I can't help but feel jealous even though I know we are mates.

"Oh, I'm good. You left so fast last time I didn't get to say goodbye. Was everything okay?" She asks.

"Yeah. Just wanted to get home," he says looking at me. Kaley sees his look and smiles knowingly. I guess she thinks he was desperate to get me home, truly he was busy saving my life. "We didn't get to talk last time, you must be his girlfriend."

"Yes, this is Lyra. Lyra you met Kaley last time we were here," Lucas says, introducing us. Kaley holds out her hand for me to shake.

"Nice to meet you," I say, shaking her hand. Her soul feels sad, not about Lucas and me but in general. It's surprising because she seems so preppy and outgoing. Inside she is very depressed and sad. I feel bad for being so mean last time. I smile at her and wish there was some way I could help her out. Her eyes go dazed for a second then she blinks.

"Nice to meet you as well. Hope to see you around again! Lucas needs a good woman in his life," she says. Her soul doesn't feel nearly as sad as I let go of her hands. Maybe she just needed someone to be nice to her. I get it. Working at Sharky's was tough on me too. Customers can be just awful.

We part ways with her, and Lucas pays our bill. His mom and dad are talking to an older couple near us and Lewis and Julie are behind us in line. Once we pay, we wait for everyone else to finish up and follow us outside. Everyone says goodbye to us, and I get hugs from Kim, Lewis, and Julie. Jon smiles at me and wishes us luck on our trip but doesn't reach out for a hug. I get it, he doesn't trust me, and I don't blame him. I make sure to program everyone's number into my new phone and give them mine as well. It'll be nice having a phone again. We walk over to our truck and Lucas helps me up, then climbs in himself.

"Ready?" He asks, buckling up. I wish he would let me drive but he is determined to do it.

"Yup. Let's go," I say, blowing out a breath. I get out my phone and set my background as my favorite picture. I also program Aurora's number into my phone and text her, letting her know to text this number and not Lucas's to get ahold of me.

"So, you like your phone?" He asks me, driving fast again. Sigh.

"You know I do," I say looking up at him from under my eyelashes.

"Don't look at me like that. I'll pull over right now," he says, voice deepening. Oops. I didn't mean to look at him like that. I just can't help it, I see him and instantly I'm turned on.

"Sorry," I mumble, looking out the window.

"Don't be. We are mates Lyra, mates who can't fully bond. It's hard on both of us. I just wish you had told me it was getting harder on you to touch me."

"I know, I'm sorry. I just didn't want to disappoint you." I place my hand over the top of his and leave it there for now. We listen to music for a bit, neither of us talking. We both know we want each other and can't act on our feelings just yet. There's no need to talk about it. I let go of his hand when I need to and watch the scenery go by outside.

"Do you think I should call my friends?" I ask finally. It's something I've been considering, even before Lucas got me a phone. I miss Mira and Ryan. I should probably call my dad as well. He should have been here a long time ago, I'm concerned the council has him.

"I think it'll be alright. Honestly, the council knows where you are already." I look over at Lucas, his fists tight on the steering wheel, and nod. I dial Mira's number by heart and hope she picks up.

"Hello?"

"Mira! It's me. Don't hang up," I ask fast, Lucas glances at me curiously but doesn't comment. I don't think I really explained to him that we aren't on the best of terms right now.

"Where are you?" She asks, her voice doesn't sound as angry as the last time. More reserved, and maybe a little concerned? It could just be my imagination because I want her to worry about me because that means she still cares.

"I'm up in the mountains, staying with a... friend," I say, looking at Lucas. If Mira could see him now, she would know he's way more than a friend to me.

"Are you coming back? Why did you just leave all of a sudden? Ryan has barely spoken to me, I can't believe you just left him like that." Okay, now she sounds angry again. Fantastic.

"It wasn't like that Mira, and you know it. I told you I never liked Ryan, and I didn't. He kissed me and I left. I told you Ann threatened me," I say, huffing. I can't believe she still thinks I had feelings for Ryan. Sure, after the kiss I was a bit confused. I had never kissed someone before for God's sake!

"And you left because of her? What's she going to do?"

"Maybe you should ask Ryan, he told me he would talk to you when I left. Explain things. I don't know what all I can tell you, Mira. My life just exploded, and I can't go back to how it was before."

"So, you aren't coming back, just like that? You are abandoning your friends and you don't even care," she yells. I can hear her crying through the phone and pacing. She does that when she's upset.

"Of course, I care Mira! I just... I just don't know what the future holds. Talk to Ryan. Go to him and kick his ass until he tells you what's going on."

"Okay," she says, calmer now. "Maybe you shouldn't call me again. It's just too hard to talk to you right now. I'll call you when I can."

The phone goes dead, and I stare down at it, sighing loudly. I can't believe she's still so upset about everything. If she would just talk to Ryan, that might fix things. I don't even know why I'm so adamant about all this. I've never had friends before and I've been alright. Why do I need them now?

"What was all that about?" Lucas asks, eyes on the road but his hand reaches over and squeezes my knee in support.

"She's upset about Ryan kissing me still. She feels betrayed and confused that I just left after everything. I think she expected me to come knocking at her door and apologize, instead I up and leave in the middle of the night. I guess it's a lot to take in."

"Just give her time, she'll come around. If she doesn't, she's not a good friend, anyway." I look at Lucas, glad to have him in my life. I don't know what I would do without him.

"I guess I'll call Ryan, warn him about Mira asking him questions and let him know I'm safe. He wanted me to contact him when I could," I say, looking at Lucas for a reaction. I know I wouldn't be happy if he was calling someone he once kissed, but he looks relatively relaxed about it.

"Sure," he says, not looking at me. Alrighty then! I dial Ryan's number and wait for him to pick up. It finally goes to voicemail, and I relax back into my seat. My phone rings almost immediately.

"Ryan," I answer, knowing it's him. The other end of the phone is silent, then I hear a breath of relief.

"Ly, I didn't know if you were okay. I've been worried for days! Where are you?" He whispers the last part and I wonder who all is listening.

"I'm... around. I'm sure the council knows where I am anyway, they sent someone after me a few days ago but I'm fine," I reassure him.

"Yeah, I know. Some dude showed up the next morning before dawn with a harpy. They searched your house, and he sent her off to find you. I've been worried sick! But the guy is still sniffing around, so I assumed you either got away or they haven't managed to find you yet."

"I got away. The wolf pack here is protecting me, they will at least think twice before coming after me again. Did the harpy come back? Lucas injured her, but we weren't sure if she was able to make it far," I say, not realizing I mentioned Lucas's name. He's become such an important part of my life now.

"Lucas?" Ryan asks, sounding a little upset. Oops. Apparently, I'm upsetting everyone today. Way to go Lyra!

"Yeah, he's my.... He's my mate, Ryan. I didn't know it until I got here." I feel kinda bad, I wish I had more time to explain things to him and break it to him gently.

"Ah," he says, voice quiet. Then he takes a deep breath and releases it. "That's good. True mates are hard to come by, if you have one, I'm not upset by it. That means he was made for you, Lyra, and you were made for him."

"Thanks, Ry, I was worried you might be upset. We didn't have much time to talk about everything before I left."

"It's okay, I'll be fine. Promise," he says, and I believe him.

"So, Mira. She's going to be calling you for information. I'm not sure what I should tell her honestly, but she's upset about everything still and wants answers."

"I've been avoiding her," he says, sounding sheepish. "Do you think she can handle the truth? She's always been so...."

"So, Mira?" I offer, and we both laugh.

"Yeah, she's Mira. I think it'll be alright, I might have to skirt around some details, but I'll work it out. Don't worry about it. You just stay where you are, I'm not sure how long the council will sniff around for."

"I can do that. You be careful though, I don't want anyone getting hurt for me."

"Don't worry, they won't hurt me. Mira is calling me now, I'll talk to you later. Stay safe," he says, before disconnecting the call.

"That went well," Lucas says, voice tight. Yeah, I knew it was harder on him than he was letting on.

"Yeah, it did. I'm just glad he didn't seem too upset about everything. I really value his friendship," I say, making sure to emphasize friendship. Lucas grins, picking up on my tone.

"I know I have nothing to worry about, I'm just overprotective and exceedingly jealous. You know how I feel about you," he whispers, looking at me.

"And you know how I feel about you," I say, pushing my feelings for him to him. His eyes widen, and he grins. I feel his all-consuming love for me fill my senses, and I smile back at him. We might not be ready to say the words just yet, but we both know how the other truly feels.

The trip is uneventful. I kept expecting that Harpy chick to show up and attack us, but it was quiet. I tried calling my dad once, but his phone is off and went right to voicemail. Which is typical for him when he's on fishing trips. A part of me hopes he's still on the boat, but I know he's not. Deep down, I know he wouldn't be away this long. We listened to music and made good time getting to Athens. Once we reach city limits, I look up her practice address and give Lucas directions to get there. Pulling up, we park, and I practically jump out of the truck before he even opens his door.

"Be careful! You could break your ankle," he says, coming around and taking my hand. We walk up to the front door and see a sign, 'Out for delivery, come back tomorrow'.

"Just our luck!" I say, frustrated.

"Babies come when they want to, can't blame them," Lucas says. We walk back to the truck and just sit inside in silence until Lucas breaks it. "What do we do now?"

"Let's find a hotel for the night. No point in going back home and coming back tomorrow. We can stay overnight and come back in the morning. Their practice opens up at eight." Lucas nods and starts the truck while I look up hotels in the area. We choose one and I give Lucas directions. We decide to stay in town at a hotel called Hotel Indigo. I know Lucas will insist on paying so when we pull up, I jump out and run inside to get us a room. I hear him call after me, but I don't turn around, I'm not letting him keep paying for everything. Walking up to the front desk, I talk to the nice gentleman and get a room with two queen beds in it. When he asks for my license and credit card though, I'm at a loss. I try to talk him into accepting cash but he's adamant he can't do that.

"She's with me. Here," Lucas says, coming up behind me. He has our suitcase in his hand and smirks at me. He knows he's won this round. Ugh. The man looks up at Lucas, then back at me and smiles.

"Are you sure you don't want a room with a king size bed?" He asks, winking at us.

I would kill to share a bed with Lucas but know we can't. They talk for a few minutes and I look around the nicely decorated lobby. A sign down the hall says there is a pool and a cafe. Sweet.

They finish talking and he hands us our keys, he gives us his spiel and tells us our room is 301. We thank him and head to the elevator. I stab the button for the third floor and cross my arms. I know I'm pouting but I can't help it. He always pays for everything. Lucas remains silent, watching me with a smirk on his face the whole time. I want to smack that smirk off.

The elevator dings and we walk to the end of the hallway. He really would give us the farthest room. I take my key and insert it into the door before stepping inside. This is not the room I requested. We walk into an open kitchen and living room, there are French doors leading to a balcony as well. Everything is decorated in red, grays and whites, similar to Lucas's house at home. There're two doors off to the side and I walk inside one, there is a king size bed and a door leading into a huge bathroom with a walk-in shower and a soaker tub. Oh man, I can't wait to sink into that. There's another door leading out of the bathroom and back into the living room. So, there's only one bedroom. I walk back into the bedroom and see Lucas sitting down on the bed.

"Why did you upgrade us to a suite? Especially one that has only one bed," I ask him, hands on my hips. He looks up at me and smiles innocently.

"You don't think you suck souls when you are unconscious or asleep. I've been wanting to try sleeping beside you for a few days now."

"Are you serious? You want to risk me killing you based on that? That's stupid Lucas. I'll sleep on the couch," I say, marching out of the room.

"Lyra wait! I know it's a risk, and it's one I want to take," he pleads, following after me.

"It's not one I want to take! Imagine if you were me, Lucas. Imagine waking up from the best sleep you've ever had and turning over to see me and I'm dead. And you know it was you who did it and now you have to live with yourself. I can't do that!" I say, beginning to cry. He's not the only one who wants to sleep together, I do too. Hell, I dream of it. But I'm not risking it, he's too important to me. Lucas comes closer and wraps his arms around me.

"It's okay. I get it but it's not just your decision. I didn't tell you last night because I didn't want you to worry, and it's creepy, but I kinda came in there and tested it out…" He says, looking down at me. "I came in your room and held your hand for a few hours."

"What! You could have died. What were you thinking!?" I scream, slapping his arm hard. What an idiot.

"I already knew it didn't work before, I decided to test it again. I also would have known if it started working when I became stupid dazed. I was prepared to yank my hand away if needed," he says, rubbing down my arms reassuringly. "It's done Lyra. I already did it. We can't change that now. I know this will work. We can both wear pajamas to bed, socks and everything. It will be a little hard-wearing full sleeves and long pants when I normally sleep naked- but it's worth it. Please just try it."

"Lucas..." I start, looking at him. His eyes are begging me. I want to give into him so bad but I'm not sure I can. This is such a big risk. I pull away and look out the balcony doors. He's right, he already tested it out. He knows I won't hurt him in my sleep and I'm a heavy sleeper. Once I fall asleep, I'm out until my alarm goes off or I wake up on my own for the day. "Fine."

"Really? You agree?" He asks, coming up behind me and settling his hands on my hips. I nod my head and he puts his chin down on my shoulder, looking outside. We stand like that for a while, neither of us wanting to be away from each other. Finally, I pull away and go back into the bedroom. I go through the suitcase and unpack our clothes into the dresser across from the bed. I sort through them, looking for sleepwear that will work for tonight and didn't find much. It's freaking June, why would either of us think about grabbing long shirts and pants? Oh! Apparently, Lucas thought of it because he packed three pairs of long pajamas. He was planning this all along. I turn around, about to run out into the living room and yell at him, only to find Lucas leaning against the door jamb. I didn't even notice him come in here.

"What?" He asks.

"Have you just been watching me this whole time?" I ask.

"Perhaps. It's sexy watching you be all domestic and put away my clothes. It's almost like we are already married."

"Funny... Wait, already married? Do you want to get married? I mean, not now obviously. Like in the fu-" I'm cut off by his lips on mine. I know he's trying to distract me but it's working. He pulls away too soon for my liking and backs up.

"Yeah, I want to marry *you* one day," he says. I totally notice him emphasizing 'you'. He smiles at me and tucks a loose strand of hair behind my ear. "Do you not want to get married?"

"I've never really thought of it. I was so focused on just finding my soulmate one day that I never even considered what would happen after I found you. Then I found out we are literally soulmates and practically married already. I wasn't sure if you wanted to do the whole legal thing or have a wedding."

"Really, I never wanted that. Growing up I wanted to have a relationship like my parents. Find someone I cared about and mate with them, marriage is really unnecessary when you mate with someone. To have a soulmate is amazing but to be able to choose someone... choosing them over having someone 'set in the stars' for you, is more meaningful. At least that's how I thought. Then I had dreams of you and saw you in the library. I knew I'd choose you. It didn't matter if we were meant to be or not. I could still have a choice in the matter. And I will choose you, Lyra. Not because we were destined to be together but because you mean everything to me. I couldn't imagine my life with anyone else. And yes, I want to marry you. Our relationship may be deeper than a marriage, but I want everything with you."

"Are you sure? That could still be the mate bond working," I ask. I didn't know I was insecure in our relationship until now. I needed to hear him say all this.

"Feel this," he says, coming over to me and grabbing my hand. My hand tingles and warmth spreads throughout. "You feel the warmth and that zap of energy between us? That's the mate bond. Us liking the same music and food, laughing at stupid shit and just enjoying one another. That's not the bond Lyra. I told you the bond only takes you so far. Us falling in love is on us, not on that."

We stare into each other's eyes and I know he's right. Even if I didn't feel that when I touched him and I had never had dreams of him, I would still choose him. I could have met him in a store one day and instantly been attracted to him. Not because of the mate bond but because I generally find his looks attractive. We don't need a bond to feel this way. And knowing that makes our relationship so much deeper than a mate bond or simply dating. He's right, this is deeper than a marriage will ever be, but I want everything with him too. I want the mate bond, to be in love, to mate fully, to marry him, to one day have kids. Everything.

Knowing that we both feel the same way, I feel much better about everything. We can overcome my power and the council. We *will* make this work. No matter the consequences.

Chapter 19

Lyra

The first thing I notice when I wake up is the warmth surrounding me. I peel my eyes open and search for the tv light, but instead, I'm met with darkness. The couch feels more comfortable than it did last night as well. I shut my eyes for a second before they spring open. Dammit, Lucas! I scoot away from him but he's already reaching out for me in his sleep. Thank God he's alive at least.

"Lucas!" I hiss, kicking him with my foot. He groans and tries reaching for me again. His shirt is off too. How could he be so stupid?

"What baby?" He mutters, finally giving up on reaching for me and instead sits up on his elbows.

"Why am I in bed?" I ask him. I refused to sleep in the bed last night. I thought about it throughout the day and I just didn't want to risk him.

"I wasn't sleeping in the bed without you. So, I brought you in when you fell asleep. And look, nothing happened," he says, trying to come closer to me.

"But what if something did happen! That's the point, Lucas, we don't know. I could have woken up just now and found you dead beside me." I didn't even realize I was crying until he reached over and wiped my face. He pulls me in for a quick hug and I let him, needing the comfort. I know I'm probably overreacting, but I'm terrified of killing him.

"I knew you wouldn't hurt me, not while you are asleep at least," he says, stroking my hair.

"You aren't even wearing long sleeves like we talked about," I say drily.

"You are lucky I'm wearing boxers," he says laughing. I swat at him and climb out of the bed. "Where are you going?"

"To eat the leftover pizza from last night," I say, walking into the living room and kitchen. We ordered pizza last night for dinner and ate two whole boxes, it's a good thing we ordered three just in case. I grab a slice of pizza and turn around when I hear Lucas coming out of our room. I thought he would have put on a shirt, or even some pants, but he's still in just his boxers. And man does he look delicious. My mouth is salivating, and it isn't over the pizza currently dangling from my hand in front of my face.

"See something you like?" He asks, smirking at me and sauntering over.

I hum a yes and he takes a bite of my pizza. Even watching him chew food is hot. I set the pizza down and pounce on him, kissing him with all I have. His tongue swipes across my lips, asking for entrance, and I open for him. He tastes like pizza and fresh water; I can't get enough. My hands are in his hair, pulling him closer and he picks me up by my ass and sets me onto the countertop. A part of me knows this is going too far, but when I try to pull away his hand sneaks under my tank top and my mind forgets why we should stop. In all the times we've made out, he's never touched me like this. His hand grazes my belly, heading upward and then cups my bare breast in his palm. The feel of his rough skin against my nipple has me breaking away, gasping for air. His lips don't leave me though, they trail along my jaw and his teeth nibble lightly on my ear. We don't even hear the knocking on our door, both too enthralled with each other.

The door flies open and crashes onto the floor. We both pull apart, gasping for breath, and Lucas sets himself in front of me, ready to fight off whatever comes at us. The room is silent, and I lean my head around Lucas's wide shoulders, trying to get a glimpse of who is here but I see nothing.

"Leave," Lucas growls out into the silence. We continue to hear nothing then pain explodes inside my head. I drop down to the ground and cover my ears from the screaming, I belatedly realize it's coming from me. This pain is worse than the one Ann inflicted on me and I can feel tears streaming down my face. I try searching for Lucas but all I see is red. Then it stops.

I hear muffled voices, but I can't understand what they are saying, my ears are still ringing and I lay on the floor trembling. I feel hands on my face, and someone lifts me into the air, I think it's Lucas, but I can't be sure. I rest my head back and keep my eyes closed, they sting when I try to open them now, and drift to unconsciousness.

***

Coldness on my skin wakes me. My eyes spring open and race around my surroundings, wondering where I am. I relax when I see Lucas lying beside me on the bed, holding my hand. What happened? All I remember was an indescribable pain and then nothing. I slowly take my hand away from Lucas and try to sit up, but my body aches and I fall back onto the bed. My movement wakes Lucas, and he yanks himself up, looking around for danger before his eyes settle on me.

"You're awake!" He exclaims, coming closer to me and touching my face. There's a wet washcloth on my forehead, that must have been the coldness I felt, and he takes it off. "How are you feeling?"

"Awful. My whole body aches and there's still ringing in my ears. My eyes sting too," I say quietly, not mentioning my throat is sore from all the screaming I did. "What happened?"

"It was my fault." I hear across the room and I look over to the door, alert. My Aunt Karen is standing there, looking solemn. "I didn't know it was you."

"Aunt Karen!" I shout, trying to get up out of the bed. Lucas grabs my body though and pushes me back down on the bed. I glare at him but he's too busy glaring at Karen to see. I look between the two of them, wondering why he's so hostile. "Lucas, let me go to her. She's my Aunt."

"No," he growls. "She almost fucking killed you Lyra."

"I didn't know it was her here. I told you this already," she says.

"I don't care if you thought it was someone else, it wasn't. You should have waited until you knew who was here before you attacked like that," Lucas says to her, still glaring.

"What happened exactly?" I ask them. They both turn to look at me and their faces soften.

"I picked up on you coming to my practice yesterday. I have wards around the place so when you got close, I knew. I didn't know it was you exactly. It places a trace on whoever enters so

I followed the trace to here. I figured I had some time before you left since you checked into a hotel. I followed you here this morning and acted without knowing who exactly was in here. I'm sorry Lyra, I didn't mean to hurt you," she says. She sounds sincere to me and I already forgive her.

"See Lucas! She's fine. Let's all get along now," I say, looking up at him. He still looks livid.

"I can't just forgive her so easily! You've been asleep for hours Lyra. You were bleeding from your eyes, ears, and mouth. I can't get over seeing that. You could have died," he says, slowly going from angry to sad. His face scrunches up like he's going to cry, and I reach my hand up touching his cheek.

"So, you are mates?" I almost forget Karen was here. I turn to look at her and nod.

"Yes, we are," says Lucas. "We came here for answers."

"Why didn't dad tell me he was a wolf? Or that you were a witch? I had to learn everything on my own and I still don't know what I am!" I know I kinda sound like a whiny baby right now, but I still feel betrayed that no one told me the truth.

"Tell me what happened first. Why isn't your dad here? You shouldn't have found out anything from anyone but him."

"Dad left on a fishing trip. While he was gone a lot of shit happened." I say, looking at her. She gestures for me to go on. "Long story short, I kissed a friend of mine and something weird happened, I was later told I was sucking his soul out of his body. Some chick broke us apart and threatened to kill me. Said I had a few hours to get out of town before the council was called on me. I went to Miss Lynn's house, and she told me about dad, that my friend was a wolf shifter and the girl who threatened me was a witch. She called me special but wouldn't tell me what I was and sent me into the mountains to get protection. I got to the mountains and met Lucas here, was attacked by a freaking Harpy, found out Lucas is my mate, had to go see some Nymphs to heal me, and then decided to come here to find out exactly what I am because dad has still not shown up like Miss Lynn said he would," I say it all in a rush, and I'm not sure she's heard me until she comes closer and hugs me close.

"I'm so sorry you had to find out about so much on your own. This was never your dad's plan. He wanted to take you to the mountains and let your powers unfold when you were eighteen. You kissing that wolf must have set it off early. You said you were sucking his soul from him? How do you know?" She asks, letting go and stepping back.

"He told me before I left town. And it's happened since, whenever I touch someone, I can feel it slowly build up. I can let go before it happens usually."

"And does it happen to just wolves or humans too?" She asks.

"Anyone so far. I felt your soul when you just hugged me. It wasn't long enough for me to start pulling but I could feel it. You aren't entirely good, are you?" I ask her. Her soul didn't feel fully dark, but it was certainly not good.

"No, I'm not. I've dabbled in what some might one call dark magic when I was younger. It stays on your soul forever," she sighs. "So, you can absorb people's souls, I've never heard of that before though it is similar to others of your kind."

"What is my kind?" I ask her. Her eyes are dazed, far off, like she's no longer here with us.

"You are mostly like your mother. Not just in looks but her...

species," she finally says.

"You knew my mom?" I ask. She has never mentioned knowing my mom before.

"We were the best of friends growing up. She pulled me out of my darkness, and we traveled together. Her family was dark too, and she didn't want to be like them."

"What was she? Please, Aunt Karen, no one will tell me. I have a right to know about my mom and what I am," I beg her. She glances at Lucas and me, then sighs nodding.

"Okay. You have to understand this doesn't define you Lyra. You can, and will, be more than what you are. Just like your mom was. I'll tell you what you are but first I'll tell you the story of your parents," she whispers the last part. I nod.

"Your mom grew up in Arizona like I did. Our families were close, but your mom wasn't like everyone else. She was filled with dreams and happiness. She wanted more from her life than the rest of us. She pulled me from my own darkness, and we ran away together- leaving our families. We traveled for a while until we met your dad in Texas. Your mom knew instantly a wolf was around and tried to leave, she didn't want to hurt him by accident. Your dad knew she was his mate when he looked at her."

"They were mates?" I ask.

"Yes. Your dad pursued her when she ran off and convinced her they were mates. She knew it was dangerous to be around him, but she stayed. It was hard on them at first, she couldn't pull his soul out like you can, but something similar and just as deadly. I helped them figure out a way around it and once they fully mated, they had to go on the run. Your dad's pack did not support them and tried to kill your mother. They remained hidden for a few months before they were found. The only reason they didn't kill your mom, was because she was already pregnant."

"What happened to her? Dad said she died in childbirth."

"She did. The pack took her and locked her in a shack throughout her pregnancy," she says.

"What! That's barbaric. Why didn't dad try to break her out?" I yell. Lucas reaches over and touches my hand, soothing me.

"He thought they would give in. That once your mom had you and your brother, they would see they were meant to be together... he was naïve. They were never letting her live. I'm not sure what they would have done with you and your brother. If your brother was more of a wolf, they might have let him live. We will never know."

"How did dad get away with me?"

"Your mom was smart. She knew they wouldn't let any of you out alive. When she went into labor, she went for a walk outside and gave birth there. She hid you in a tree trunk and went off to give birth to your brother, but she didn't make it. Her guard found her, and she gave birth to him with your dad beside her. She managed to tell him about you before she died and when your brother was stillborn, your dad ran off to find you. He took you away and went to me. I knew you would be like your mom and would be in danger, so I bound your powers until you were eighteen."

"So, what was my mom? I need to know what I am Aunt Karen." I finally ask her. Knowing how my parents met and fought for each other is sweet but I don't know why she won't just tell me what I am.

"You are a hybrid, the first ever. The few pregnancies like your mom's all ended in death for the mother and her babies," she says, not looking at me. I know she's avoiding telling me what I am.

"Just tell me already!" I say loudly. She looks at me and takes a deep breath, slowly releasing it.

"Long ago, it's believed Apollo created the wolves. They were one of his most treasured creatures and he used to use them often. At one point, he was having an affair with Hecate, the Goddess of magic. When he ended things, Hecate was angry and wanted to get back at him. She created something to destroy his wolves. They would seduce them.... and then eat them," she says, watching both me and Lucas. Lucas looks paler than ever, he must know how this story goes.

"And?" I ask.

"They were called Empusae. Half snake, half woman. They were dark creatures who could shift into snakes as easy as breathing. They could wield dark magic and preferred to live by water."

"So, my mother was one? She hunted down wolves and killed them?" I ask, dreading the answer. I can't believe it. I look over at Lucas and he's staring down at the blanket in silence, shoulders tense. How can he be with me knowing what I am?

"Yes, she was one, but no she did not hunt wolves. Her family did, and she wanted no part of it. I told you she was different. She never wanted to harm anyone and loved your dad very much. It was hard on her in the beginning. She had to constantly fight her nature, but she did it for him," she says, patting my hand. I look down at her hands and feel her soul again, she's telling the truth.

"What does this all mean for me? I don't have the urge to kill Lucas or any other wolves."

"You will be different, you might lean more towards your mom, but you still have your dad inside you. Empusae feed on flesh and blood, you feed on souls. Are you weak at all? Showing signs of illness?" She asks me, looking over my face.

"Not really. I was feeling sick last week but Miss Lynn gave me a powder and it helped. I haven't fed on anyone's soul, I always let go before I can take it in."

"Get me the powder," she says seriously. I stand up and walk into the kitchen slowly, still feeling a bit woozy after everything. I take out the canister from our food bag and hand it to her. She pops the top and sniffs it then waves her hand over the top. The powder swirls a little on top and she nods to herself.

"This is dried blood. So, you must have to feed on that to survive," she says matter-of-factly. Blood? Gross.

"Great. Soon you'll be telling me I'll feed directly from people." Just as I finish talking, she looks at me funny. "Oh, you are telling me that."

"It's highly likely. Empusae have fangs that pierce through flesh and venom to paralyze their prey, like snakes. Let's see," she walks closer to me and Lucas watches over by the door. I notice he hasn't said anything since Aunt Karen told me what I am. I need to know his thoughts on what's going on.

"Lucas, come here," Aunt Karen says. He comes over without hesitation and she takes his arm bringing it up to my mouth and cutting it. I open my mouth wide and nothing happens. Karen taps her chin then takes a dab of Lucas's blood and puts it on my tongue. My taste buds explode, and I suck deeply on my tongue, closing my eyes and savoring the taste. I open my eyes and they are both staring at me. Oops. "Let's see your teeth."

I open my mouth and she nods, looking satisfied with herself. Lucas looks closer too. He doesn't look disgusted at least. Karen waves her hand, and a glass flies out of a cabinet, then she does some motion with her hands, like milking a cow, and I feel liquid pull out of my teeth and flow into the glass. I look into the glass and see a mostly clear liquid with a slight purple sheen to it.

"Venom. That answers both questions. So, what else can you do?" She asks me.

"I'm not really sure. I shifted into a wolf on my birthday, but I could see other animals when I was shifting. Lucas had me test it out, and I shifted into a snake. Guess that makes a lot of sense now," I say, still staring at my venom in the glass. This is weird. I look at Lucas again and he's staring at me with... I'm not even sure what that look in his eyes is. Pretty sure it's disgust or revulsion.

"You can most likely shift into multiple animals," she says smiling at me. "We will figure out the rest of your powers as they come."

"Can you help us? I can touch Lucas for longer periods of time, but it also becomes harder to pull away." I ask her.

"Yes, I can. Once you are fully mated, you won't be able to harm him. It's not physically possible. Your mom went through the same thing, the longer she was around him and got used to him the less she felt the need to feed on him. It will get easier for you."

"That's all I have to do? Just touch him as often as possible and eventually work up to mating?" I ask incredulously. That sounded too easy.

"That and when mating you'll have to fight your base instinct to bite him."

Yup. I knew it was too easy. Lovely.

Chapter 20

Lucas

An Empusae. Damn. I knew Lyra was something different, but I wasn't expecting that, that's for damn sure.

I've been taught my whole life about them. That they were made to seduce us and kill us. All of them are extremely beautiful, with red hair, and are attractive to wolves naturally. I haven't heard of one killing a wolf in a long time, many have stopped hunting us and instead kill whoever they like.

Looking over at Lyra, it's not as surprising as I originally thought. She is beautiful, almost otherworldly, and has curly red hair. Her eyes are gray and occasionally when feeling deep emotion, I notice her pupils slant like a snakes would. It all makes sense now. Damn.

So where do we go from here? Lyra and her Aunt Karen are talking in the kitchen, Lyra is showing her the canister.

"This is dried blood. So, you must have to feed on that to survive," Karen says to her. Even that makes sense now. I remember back when we hunted, and Lyra naturally sniffed out a rabbit and ate it. Normally, it's hard for wolves to hunt that first time. Getting used to taking something's life and eating raw meat. Lyra took to it too easily. She was made to do just that.

"Lucas, come here," Karen demands, bring me out of my thoughts. I step forward and she takes my arm gently and cuts it with magic, nothing happens to Lyra. Karen shoves her finger into the wound and then swipes it across Lyra's tongue.

There it is. Lyra's mouth closes, and she seems to be sucking on her tongue... I can give her something else to suck. She releases a loud moan and I instantly think of the two of us in bed together. Fuck I want her so badly. I don't care about what she is. She is still the same woman I want to spend the rest of my life with.

"Let's see your teeth." Lyra opens her mouth wide at Karen's words. I look closer and can see two sharp fangs protruding from her mouth. Karen waves a hand and a glass flies through the air, she holds it in front of Lyra's mouth and then does a weird gesture with her hands that I barely notice. I'm too enthralled looking at Lyra's pretty mouth. Light purple liquid seeps from her sharp teeth and into the glass. Seeing Lyra with her fangs exposed doesn't scare me like I thought it would. Instead, I feel intense arousal. I want to take Lyra into the bedroom and throw her onto the bed right now, Karen be damned.

When Karen tells Lyra she will have to fight her instincts to bite me during sex, I want the opposite. I want her to sink her fangs into me and mark me, just like I want to mark her. I stare at her darkly, wondering if she has any clue of where my thoughts are. She doesn't seem to. She looks embarrassed and sad.

"Lyra," I say, growling lightly. Both Karen and her turn to look at me now. "Bedroom. Now."

I storm into our room and wait at the door for Lyra to join me. I slam the door when she enters and press her against it, staring at her mouth. Her fangs are still elongated and damn she is irresistible. I lean forward and capture her lips with mine.

"Lucas we can't," she whispers.

"Why not? I want you so badly right now," I say gruffly, kissing down her neck and nipping at her where I want to sink my teeth.

"I don't want to hurt you and my Aunt is right outside the room. How can you even look at me now?" I stop kissing her neck and stare at her. Her eyes are filling with tears and she won't look me in the eye. I can't have her thinking this way.

"You are still you. And honestly, none of this is surprising to me. It makes a lot of sense actually," I tell her, wiping her tears and forcing her to look in my eyes. "I find you more attractive than ever."

"Really? Even though I have freaking fangs?" She asks, looking at me like I'm crazy. I groan, looking at her mouth. They are still peeking through.

"Especially with the fangs. Seeing them turns me on. I just want to throw you on the bed right now and have my way with you," I say, my voice going even deeper, and I kiss her again. She needs to know how much she means to me. "I love you. I know we've only known each other for less than a week, but it feels like forever. I've had dreams of you for years now. I know who you are on the inside, and I want you to be mine. I accept you as you are Lyra. I don't want you to change yourself for me."

"Really?" She asks, tears filling her eyes again. This time there's a hopeful look in her eyes and a slight smile on her lips. I nod. "I love you too Lucas. So much."

I lift her up and she wraps her legs around me. I go to kiss her again but there's a knock on the door. I forgot about Karen. Fuck.

Sam Miller

"I'm still here and we still have more to talk about," she says through the door. I look at Lyra and she looks mortified, cheeks flushed a deep scarlet. I imagine this is like being scolded by a parent to her. I let her down and we walk out the door. I make sure not to touch her for now, if I touch her, we are going back in that room and not coming out. I don't even care if she takes my soul.

"You're so much like your parents," she says to Lyra and I.

"Please don't say that. I really don't want to know," she begs, groaning into the palm of her hands. Karen laughs.

"I'm just saying! Your dad was like that with your mom too. He loved seeing her fangs like that. They were good together," she says, looking wistful. "You guys can stay here, or you can come back to my house. You'll need to touch as much as possible to build up an immunity, but I need to be near you to make sure it doesn't go too far."

"I'm all for touching as much as possible," I say, swinging my arm around Lyra's waist. She looks up at me and smiles. I press my hand under her shirt and settle it on her bare waist. Lyra looks down at my hand and back up at me with a raised eyebrow. "What? She said to touch as much as possible. That's what I plan on doing."

She doesn't know it yet, but I plan on us fully mating in the next week. I know we have to be careful but damn I want her all the time. I don't know how much longer I'll be able to last without taking her.

Chapter 21

Lyra

I t didn't take long to decide we were staying with my Aunt Karen. I loved the hotel we were staying at, but if Lucas and I are going to touch as much as possible, then we need to be close to someone who can stop both of us from taking it too far. I'm nowhere near ready to complete our bond- I mean, I am, but I can't control myself fully just yet.

We moved our stuff over yesterday morning and met Aunt Karen's family. I had met her husband, Andrew, before, but this was my first time meeting her daughters: Ava, who is five, and Emma, who is almost two. Lucas loves the girls and offered to watch them for us today. Surprisingly, Aunt Karen agreed easily, and we left them alone so we could spend some time together- just the two of us.

The car ride is mostly silent, the two of us are lost in our own thoughts. I'm still reeling about everything I've learned and while I understand why no one told me the truth, I'm still a little hurt. We pull up at the Georgia Square mall and neither of us has said a word yet. It's not until we are walking inside that she turns to me and drags me away from the door.

"I don't like this tension between us. I'm sorry about not telling you the truth. Your father thought it was best for you not to know yet, and I agreed with him," she says, eyes pleading with me to forgive her. I cave instantly. We can't change the past, we can only move on.

"I know. You guys probably made the right decision, I'll have to get over it. There's no point in me being angry at you now, we can't change what happened," I say, leaning forward and hugging her close. She smells like apples like she has since I was little. "I missed you."

"I've missed you too," she whispers, hugging me tightly. We finally separate, and we both have tears in our eyes. Women. "Now let's get you inside so you can pick out something nice for Lucas."

"Something for Lucas? I thought we were shopping for me," I joke, following her inside. She looks back behind her and winks at me.

"Something for you to wear that Lucas will like," she says, leading me towards a lingerie store. My eyes widen and I glance between her and the store. I plant my feet firmly on the ground, refusing to go inside. "Come on. You're an adult now, with a mate I might add. If you are anything like you were before, you still wear granny panties."

I refuse to acknowledge her, but my cheeks heat in embarrassment. She laughs and drags me into the store. For an older woman, she sure is strong. Must be from handling two young children. I stop dragging my feet, eyeing the manikins and the different pieces of clothing. Some are bright, others are more subdued. My eyes are drawn to the cool colors, purples, blues, greens. I walk over, eyeing the different styles and Aunt Karen comes up behind me, pointing at a pair of see-through ones. My eyes widen even more, and my cheeks flush. I can't believe I'm looking at sexy underwear with my Aunt.

"Get these," she says simply. She eyes my hips and picks out a size 16 without comment. Damn, she's good. That's exactly what I wear. Stupid hips. We go through and pick out a few more pieces, she even grabs some for herself. Ew. We go back to try them on in different dressing rooms and she insists that she see the purple pair on me. Finally, I agree and let her into my room.

"Those," she says, eyeing them and circling me, "are gorgeous!"

"Do you want me to have children soon? Because that's what you are asking for," I tease, looking at my butt in the mirror. These do look awesome. Seeing her face though, I turn around. "What's wrong?"

"Well…" she starts, looking uncomfortable, "it's just that Empusae aren't known for having children often."

"What do you mean? Mom had me and, obviously, someone had her," I say, not understanding. Aunt Karen sighs and takes a seat in the dressing room.

"Empusae have issues conceiving. Then when they are pregnant, it's even harder to carry pregnancies to full term. They feed on people and their bodies naturally absorb their babies in the womb." I gasp, my hands flying to my mouth and I lean against the wall. That's just awful! "You might be different though, you're a hybrid. Wolves don't have fertility issues and your mom got pregnant with you and your brother very fast. I wouldn't be too concerned, but it's something you should know."

I nod, calming myself down. She might be right. I am different from my mom. Standing back up, I eye myself in the mirror again. Wondering if my belly will ever protrude with a child. It's something I've never really thought about before, but I want that with Lucas. So badly.

Aunt Karen leaves the room and I try on a few more things before giving up. I'm just not as excited as I was before. I randomly pick a few items, making sure to get the purple one I really liked and check out. Aunt Karen insists on paying and she takes me to lunch afterward. I try not to look into the window of a children's clothing store as we pass, but I can't help it. I can't help but imagine a little boy dressed as a superhero, or a little girl as a firefighter- because really, girls can be anything they want, not just princesses. My eyes run over the window displays, looking at the all-gray crib decked out in moon items. I want this. I want this more than I thought I would.

Chapter 22

Lyra

L ater that night, I sit on the couch and watch the three of them play on the floor. Lucas is wearing a loose gray t-shirt and black basketball shorts, probably the most casual I have ever seen him. He also has pink glitter covering him from head to toe. Ava is sprinkling glitter everywhere and Emma is trying to hide behind Lucas, so she doesn't get covered. I smile watching the three of them laugh.

"No fair!" Ava yells as Lucas lifts Emma up into the air. She stomps her bare feet and jumps into the air, trying to reach Emma. She's wearing a pink dress and purple leggings. "Put her down! I want to make her sparkle!"

"No!!!" Squeals Emma. She climbs as high as she can in Lucas's arms and screams. At two, she's small for her age and easily fits into her little blue dress.

Lucas turns to me and drops Emma beside me before picking up Ava and tickling her. Ava giggles loudly and snorts. Emma snuggles up beside me and watches them curiously. She's still young and learning about the world around her. She takes her thumb and shoves it into her mouth, sucking on it. I shake my head but ignore her behavior, Aunt Karen isn't the biggest fan of letting her suck her thumb, but she's only two!

"Okay, Okay!! I give!" Ava says, out of breath from laughing so much. Lucas lets her down and lies beside her on the floor; Ava isn't the only one worn out it seems. Ava has a mischievous smile on her face, and before I can warn Lucas, she jumps on top of his stomach causing Lucas to groan loudly. Ava giggles and bounces on his stomach, I'm pretty sure Lucas is not breathing at the moment.

"Lyra! Help me, baby, please," he manages to groan out. I laugh and stand up from the couch, bending down and catching Ava as she bounces up.

"Alright, little Miss. We are all done trying to kill Lucas," I say to her, plopping her down on the couch beside her sister.

"Aw! You always take his side. Why don't you pick my side for once?" She asks, her bottom lip jutting out in a pout. Her face looks ridiculous with pink glitter spread over her cheeks and eyelashes.

"You know I love taking your side Ava, but Lucas has had enough for now," I say, smiling at her. I lean closer to her ear and whisper, "How about I help you get him later?"

She quickly nods her head and jumps off the couch, racing to her room to play. Emma climbs off the couch and tries to go after her but I swoop down and pick her up in my arms. She loves to play with Ava, but someone has to be watching Emma at all times.

"No, ma'am. You are staying with us until your mama gets back," I say to her. She fights my hold, and I set her down in the corner of the room which is set up with toys for her to play with. Once I make sure she's settled and not going to toddle off, I look at Lucas who is still laying on the floor with his eyes closed.

Smirking to myself, I quietly tiptoe over to him planning on a sneak attack. When I'm less than a foot away, his hand whips out and grabs my ankle; making me tumble down on top of him. He groans again but doesn't let me go as I straddle him.

"Was me falling on top of you part of your plan?" I ask smiling, laying my palms down on his muscular chest.

"Not exactly. The plan was for you to fall beside me, not on me. Damn, woman, you are heavy," he says. I know he's joking but I slap him on his shoulder anyway, causing glitter to fly through the air. He laughs at me and pulls me down for a kiss. I imagine he was planning just a peck but once our lips touch, we can't seem to stop. It's been like this the last few days, constantly touching, and we can't seem to get enough of each other. I know part of it is the mate bond, but a much larger part is just us. We love each other and can't wait to take that final step in our relationship. I pull away first and sit up on top of him, I glance over at Emma to make sure she's okay before looking back down at him.

"You will make a great mom," he says, looking up at me with a soft smile on his lips. His face is completely relaxed and open, getting away from his family had helped him let go of a part of himself I didn't realize he was holding back.

"And you'll make a great dad," I whisper back to him. It's true. Watching him the last two days play with Emma and Ava have shown me a glimpse of what he will be like when we have children... if we can. I don't allow my mind to think of that right now. I know it's hard for Empusae to get pregnant, something Aunt Karen mentioned, and I'm not sure how that will change with me being a hybrid. Either way, we aren't ready for children just yet. "Wanna watch a movie now?"

"Sure. You pick and I'll make us some hot chocolate and popcorn," he says as I stand up. I walk over to the wall of movies and debate on which genre I'm wanting to watch tonight. A part of me wants to pick a romance movie because come on what girl doesn't want to watch romance with her hot boyfriend? But instead, I pick a Harry Potter one. Again. I pop it into the DVD player and pick up Emma. It's almost eight at night and it's time for her bedtime.

"Hey, I'm taking Emma upstairs first and putting her to bed. Don't start without me!" I yell into the kitchen so Lucas can hear me. He walks out before I can walk up the stairs and gives Emma a kiss on the cheek.

"Goodnight little one," he whispers to her and pecks me on the cheek as well. God, he makes my ovaries freak. I smile at him and walk up the stairs to Emma's room. Emma has a curious soul, unlike her sister who is always happy. I try not to touch either of them for long periods of time, but it's nice being able to feel someone's soul and know how they are feeling in that moment. I walk into her room and change her diaper and her clothes before laying her down in her bed. Thankfully she's a great sleeper and doesn't need anything else. I make sure the baby monitor is on, then turn off the light and shut the door behind me.

Walking down the hall, I stop in Ava's room and make sure she's still good. She has another hour before her bedtime so I can come back later to put her to bed, but when I open the door, she's sound asleep on the floor still fully dressed.

"Ava, honey," I whisper, rubbing her back lightly. She stirs and looks at me, bleary-eyed. "You need to go to the bathroom and change into your PJs before bed." She grumbles some but eventually follows me into the bathroom. I help her do her business and change her clothes before I tuck her into bed. She's back asleep before I even make it to the door. I stop by my room and change into shorts and a tank top before heading downstairs.

Lucas is on the couch waiting for me, the title menu on the screen in front of him. I plop down beside him on the couch and snuggle under the blanket with him. He's shirtless now, must have taken it off because of all the glitter and thrown it somewhere. I press my bare skin into his and lean my face up to look at him.

"Why did you lose the shirt?" I ask.

"Needed to get the glitter off me, plus I wanted more practice," he says, grinning down at me. His eyes are darker than usual and I know just what he means by practice. "How is Ava?"

"She was passed out on the floor when I went up there. I woke her up and got her in bed. Now, it's just you and me until Aunt Karen and Andrew come home," I say, looking at his lips. Before I can even blink, I'm lifted up and dropped on his lap. He captures my lips and tugs me as close as he can, his hands under my tank top and spanning my back. I grind my wet heat against his hardened length through our clothes. He groans loudly and grips my waist, trying to create more friction between us. I know he wants me just as bad as I want him.

"Lucas," I breathe out, pulling my lips from his. He drags his tongue down my neck and I almost cum on the spot. "Don't stop."

He pulls away and looks into my eyes. Seeing that I'm sure, he lifts my tank top over my head and leaves me bare from the waist up. Even though this is his first time seeing my breasts, he barely glances down at them before crushing our naked chests together and kissing me furiously. I grind myself down on him again, enjoying the jolts of pleasure flowing from my center and to the rest of my body. He pushes his hips into mine repeatedly, neither of us caring we are dry humping like little teenagers; we need this release more than we need to breathe.

Without thinking, I bring my mouth to his neck and graze my teeth against his jugular. Lucas groans and pushes his neck closer to my mouth. Giving into my instincts, I sink my teeth into his neck and pull. Both of us explode in pleasure and shake with our orgasms. I've masturbated before but never has it felt like this. I take in another mouthful before I jump back and look at his neck. There are two puncture wounds staring back at me. I look at Lucas's face and it's frozen in pleasure, eyes still closed.

"Lucas!" I say, jumping off him. I bring my hand to my mouth and bring it away, blood along my fingers. I freaking just *sucked* his blood! Lucas looks at me in a daze and smiles.

"It's okay Lyra, I don't think you put any venom in me. I feel fine," he assures me, reaching for my hips. I back up and frantically throw on the shirt I found on the floor, conveniently it's Lucas's.

"It's not okay! I didn't even think about it before biting you. I could have killed you!" I yell, pacing back and forth in front of him. Lucas watches me pace, then stands up and grabs me into his arms. I fight him for a second and then I relax in his arms, sobbing. "I can't hurt you. I couldn't live with myself."

"I know. It's okay. I love you and you didn't hurt me. We just got carried away," he whispers, stroking my hair. I feel my body relax even more and he picks me up in his arms. "I'll take you up to bed. I'll come in when you're asleep okay?" I nod and he walks up the stairs, carrying me the whole way. He places me on our bed and turns off the light, walking away.

This is becoming our routine now. I go to sleep first and then Lucas comes in after to sleep beside me. At least we know he's safe when I'm asleep. I pull off my shorts and leave on Lucas's shirt and my underwear, bringing the blanket up and around me. I snuggle into Lucas's pillow and close my eyes.

I don't know what we should do. Every day we get closer and closer to going too far. I know Lucas and Aunt Karen both have faith in me not to hurt him, but I don't believe in myself. Lucas drives me crazy when I'm around him. Hopefully, Miss Lynn will be here soon, and she can help me control myself more. Maybe she knows some secret Empusae power chant or something. I'm willing to try anything to not hurt Lucas.

***

I wake up and roll over in bed, expecting to find Lucas beside me but he's not. I open my eyes and look around the room, but he's nowhere to be found. Frowning, I get up out of bed and go downstairs to search for him. I'm always the first one to wake up, this is weird.

Walking into the living room, I hear voices coming from the kitchen and dining room. I walk in and see everyone gathered around for breakfast. I glance down at my lack of clothing, still wearing Lucas's shirt and my underwear, and blush bright red. His shirt goes down to my knees, but still. Lucas looks up at me and smiles, gesturing with his head to the seat beside him. I tentatively walk over and take my spot, refusing to look up at anyone else.

"Oh, don't be shy. It's not like we are all fully dressed either," My Aunt Karen says. I glance down at her wardrobe choice and see she's also wearing a man's shirt and long sleep pants. Everyone at the table is still wearing their PJs, except Uncle Andrew who is dressed for work. I feel Lucas's hand on my thigh, and I look up at him. He smiles reassuringly and loads my plate up with food. I dig in without thought. I don't think I've ever felt this hungry before.

"Something must have helped your appetite," Aunt Karen says, watching me stuff my face. Lucas chokes out a laugh and I glare at him.

"Don't know what you mean," I say stiffly, going back to my breakfast.

"I'm sure you don't," Aunt Karen says, then looks down at my lips. "You must have worn a dark lipstick to bed last night, your lips are stained like blood." I gasp and bring my hand up to my mouth, trying to rub it off. My hand comes away slightly red tinted. Damn.

"It's not that bad, baby," Lucas whispers in my ear, scooting closer. He takes a napkin from the center of the table and dunks it into his water glass, bringing it out, he dabs my lips clean and then pecks me. "All good."

I stare at him like he's completely insane. I don't know how he was so cool about everything that happened. I figured he didn't freak out last night because he came in his pants, but now in the light of day, I thought for sure he would be upset with me. He goes back to eating his breakfast and I face forward, looking at my plate.

"Alright, I'm off to work," Uncle Andrew says to the table. He bends down and gives the girls a kiss, then leans over and kisses Aunt Karen soundly. He works on the weekends as a construction manager. It works out well because Aunt Karen works Monday through Thursday at her clinic and is on call during any deliveries. Someone is always home with the girls during the summer.

"Bye! Love you," Aunt Karen calls out as he walks out the door.

She smiles softly and then turns to me. "We should talk." Well, that ruined my appetite. Pushing away from the table, I follow her into the living room while Lucas watches the girls. "What happened?"

"Do you want specifics?" I ask her snidely. She doesn't look impressed.

"Please don't. Just tell me the basics," she says, sighing.

"Well we were about to get it on, on your couch by the way, when I was filled with such pleasure, I bit Lucas," I say, looking her in the eyes. I might be embarrassed by what I did but I don't regret being with someone I love.

"I said the basics," she groans, her brown eyes looking up at the ceiling. "You must not have released venom, otherwise he would have been knocked out cold on the couch for hours."

"I don't think so. I didn't even realize what I was doing, I was just following my instinct and bit down. Then freaked out and Lucas had to calm me down."

"Better than what your mom did," she says snickering.

"What did my mom do?" I ask curiously, a part of me wanting to know more about her and another part not wanting to know this specific detail.

"She bit your dad less than a week of being with him. And she released venom. She called me crying hysterically. She had no clue what to do. I rushed over to her hotel room and there was your dad, naked ass in the air, passed out cold on the floor." She's full-on laughing now and I can't help but join in, even though I really didn't need to know about all that.

"Okay, not as bad as my mom," I say, still laughing.

"It's going to happen Lyra. It's okay. If you inject venom, he will just pass out and be good as new in a few hours. Otherwise, he will quite enjoy your biting him and so will you. It does help you desensitize though. Your mom and dad were able to mate within days after that happened."

"Really? That would be great! I feel like I'm half a person right now, like my whole life is on hold until this happens," I say.

"I know. Your parents were the same way. How long can you go now without siphoning his soul?" She asks.

"I'm not sure. I lose track of time with him," I say, blushing.

"That was over ten minutes last night," Lucas says, coming into the room holding Emma in his arms and Ava following closely behind him.

"Stupid wolf hearing," I mutter. Lucas looks over at me and smirks. I know he heard me. Great.

"Well, I'm taking the girls to the park. Would you guys like to join us or stay here and have some alone time?" Aunt Karen asks. Before I can even think about it, Lucas tells her we are good and to go without us. I guess he has plans. Aunt Karen looks between the two of us and smiles knowingly, then takes the girls upstairs to go get ready.

"Do you plan on us leaving the house or staying here?" I ask him.

"Definitely staying here," he says gruffly, coming over and pulling me into his arms. "I know we didn't get to talk last night, but I wanted you to know that was hot as hell and I want a repeat of it ASAP."

"Does this repeat require clothes, or can we be naked this time?" I tease.

"The fewer clothes, the better."

I laugh and run up the stairs to our room, Lucas following closely behind me.

***

We weren't able to take it all the way. Unfortunately. If I had it my way, we would be fully mated right now. Sadly, I felt that awful tingle appear just after I came on Lucas's face. I had to push him away forcefully and then hightail it out of the bedroom. Thank god no one was home. Otherwise, they would have gotten an eyeful as I ran naked through the hallway. At least I didn't bite him this time- though he did bite my thigh, and it felt delicious. I walk back into the bedroom and Lucas is gone. I dress quickly then head downstairs.

"I want you to mark me like that more—" I step into the living room and shut my mouth. Lucas is sitting there in sweatpants and Miss Lynn is sitting across from him looking highly amused. "Miss Lynn!!" I say running over to her and hugging her.

"My dear! You are looking well. And you found your mate! I'm so happy for you," she says, hugging me back and rocking me back and forth.

"I'm so glad you're here. I have so many questions." I say, tearing up a little and sitting beside her. I look over at Lucas and his face is grim. "What's wrong?"

"Nothing. I just feel weird around her. No offense," he says to

Miss Lynn, who shrugs it off.

"None taken! I know wolves feel off centered around me and that's normal. Especially since I had my fangs removed," she says.

"Wait, your fangs are removed?" I ask her, flabbergasted.

"Why, yes, many Empusae turned themselves over willingly to the council about fifty years ago. There was a mass war between us and wolves and some of us didn't want that. Our fangs were pulled out, so we were no longer a threat to wolves. It changes our scent so we are no longer attractive to them and we can't hurt them. That's why I had the powder dear, that's the only way I can survive now. Some still view us as a threat. Which I understand, we were created to kill them."

"Is that something I can do? I don't want to hurt Lucas," I say.

"No way in hell," Lucas growls at me. Miss Lynn looks over at him and smiles.

"I think he's partial to your fangs dear and I'm not sure that would even work. Wolves have amazing healing powers. Your fangs might just grow back," she says. That makes sense, I guess.

"Do you know what happened to my dad?" I ask her. Lucas's family has called us daily, and he still hasn't shown up. Miss Lynn looks down when I ask her. "What is it?"

"The council took him. They weren't aware there was a hybrid. It's a crime against the council to hide one. When they were told about you, they knew you must be a hybrid. There is nothing out there with powers such as yours. They ambushed your dad as soon as he got home. I tried to intervene, but they threatened to take me as well since I knew about you and didn't report it.

I'm so sorry," she says to me. My eyes fill with tears and Lucas comes over to me and wraps me in his arms. I cry into his shoulder while he strokes my back.

"It'll be okay. We will get him back. There has to be a way," he says.

"The only way to get him back is to travel to the council and turn yourself in. They might let him go in your place, they might not. But that's not what your dad would have wanted. He would want you to stay with your mate and be happy."

"Can't I have both? Can't I be happy with Lucas and have my dad?" I ask her.

"I'm afraid not. Not unless the council is overthrown. You have the backing of Lucas's pack, but you will need much more to do that. You'll need more shifter packs and other mystical creatures."

"What other creatures are out there?" I ask.

"Many. There are still big Empusae clans, witch covens, harpies, sirens, some giants, and more. Most are hidden but we could find some if that is what you want to do. Not all will join you. Most are scared of the council and some will be too scared to stand against them. Unfortunately, the ones who aren't too scared will be the ones you don't want to work with. Like your mother's clan. All those Empusae use their gifts for evil, killing wolf and men alike. There are not many of the good ones left, and many who are no longer have fangs and cannot fight. This would be a tough road to go down if you choose it," she says seriously. I had no idea there were so many creatures left.

"I'll do anything to find my dad," I say finally. I'm determined to find him. I can't leave him alone in some jail cell because he was protecting me.

"Then we need to decide on a home base, I would suggest your home, Lucas. We will be protected by your wolf pack; the council won't go near us inside those walls."

"Okay, so we go back to Sylva and then what?" I ask.

"I train you. You are weak until you fully mate; your mind too preoccupied. Once that's done, I'll begin training you and we can start searching for others to help," she says.

"How am I supposed to mate with him fully? I can barely touch him for ten minutes before I start to pull his soul from his body," I say, exasperated.

"Carefully. You need to be touching more," she says, looking at the distance between us. Lucas instantly grabs my hand, and she nods in approval. "I mean touching all the time. As soon as you feel yourself losing control, let go for a minute and then go right back to touching him. Push your limits. That's the only way you'll get better. You need to have at least thirty minutes of touching before you can go all the way. That's usually what Empusae need to make sure we are in control. If you work on it all day today, you might even be ready tomorrow."

"Aunt Karen said mom and dad were able to mate within a week after she... uh... bit him," I say carefully, Lucas looks at me curiously and I shake my head, begging him not to ask. While it was nice to know something about my mom, I really don't want to repeat what I found out.

"Yes. Biting someone and drinking from them, brings a little bit of that person into you. It makes it easier to be around them. You are lucky. Empusae have an intense need to drink and once we start drinking, it's almost impossible not to eat them. So, it's a bit hard to not kill someone."

"Have... have you killed someone?" I ask her tentatively.

"Once," she says, looking away. "I wasn't planning on going with the other Empusae to have our fangs removed. I had heard of the movement for a while, but I was content in my life and wasn't concerned. I started seeing a human boy, and we became close fast. I fought every instinct in me not to hurt him. Eventually, I gave in to my instincts, thinking if I bit him it would make it easier on me.... I was wrong."

"I'm so sorry," I say. Her eyes look haunted. Her cheeks sucked in and lips pressed together. I couldn't imagine liking someone and accidentally killing them. I would walk myself to the council after that too.

"I've come to accept it. I went to the council after that, had my fangs removed and moved to Cedar Island where I've lived the rest of my life. I was doing the motions until you came along. You gave me purpose again and I want you to learn from my mistakes. Just be careful. You've already tasted Lucas's blood; the hard part is over now, and you didn't succumb to blood lust," she says gently. I nod at her words and try to wrap my mind around everything. So much has changed in my life in such a short period of time.

"The plan is to go home then?" Lucas asks, we look at him and nod. He pulls out his cell phone and calls someone, I assume his dad or brother. "Hey. We are coming back either today or tomorrow," he pauses and glances at me. "Yes, we know what she is now. I'll tell you when we get back. And expect us to have some company. No one dangerous but it will put the pack on edge."

Lucas hangs up the phone and sits back down beside me, touching my arm and grabbing my hand. He's taking this touching constantly thing very seriously.

"How is everyone?" I ask.

"They seem fine. I just wanted to warn them someone else was coming with us. I don't want to explain what you are on the phone," he says, sighing.

"Are you embarrassed by it?" I ask, looking down at our hands.

"Of course not. I love you, all of you. It's just something easier to explain in person than over the phone. That's all," he says, touching my cheek. He leans in and kisses me fast, then Miss Lynn clears her throat; reminding us she is here.

"Sorry," I mutter, looking over at her.

"Don't mind me, dear," she says chuckling. "I don't mind seeing a show, but shouldn't I pay first?"

"Very funny," I huff, rolling my eyes. Lucas laughs and stands up, holding his hand out for me. I stand up with him and take his hand.

"Let's go pack. We can have everything ready to go so we can say goodbye to Karen and the kids when they get back," I nod and we walk upstairs together, throwing everything in our suitcase. By the time we are done, we hear noises downstairs and wander down. Miss Lynn and Aunt Karen are at a standoff in the living room while the girls cower behind their mother.

"Aunt Karen, this is Miss Lynn," I say, introducing them.

"I know," Aunt Karen says, not looking away. "We just don't get along the best is all. Can't help it."

252

"Well try," I say, frustrated at the two of them. "We are going back home."

"What? Why? I don't sense that you two are mated yet," she asks me, looking at the two of us.

"We aren't. Not yet at least. The council has my dad and will be coming after me. I can't risk your family; the pack can protect us, and we can work on a plan to get him out," I say. Lucas sets our bag down on the floor and wraps his arm around my waist. I lean into him for support. I don't know what I would do without him.

"Are you talking about overthrowing the council?" She whispers, looking between the three of us. I nod and she turns to the girls. "Ava, take Emma upstairs into your room and play with her, will you?" Ava does as she says, she loves watching Emma and not often is she allowed to. "Talk."

"There's no other way to get dad free. I can't leave him there. All he did was protect me and it's not fair," I say, my eyes getting wet.

"Life isn't always fair," she says looking at me. "This will be tough, but we have more people on your side than you know. There are many witch covens who are unhappy with the way the council is running things. We no longer believe they are communicating with the Gods and are acting for their own benefits."

"So, you'll help?" I ask. I sound like I'm begging her. I probably am. I love my dad and will do anything to save him.

"Of course, I will. I'll contact some people and send them your way. When the time comes, I'll come too. I need to finish some things up here first, make sure my family is protected."

"You are more than welcome at the pack, all of you," Lucas says sincerely. "We have plenty of empty houses and we can protect them."

"Well," Aunt Karen says, thinking. "That should be fine. Expect us within the week. I need to tie up some loose ends here and then we'll be on the way. Thank you for the offer, Lucas."

"You are family now. We do anything for family," he says, smiling at her. My heart melts. I really got lucky when fate chose a mate for me. I guess I can't blame it all on fate. I chose my own mate, and I picked the best one possible.

Chapter 23

Lyra

W e waited until Uncle Andrew got home to say good-bye before heading back to Sylva. Miss Lynn didn't have a car, she took a bus to get here, so she was riding back with us in Lucas's truck. Thank Goodness he has a back-seat! I couldn't imagine sitting in between the two of them on the way back or having Miss Lynn sit between Lucas and I. We loaded up our suitcase, and the big bag Miss Lynn had, into the bed of the truck and we were on our way.

"Any preference for music?" Lucas asks Miss Lynn, looking at her through the rearview mirror.

"No dear. I'm going to take a nap. It's been such a long day, you don't mind, do you?" She asks sweetly.

"No way! Go ahead and sleep. We don't mind Miss Lynn," I say, turning around in my seat and smiling at her. She returns my smile and curls up in the seat. She had brought her own pillow from home and Lucas always kept a spare blanket in the back-seat in case he ever broke down and needed it.

We ride in silence for the first few minutes before we both hear Miss Lynn's breathing even out and we know she's asleep. I turn to Lucas and lay my hand over his bare knee, thankful that he chose to wear loose shorts again. It makes touching so much easier when there's less clothing between us.

"I can't wait to get you home alone," he mutters, turning his head to look at me.

"Eyes on the road Casanova," I say smiling at him. He turns his head forward and I move my hand a little higher, squeezing his thigh. He glances at me again, but his eyes don't linger on me for long.

"Keep doing that and I'll pull over. Think she will sleep through us screwing in the bed of the truck?" He asks seriously. I turn to look at him, expecting to see a teasing look on his face, but instead, he looks as serious as he sounds. His face is tense, and his eyebrows are high in thought.

"Not this time. We aren't losing our virginity in the back of your truck," I snort.

"How about in our bed when we get back?" I look over at him again and he's smiling at me. I lean over the console and kiss him quickly, then turn his cheek so he's facing the road again.

"We won't be getting back unless you pay attention to the road. It's getting dark out and deer are everywhere," I say, looking out the window to emphasize my point.

"Fine. I'll pay attention. Just move your hand a little higher." I glare at him and he laughs, shaking his head. "Kidding! Geez. You can keep it where it is, no matter where you touch it's going to be distracting. Just don't touch my dick or all bets are off."

"Deal," I say laughing. "When did your bed become our bed?"

"It's been our bed since I met you," he says, smiling. I smile at him and wish we were home now. "We can choose a different house if you want. There are plenty of empty ones in the community. Even some bigger ones on the edge that are away from everyone else. I think one or two might have a pool already."

"I don't mind the house you chose. We can take a look though. Maybe we will find one we both like better than your home now," I say, my thoughts imagining us picking a house of our own. It would be nice to have something we both chose. Something we can raise a family in. I peak over at Lucas, his eyes set on the road, and think of our future children. Maybe they will have my red hair and his ice-blue eyes, or vice versa, his black hair and my gray eyes. Either way, they will look adorable.

"What's that smile on your face for?" I look over at Lucas, who is glancing between me and the road.

"Just thinking maybe you are right, we should choose a house together. Something big enough we can raise a family in. And what our kids will look like," I say, smiling softly. Lucas's eyes light up and his face transforms with boyish delight.

"See? I told you we should pick something else. It will be ours, not that my place isn't ours already, but you know what I mean. When would you like to have kids? I'm not in any rush, just curious."

"I don't know. I want at least a year of just the two of us. Enjoying each other and making plans. I don't even know if I want to go to college or even if I can."

"Of course, you can if you want! You can do an online school or just take a break for now. We can pick a place with enough space to have our own offices, and you can do school work or start a job online. Once everything with the council is settled, you can work away from the community. I just don't trust it right now," he says.

"Yeah, I understand that. I was considering doing something with water, like maybe a swim instructor at the local pool. I can teach the community kids how to swim, I know it wouldn't give me money, but it would be something to do during the day. I also love to write, maybe I could write a book or something."

"Whatever you want to do, is fine with me. We aren't strapped for money, I make a good bit designing new buildings. Plus, I have a heavy trust fund set aside that I have never touched. You can stay at home and teach the neighbor kids if that's all you want to do."

"You are so sweet. I love you," I say, leaning over and kissing his cheek. I lean back in my seat and watch the trees go by fast. "What happens if we can't have kids?" I ask quietly, not wanting to ruin our moment but needing an answer all the same.

"Don't worry about that now. There's no reason to stress over something we can't control now or later. When the time comes for kids, we will face it then. And if we can't have any, maybe we could adopt?" He asks, glancing over at me quickly to gauge my reaction. That wouldn't be a bad idea, I'm open to it. "I've heard of families in the community taking in children before, some even wolf. There are no laws about adopting a human baby, so we have a lot of options. No matter how we have a child, it will be ours and you'll make the best mother."

I smile at him and close my eyes for a second, imagining our life. He's right, no matter how we have a child, it'll be ours. I open my eyes and look at him sideways.

"Even so, we should get plenty of practice in just in case. Sound like a good plan?" I tease. A wolfish grin spreads over his lips.

"Damn right."

***

We pull up at the community gate close to eight at night. The sky is pitch black, and the moon is full. Miss Lynn woke up less than an hour ago and the ride has been mostly quiet since. I stretch as Lucas lines up with the gatehouse and waves to Bernie, the night guard. Bernie waves back and opens the gate for us. We drive through and go straight to Lucas's house.

"Are we not going to your dads?" I ask curiously.

"Not tonight. When I called him at the gas station, I told him we would crash as soon as we got home. We aren't up for all those questions tonight." Nodding, I jump out of the truck and head to the bed. "I got it, baby. Go ahead inside and get Lynn set up in your old room."

Lucas throws me the keys and I open the door, waiting for Miss Lynn to catch up. She smiles at me and I lead her upstairs to the guest room. I quickly clear out some of my stuff from the floor and throw it in Lucas's room to go through later.

"Light reading?" She asks me, indicating the Greek mythology book.

"Yea. I borrowed it from Lucas. I was curious about the different creatures and myths," I say, taking the book and tucking it under my arm.

"Most of that isn't myth though dear. You should read it more in depth." Lucas comes in and drops Miss Lynn's bag on the bed with a thud.

"What on earth do you have in that blasted thing?" He grunts.

"My whole life has been uprooted, young man. I have everything I need in this bag." She reaches over and unzips it, inside looks like a black hole. I step closer, trying to get a better look, and I see what looks like shelves.

"No freaking way! Is that like Harry Potter?" I ask excitedly. Miss Lynn just blinks at me in confusion. "Like an extension charm or something so that a bag is bigger on the inside."

"Of course! How did you think I would have only one bag?" She says.

"That's so cool!" I exclaim, coming closer. "How does it work? How do you make your own?"

"I had this one made for me a long time ago by a witch. Empusae have natural magic, but it's almost always very dark. We can't perform the simplest of spells. Can't tie my own shoe with magic but if I want to blow it up, no problem!" She says laughing. I look at her, wondering if she's serious and decide she is. I shrug and walk to the door to stand by Lucas.

"Well, we are off to bed. Do you need anything else?" I ask, hoping she says no so I can go sleep. I'm exhausted and want to snuggle with Lucas before bed.

"I'm all good. Thank you, dear. Goodnight you two. I'm a sound sleeper, by the way, give me thirty minutes and not a single sound will wake me up!" She says, winking at us. Not only do I blush red, but Lucas does too. There's something about an old woman insinuating you are having sex that makes even the most open people embarrassed. Lucas quickly leaves the room, and I shut the door following behind him. I barely walk in the room before I'm thrown on the bed, on top of all the clothes I had just thrown on it.

Lucas stands at the end of the bed, grasping the bottom of his shirt and slowly pulling it off. His eyes look more wolf than man, and I totally feel like I'm his prey tonight. His shirt off, he comes towards me and grasps one foot in his hand. He pulls off my flip flop, fingers trailing up my leg and to my shorts. His fingers trail back down and grasp my other foot, taking that shoe off as well. He reaches up both legs and unbuttons my shorts in two second flat, sliding them down my legs and revealing my blue, see-through panties. Lucas groans at the sight.

"I didn't know you owned such sexy underwear," he says, staring in between my legs.

"I bought these for you when I went shopping with Aunt Karen yesterday morning. There might be more in my bag," I tell him boldly. I've always been a brave person but when it comes to my sexuality, I'm usually shy. Tonight though, I'm full of confidence.

"If she wasn't across the hallway, I would rip those off with my teeth," he growls, throwing me over his shoulder, my ass in the air, and walking into his en-suite bathroom.

"Promises, promises," I mumble, swinging along his back. He slaps my ass hard with a loud smack before depositing me on the bathroom floor.

"Don't make me do it Lyra. I will. I'm on a thin rope right now," He groans. I decide to stop teasing him and look around his bathroom as I've never been in it before. He has a small shower stall, big enough for one person, and a single person tub. I frown at them both. "Yeah, not the greatest bathroom."

"Can we pick a house with a two-person shower and tub? Please?" I beg, turning around and facing him.

"Anything you want. And if no houses have that, I'll design a new bathroom, and have it made for you," he says, stalking towards me. His hands linger on the bottom of my shirt and then takes it off me, leaving me in only my blue underwear. "Is there a reason you never wear a bra?"

"Do I need one?" I ask innocently as he stares at my breasts, eyes lingering on my dark nipples and trailing down to my underwear.

"I prefer you not to wear one. They are perfect," he says, reaching out and holding one in his hand. His head lowers and sucks on my other breast and I gasp. My hands rise and tangle in his hair, pulling him closer to me.

My legs feel like jelly and my eyes are slammed shut. His lips let go of my nipple and trail upwards as his fingers tweak both nipples now. His lips find mine and he kisses me deeply, passing his tongue through my lips and tasting me.

"Please Lucas," I plead, needing a release. He lets go of me all together and turns on the bath behind me, adjusting the temperature. I stand there in shock, staring at him. He turns around and smirks at me.

"Do I need to take the panties off too, or can you manage that?" He asks. With a huff, I bend over and yank my underwear off my legs and kick them at him. He pushes his shorts down as well and even though I'm mad at him, I can't help but stare at his hardened length. I've never seen an intact man before, all the porn I've watched the guys were cut. I'm absolutely fascinated with the extra skin covering his glands. "What?"

"Huh?" I mumble, still staring at him. The last few days we have gotten very comfortable with each other, but I hadn't seen his penis until tonight. Without thought, I drop to my knees and study him closer. He inhales sharply but doesn't pull away as I gingerly reach out and grasp him. I hear him curse and he pushes it towards me. I open my mouth and engulf him, bobbing up and down and paying special attention to his extra skin with my tongue. His hands reach around my head and twist into my hair, guiding my bobbing along. I let him set the pace and watch his reactions to each new thing I try; I want to know exactly what he likes in bed, or out of it in this case.

Before long, he's pumping in faster and I can barely continue sucking on him. I know he's close to coming and I want it in my mouth. He tries to pull away at the last second, but I push my mouth forward; refusing to let go. His cock goes rigid in my mouth and begins to pulse, filling me with his juices. Definitely not my favorite thing in the world, but knowing I brought him pleasure is everything. He stands there for a second, breathing deeply, before looking down at me with half-lidded eyes. I smile coyly at him and lick my lips. I've never been so bold in my entire life.

"Damn. I certainly wasn't expecting that," his words are barely coherent. I smile up at him and stand up. He looks over my shoulder and practically dives for the bathtub- which is almost overflowing. Oops. He gives me a dark look and motions for me to come closer. Letting out a little water, he sits in the tub and scrunches his body up, I'm sure he's uncomfortable but I don't comment. I step into the tub, my back pressing into his chest and relax my body into his, already feeling his dick pressing into my back, half hard again.

"Why are we taking a bath together when this is clearly made for one person?" I ask, resting my head on his firm chest. His hands work their way through my hair, unknotting it in places.

"Because I want to wash you before bed," he says, grabbing an empty wash cup and filling it. He pours it onto my hair a few times, making sure it's soaking wet before reaching over and grabbing my shampoo.

"How do you have my shampoo in here already?" I ask as he lathers it up in my hair, fingernails scraping against my scalp.

"I smelled it the first day and made sure to have some in here for when you'd be joining me," he says, massaging my head. My eyes are firmly closed, and I can't help but let out little moans of pleasure.

"Not creepy at all," I say sarcastically. He snorts behind me and I grin. "You were so sure I'd be bathing in here with you?"

"Yup. You are my mate, I knew you'd be in here eventually and I wanted to be ready," he says, lifting the full cup of water and dumping it on my hair, rinsing out the suds. He grabs the soap and lathers it in his hands before placing them on my body and working his way downward. He stops briefly at my nipples and tweaks them once, eliciting a loud moan from me. He continues downward but avoids where I want him most. I keep expecting his hands to wander in between my legs but they manage not to touch me there once the whole bath. Before I know it, he's pulling the plug and pushing me up so he can exit the tub. I continue to stare at him as he grabs a towel and dries me off first before grabbing another one for his own body, he never stops touching me the whole time. Without a word, I lead us into the bedroom and grab one of his shirts and another pair of underwear. I know I'm acting a little childish, but I can't help it! He knows I want him badly.

Before I can dress, he wraps an arm around me and gently takes the clothes from my hands. "Nope," he whispers against my neck, causing me to shiver. So, he does have plans for me still. Damn right. He shoves the clothes off the bed fast, then turns me to face him and pushes me back onto the bed. He crawls on top of me and kisses me gently before lowering himself to where I want him most.

All I feel is his breath against me at first and feather-light kisses along my inner thighs. I have to bite my lip to keep from crying out and begging him to lick me. Without warning, his tongue is on me and rubbing in deliciously tight circles. I cry out, hoping I'm not too loud and cover my mouth with my hand. He teases around my swollen bud, then flicks across it fast. I know he's teasing me and I'm loving every second of it.

I gasp and one hand grips the sheet under me, the other one is fisted in his hair tightly. I don't want him going anywhere until he finishes what he's started. I feel myself spiraling upwards and just as I'm about to cum, he pulls off my bud and licks my swollen lips.

"You asshole! So, help me God, if you don't--" He cuts me off by diving right back on my clit, and this time he doesn't stop until my teeth are lodged into my arm to keep myself from screaming. My eyes are wide and I'm panting around my arm, trying to catch my breath. Lucas crawls over top of me and gently pulls my arm away, looking at my puncture marks in fascination.

"If she wasn't in the next room, I'd take you right now," he growls at me, pressing his hard length into my thigh. I'm half tempted to say fuck it and move my hips until he's positioned where I need him to be. Sadly, he's right though and I don't want my first time to be across the hall from someone I see as my grandmother. I groan and flop back onto the bed, Lucas watching me intently. "How are you feeling?"

"Fine," I say, wondering why he would ask such an odd question. Then I sit up, my head almost colliding with his nose in my haste. "How long has it been?"

"Over thirty minutes," he says, grinning at me.

"Are you sure?" I ask, looking around for a clock but not seeing one. Lucas laughs at me and I glare at him.

"My clock was moved to your room, remember? I just estimated, let me check my phone." He says, getting off the bed and grabbing it from the dresser. He whistles loudly. "Over forty actually."

I jump up from the bed and embrace him, wanting him now more than ever. We did it! That is the longest we have ever touched.

"Not now, tomorrow. We can move her to my dad's place and give us some space. You get some sleep, I'm going to head to my office for a little bit before I come in."

Lucas kisses me goodnight and walks out of the room. I'm tempted to follow him, but I slip on the shirt and underwear I originally picked out and climb into our bed and snuggle with his pillow. Excited for the day to come.

Chapter 24

Lyra

The room is pitch black when I awake. Lucas's arms are wrapped around me and I lay there, enjoying the feeling of him. I'm not sure what time it is but something woke me up. I slip from the bed carefully and tiptoe out the door, shutting it quietly. My feet pad softly against the wood floor as I walk down the hallway, towards the stairs. There's a glow reaching up from below and I make my way down silently.

"You can't sneak up on me dear." I hear Miss Lynn say from the kitchen. I turn the corner and see her standing by the kitchen sink, coffee mug in hand. I take a sniff, but don't smell coffee beans from here. "Oh, this is tea. I can't stand coffee."

"Makes sense. What are you doing up so early?" I ask, coming to stand beside her. She's wearing a red satin robe and her hair is flowing loosely around her head.

"Up for a swim. You didn't think you were the only one who enjoyed swimming, did you?" She asks me, her eyes twinkling.

"Is that an Empusae thing then?"

"Why, yes, it is. Empusae are naturally drawn to moisture- as are many snakes. We prefer being near water, if not in it. I can't swim in the ocean much anymore; I'm just not strong enough, but a pool will be just fine. I'll be out there for a few hours. You will have plenty of time to do... whatever it is you need to do," she says, winking at me. My face heats and I want to hide, of course she heard us last night. I knew there was no way she couldn't have.

"Oh, God. This is embarrassing," I mutter, hands covering my warm cheeks.

"Not really. Sex is a natural thing. Go get your man. I won't be able to hear a thing from out there."

Before I can respond, she walks swiftly to the door and walks outside. I shake my head and look up at the ceiling, wondering if I should do what she says. It would definitely be a surprise for Lucas, and I want us to mate as soon as possible. Decision made, I race back up the stairs as quietly as I can and enter our bedroom. It's still dark inside and I strip out of my clothes, listening to Lucas breathe deeply in sleep. I pull back the covers and swiftly climb in beside him.

He doesn't even stir as I settle in against him, molding my body to his side. He's sleeping naked again, I assume this is his normal when he's not sleeping in someone else's house or in a hotel room. I rest my hand against his chest and slowly drag it downward, nails grazing against his skin. His cock is already hard for me and I wrap my fingers around it softly. He still doesn't move.

Rising up, I bring my mouth to his shoulder and bite down gently. Dragging my lips over and upwards, I place my mouth on his neck, sucking gently at first and progressively harder as I pump his hardness in my hand. He moves a little in his sleep, and his breathing picks up, otherwise, he remains out of it. Deciding to give him an extra special wake-up, I trail my lips down the same path my hand took until I'm under the covers on my knees. I take him in my mouth instantly and lightly suck on the skin. His pelvis pulses up to meet my face and I smile around his dick. Finally, I'm getting a reaction out of him. I bob my head up and down, my hand wraps around the base, still pumping along with my mouth. His hands push back the covers and grab my hair, pulling me away from him, and he brings me up so I'm straddling him.

"Good morning," I say, grinning smugly down at him. His hands are on my hips and his dick is pressing excessively into my ass cheek. Just a little maneuvering and he'd be filling me.

"Very good morning. I thought I told you the next time we wake up naked together, there would be no stopping," he mumbles, still half asleep. My hands move from his pectoral muscles and grab onto his shoulders, I push myself back a little and line him up perfectly. His eyes widen, fully awake now.

"That would be the point," I say, moving slowly down and allowing him to fill me slowly. His hands on my hips tighten and I can feel his body tense, trying to hold himself back and let me set the pace. I brace myself for any pain, but I feel none. Ever so slowly, I continue moving down until he's fully seated inside me; stretching me completely. I moan and sit still, trying to accommodate his large size. Lucas's eyes are watching me darkly from below; I know if I don't move soon, he will take over.

Using his shoulders as leverage, I slowly move up and down; feeling pleasure in every movement. I lock eyes with Lucas, opening myself up to him as he is doing with me. Allowing each other to see the emotions playing on our faces and through our eyes. Lucas's eyes are darker than I've ever seen, and his body is still tightly wound.

"You are holding yourself back, let go," I say, bending closer to his ear and nipping it. He flips us over and I look up at him, giggling. My laugh is cut off though as he drives into me hard and I moan loudly.

"Too much?" He asks me, ceasing his movements and I shake my head; it'll never be too much with Lucas. He plows into me again, hitting a spot in me I didn't know existed. My hands tighten around his shoulders and I pull him down to me, kissing him fiercely. Our tongues fight for dominance and eventually Lucas wins, his tongue entering my mouth. I feel that now familiar pressure building low in my belly and I tense up. Lucas pulls away, looking into my face. He goes faster and buries his head in my neck, as my mouth goes directly to his and I fight my instinct to sink my teeth into his skin.

When I feel Lucas's teeth against my neck, I begin to shudder; no longer able to hold back my orgasm. My fangs elongate and I find myself staring at his pulsing vein. God, I want to bite him so bad.

"Do it," he demands into my neck, his teeth still nipping gently. I know I shouldn't, but I let my mouth open and bite down. My whole body explodes, my orgasm rocking through me and Lucas's blood entering my mouth. Lucas clamps down on my neck too, prolonging my orgasm, and he cums inside me. Mine.

"*Fuck.*" I hear Lucas say, but there's no way he can talk with his teeth in my neck.

"*Lucas?*" I whisper back in my mind, releasing his neck and licking it clean.

"*Yeah, baby?*"

"*You do know we are talking with our minds, right?*" I ask him. He laughs out loud and inside his head, it's a different experience.

"*I'm aware. I told you this sometimes happens,*" he says mentally, pulling himself out of me carefully and laying on his back. He pulls me half on top of him and I snuggle into his side, completely content and satisfied.

"We did it," I say out loud, not used to our mental connection outside of our wolf forms.

"We did. Damn that was amazing," he says, still sounding a little asleep. I push myself up and look him in the eyes.

"Are you okay? I didn't hurt you, did I?" I ask him, turning his face so I can see his neck. The two puncture wounds are already healing.

"The opposite. You've made me a very happy man," he says, turning his face and kissing me. "How do you feel?"

"A little sore but in a good way," I say, laying my head back down on his chest.

"I mean the soul thing. How is that?" He asks me. His hand is running through my hair and down my back. I didn't even think of my powers. I try to feel the connection to it I always feel when I touch someone, but it remains dormant. The only feeling I get is Lucas's soul and his feelings, he's completely happy and a bit tired.

"I don't feel it. I just pick up on your feelings though."

"What am I feeling?" He asks me, I feel him move under me and look down at my head. I look up and catch his eyes with mine.

"Love and happiness," I whisper. "Same as me."

"I love you Lyra," he says, leaning down and kissing me again.

"I love you too Lucas," I sigh happily.

***

We lay in bed for almost an hour, just enjoying each other's company. I convince Lucas we can wait until later to go again, I don't want to keep Miss Lynn waiting outside all morning.

"Where is she anyway?" He asks me, pulling up a pair of shorts with no boxers. At my look, he grins. "If you aren't wearing a bra, I'm going commando."

"I don't mind," I say, eyeing his abs before he tugs on a shirt. "Miss Lynn is in the backyard swimming. She told me to get busy with you."

"Glad to know someone is looking out for my sexual health," he jokes. I swat at his arm and he grabs me, pulling me into his chest. "Have I told you I love you yet this morning?"

"Hmm. A couple of times I think, but you should say it again." I grin up at him. Standing on my tip toes, I kiss him soundly.

"I love you."

"I love you too," I say to him, before dancing out of his arms and throwing on clothes, this time my own. I choose a sky-blue summer dress, with thin straps, and throw it on over a pair of purple underwear this time. I have to swat at Lucas again as he reaches out to touch my ass. "No touching!"

"How many pairs of underwear did you get for me?" He asks, trying to peek into my bag. I zip it up and throw it on the floor.

"Plenty. You'll just have to wait and see," I tease him.

"When are you going to unpack? I have half the drawers cleared out already," he says, walking over to the dresser and showing me the empty ones.

"Well... I was hoping we could go look at other houses," I say, biting my lip. Lucas looks over at me and smiles.

"That sounds like an excellent idea. I wasn't sure when you wanted to start looking. I'll talk to dad today, he knows more about which ones are open and would fit us. Ready to head downstairs? I'm starved." I nod at him and follow behind him.

When we arrive in the kitchen, smells of bacon and brown sugar hit our noses. Miss Lynn is at the stove cooking breakfast, I assume oatmeal by the smell. She looks behind her as we enter and smiles at us.

"Good morning!" She chirps. "I just came inside a few minutes ago, I didn't hear anything, so I figured it was safe to be inside."

"Oh... Thanks," I mutter, a blush rising on my cheeks. She certainly doesn't beat around the bush. I take a seat at the island and Lucas grabs some coffee for the both of us. He places black coffee in front of me and turns around, grabbing the sugar container and the caramel creamer from the fridge. I fix my coffee the way I like it and glance at him, taking note of how he takes it. Same as me. We really are a lot alike.

"Sleep well?" Lucas asks Miss Lynn.

"Oh yes. That bed was comfortable, and I slept like a baby. Your pool is lovely by the way. Does your father have one as well? It would be nice to swim every day while I'm here," she asks.

"Yeah, he does. You might have to share with some local kids though. Not many houses have pools so the kids flock to my dads in the summer to swim. If you get up early, you should be good."

"That'll be fine. I'm an early bird," she laughs, turning back to the stove and stirring the pot. She turns off the burner and flips bacon in the other pan. Pulling some bowls out of the cabinet, she pours the hot oatmeal evenly in the three of them before placing two in front of Lucas and me.

"Thank you," we say at the same time. She stands across from us and stirs in more sugar into her oatmeal before digging in.

"When should we head over to your dads?" I ask Lucas, blowing on my spoonful of food. I don't feel like burning my tongue today.

"When we are done eating breakfast is fine," Lucas says, shoveling food in his mouth. I see the steam rising from his bowl and know that it has to be hot. Lucas doesn't even flinch, just chews, swallows and shove another spoonful in. I shake my head and finally take my first bite. It's good actually, she added a hint of cinnamon to it which is how I like it. When Miss Lynn is done, she head's upstairs and leaves the two of us alone so she can get ready. Lucas washes his dishes in the sink, and I finish up my last bite before bringing it over to him.

"Do you think your parents will hate me once they find out what I am?" I ask him quietly. It's been a big worry of mine since I found out myself. His dad already doesn't like me, I'm sure this won't help matters. Lucas is quiet as he washes my bowl and sets it in the dish strainer. Finally, he turns and takes me in his arms.

"They will not hate you. You are my mate and they will accept you even if you were a tree," he says seriously, his joke falling short. "Seriously, it will be fine. The worst is over now, we are fully mated, and you can no longer hurt me. They will be fine with it."

"What about the pack? Do you think they will ever accept me?" I ask, looking into his eyes. I need to know what he really thinks.

"That I don't know. There are a lot of pack members and they are all different. Some I know will accept you, others I'm not sure. They will look to my dad to know what to do. He will accept you and they will too. If not, we will leave. I'll be happy as long as we are together."

"How do you know the exact thing I need to hear to feel better?" I ask, hugging him tightly.

"I just do," he says simply. We hear footsteps coming down the stairs and look over as Miss Lynn comes in the room.

"Hope I'm not interrupting something, I can go back upstairs or outside if you need a minute," she says.

"No. We are fine. Let's go," I say, pulling away from Lucas and grabbing his hand. I'm not sure I fully believe him that they will accept me. I am their natural enemy, something created to destroy their kind. I don't know if I could ever accept someone like me if I was them. I just have to hope Lucas is right.

Chapter 25

Lucas

I have never been more nervous in my entire life.

Walking into my family home, everyone is quiet. The normally active household knows this is serious. My mom greets us at the door with a small smile and a hug, she even makes sure to hug Lyra. I appreciate it that she approves so much of us being together. We quietly follow my mom to the formal living room, a room back behind the dining room that is only used for family meetings and pack business. Everyone is already seated when we enter, Julie and Lewis both smile at us and glance at Miss Lynn. They don't understand who she is and why she gives off such a bad vibe to them. I can't blame them, she gives me the heebie-jeebies.

"What did you learn?" Dad asks, seated beside Lewis on the sectional. Mom takes a seat on his other side, grasping his hand. She already has a feeling this is bad news.

"We met her Aunt Karen, and she explained what Lyra is," I start, standing beside Lyra and looking down into her eyes. We both know this is the moment. How they react decides our plan. We might be kicked out, forced to live among humans and hide. I'll do it for her, she's worth it. I would prefer to be free to be myself and be with my family, but if they choose to not accept us, I'm out. Taking a deep breath, I continue, "She's a hybrid obviously, half wolf and half... Empusae."

My family stares at us in shock; I'm not even sure if they heard me. The only indication is their faces. Julie's eyes are wide with shock and she glances over at Lewis, whose eyes are fixed on Lyra now. Living with him for so long I can read his expression relatively well, he is more curious and assessing then upset. Mom looks understanding and obviously wants to come over and hug us again, she will always accept me. Then there's dad. He just sits ramrod straight, not blinking. His mouth is clenched, and I can see his vein pulsing in his forehead. He's pissed. He's the one we have to worry about the most.

"Are you sure?" Dad asks me, his voice eerily calm. I glance at Lyra and squeeze her hand before nodding at my dad. I place myself slightly in front of her. I don't think dad will attack her, but I'm not taking any chances. Dad's eyes swing to Lyra, then to Miss Lynn, going back and forth. Understanding lights his eyes and I know he's put it together. "And you? You're one of them as well?"

"Yes. Though I mean no one any harm, my fangs were removed many years ago. I live a solitary life," she says, smiling gently. Her words don't seem to calm anyone in the room though. If anything, everyone is tenser than before. No one moves. Lewis glances at dad, assessing his reaction. I hold my breath, waiting for someone to say something. Finally, Lewis makes a decision and stands up.

"So, what's the plan?" He asks us. Dad looks up at him, appalled.

"Lewis-" Dad starts, but mom puts her hand on his arm. Her touch silences him and he squeezes his mouth together into a thin line, hands balled into fists. He's trying to calm himself and failing. I've seen him do this many times as a child. Usually, he has an even temper, but when something sets him off this much, he blows big.

"This isn't up for discussion. They are fully mated, I smelled it when they came in. She is family," Lewis says, not turning around but clearly speaking to our dad. "If we turn her away, Lucas leaves. You can throw them out if you want, but none of us will forgive you, and when I take over as Alpha, I'll invite them back. Might as well accept this now and save your family."

I watch Lewis, happy he is taking up for us. I feel awful tearing our family apart, but I can't leave Lyra. If she goes, I go. Dad looks infuriated and his body shakes, he's so angry. Mom keeps her hand on his arm and rubs it up and down, trying to soothe him.

"He's right Jon. I won't have you throwing them out. If they go, I'm following," mom says. Dad turns his glare to her.

"You can't be serious. She is a danger to all of us. We are lucky she hasn't killed Lucas already," he yells, shaking her hand off and rising to his feet.

"Dad, she won't hurt me. She can't now, mates remember? She physically can't do it," I say, taking another step-in front of Lyra. "Lynn is here to teach her how to control herself, we hope with her help Lyra can function in our community safely. You should know about choosing your own fate, you chose mom; it's the same thing. Lyra has chosen to be good. She is above what she was made to do, and we can't blame her for someone else's mistakes."

Dad looks at everyone around the room before his eyes settle on behind me, on Lyra. They slowly soften, his face relaxing, and he nods at her. I know this isn't personal, he's concerned for our pack. This isn't just a decision on letting us stay. It's a decision on letting Lynn stay and standing against the council for Lyra, someone who was created to kill us and our family.

"I'm sorry," he mumbles. "I know they are right. There's just a lot riding on this decision. I don't even know if the pack will allow it. Even if I give my consent, they could rebel. Or leave and then what? How can we protect you if half our pack is gone?"

"They will follow us. Our pack is loyal," Lewis says, coming up beside dad and clapping him on the shoulder. "You need to get Leo on our side though. As Beta, he has major sway within the community. If we all stand together, they will stand with us."

"I know you are right," dad agrees. "I have to worry about all outcomes, that's my job and will one day be yours. You'll be a good alpha when the time comes." He turns away from Lewis and faces us. "I apologize. You are good for Lucas, I've never seen him so happy before. We will help you. I know quite a few other packs who will join us. I need to talk to Leo, and then the rest of the pack."

***

It doesn't take long for Leo to show up and, of course, he brings Vanessa with him. They don't bother knocking and walk straight into the house. Leo is wearing relaxed clothing of jeans and a button-down, yellow shirt and Nessa is wearing a tube dress. If you can even call it that, it barely fits her. Her eyes instantly fly to me and she smiles, coming over and trying to hug me. Lyra physically puts herself in her path and crosses her arms. She's just as protective and jealous as I am, damn that's hot.

"No need to be so defensive. I was just going to hug him," she says, trying to walk past Lyra. A growl escapes her throat, and she steps in front of me again. Nessa's smile drops and she glares at her. "Move it. You have no claim on him."

"Actually, I do. He's my mate," Lyra says, her voice going deep. Nessa's mouth pops open and her eyes widen. I set both palms against Lyra's hips and pull her back into my chest. Her arms remain crossed, but I can feel her body relax a little at my touch. Bombshell looks down at my hands and then into my eyes. I suppress a growl, I don't want her even looking at me- she's upsetting my mate.

"You are mates? I mean, I've heard rumors around the pack, but nothing was confirmed," she asks and then breathes deeply. Smelling our scents, determining if we are telling the truth. Her eyes slant and she glares at Lyra again.

"That's fantastic!" Leo says, coming up behind his daughter and dropping his arm around her shoulders, squeezing a little too hard. Vanessa winces and her glare drops away, eyes looking anywhere but at us. "Isn't it Nessa?"

She nods and Leo looks satisfied. I'm sure he wanted his daughter and I to mate, who wouldn't want their child happy? But he knows it's too late now.

"I didn't expect Vanessa to join us when I requested a meeting," dad says, looking irritated. His eyes are still pinched at the sides and his mouth is in a hard line. Leo looks over at him and his demeanor changes; he knows this is serious. He whispers in his daughter's ear to go wait outside the house and she leaves without another word. She will get over it.

"What's going on?" He asks solemnly.

"Sit down. This will be a lot to take in," dad says, running a hand through his graying hair. I feel bad for putting him in this situation. Leo takes a seat in an armchair, sizing up everyone in the room. His eyes linger on Miss Lynn longer than the rest of us, but he doesn't say a word. Dad clears his throat and goes to sit beside mom. Lyra pushes me into an armchair and makes me sit first before she plops on my lap. Once everyone is comfortable, dad turns to Leo.

"This gist of it is Lyra isn't human. She's a hybrid. Her dad's a wolf and her mother was an Empusae," he pauses, waiting to see if Leo will comment. When he remains silent, he continues talking, "She has different gifts than that of her parents, she has much to overcome but isn't a bad person. She's Lucas's mate and we accept her as such. We will be standing against the council and finding others to join us. This has been building for years, no one believes in them anymore and now is our chance to take them out. I want the pack to stand together as one. We will be opening our community to outsiders, people who are willing to fight with us. Understood?"

The room is quiet. I've heard dad talk like that before, but it isn't often. He usually doesn't resort to his alpha voice unless necessary. He didn't ask for Leo's opinion, he told him what was going to happen, and he expects him to agree. I squeeze Lyra's body as we wait for Leo's reaction. He stares at dad for a long moment and then glances at us. His eyes hold anger at first, then resignation. He knows he can't stand against his alpha, to do so would be to create a bad enemy. It would tear the pack apart, most would still follow dad. It isn't worth fighting over and he knows it.

"Sounds reasonable. Are you sure she's not a danger to us?" He asks, eying her carefully.

"I won't be. That's why I have a guide here, she will teach me control," she says, finally speaking up. Leo nods at her and turns back to dad. I finally feel myself relaxing. My family is accepting us, Leo is agreeing. All that's left now is to inform the pack.

"So, what do we do?" He asks.

"We prepare for war."

Epilogue

Lyra

Four months later

I stare at my reflection in the large mirror above the bathroom sink, trying to decide what to do with my wet hair. It's a bit shorter than it used to be, I insisted I cut it once it went past my butt. I swear Lucas cried a little even though it's still down to my waist. I do a French-braid, liking the idea of it being out of my eyes for now. I have too much to do today to worry about my hair constantly.

Walking out of the bathroom, I pass Lucas lying in our bed. His nakedness covered by a blanket, but I can still make out the lines of his body from the dull light reaching in from our windows. It's still the same dark comforter he had on his old bed, he liked it too much to get another and I agreed. He already gave up his old house for me, the least I could do was let him keep his bed. It's pretty comfortable anyway, no complaints from me.

I walk to our closest and grab a long sleeve green shirt and a pair of blue jeans from my dresser. I dress hurriedly and throw on my gray boots before walking out the door. Our house is much bigger than the last one. It has four bedrooms upstairs, each with their own bathroom, and the downstairs has two offices, a large kitchen overlooking both the dining room beside it and the living room. Lucas had to add-on our offices, but we wanted plenty of room for us to do our work and for a family if that happens. For now, it's just the two of us and we are both content with that.

I turn on the living room light as I walk through to the kitchen. I make us both breakfast and start up the coffee for Lucas, throwing in hot chocolate in the microwave for myself. I set Lucas's plate of food in the microwave to stay warm and dig into my sausage links and eggs. I don't have time to wait for him today or to swim after I eat, I'm due for patrol in less than an hour.

Surprisingly, the pack accepted me without too many problems. Most of them understood the mate bond, and that we were destined to be together. There wasn't much point in being upset about what I am, they can't change it as much as I can't. What was harder for them to accept, was all the outsiders who moved into the community. Witches, other shifter packs, and even a harpy clan joined up to go against the council. We had to section off houses specifically for others; the shifters were mostly in the central part of the community. The witches took places around the southern edges and the harpies took places around the eastern edges. Our home is on the west side, away from others. The closest person to us is Miss Lynn, who moved a few houses down from us in a smaller one story home. It also has a pool, so she was quite happy with that even though it's getting colder outside. Neither of us much mind colder water, but soon enough it'll be too cold even for us.

I head into our backyard, thankfully it's one that is connected to the main wall surrounding our community. Makes patrolling easier when we can just walk through a wall. I pass through and immediately strip and shift into my wolf. Shifting has gotten much easier for me. It took a while, but slowly I've been able to change into other forms. I managed a polar bear a few days ago; I joked with Lucas that at least I would be warmer during the winter. For the most part, I stick with my wolf form. I know everyone accepts me, but I don't want to rub it in their faces that I'm different.

Running the perimeter, I circle back encountering a few other wolves on my way home. I don't reach out to them, and they don't reach out to me. I usually patrol alone for the most part unless Lucas has the same duty as me. Occasionally, I run with Julie but she doesn't have many patrols- too busy being the Luna-in-training. Lewis is never out here, neither is his dad.

I haven't managed to make many friends here, which I guess if you think about all the years I spent friendless, that isn't all that surprising. But I had hoped I would find someone I could connect with. The only person I like, outside of my family, is Aurora. We get along fairly well and we have a lot in common. We both grew up as humans, though she really is one, and we both feel like outsiders here. I try to get together with her often, but I avoid her mate: Bryden. He's not the nicest guy here, pretty lazy and expects Aurora to do everything for him. He doesn't even have a job, he just relies on the pack for expenses and Aurora, who is a midwife in training.

Their mate bond is weird too. They don't often seem to share affection typical of mates and the few times we've talked about our sex lives, Aurora isn't happy with it. I just can't understand that since me and Lucas can't keep our hands off each other. We are constantly having sex, sometimes multiple times a day, and Aurora and Bryden are lucky to do it once a month. It just seems unnatural to me, and I try to bring it up with Aurora but she shuts the conversation down each time. I've learned to just drop it and steer the conversation onto other things.

Besides Aurora, no one else in the pack really talks with me. They accept me, sure, but no one really has reached out to me to make me feel included. During patrol runs, people go off in groups to chat. I'm generally alone. I do still talk to Ryan occasionally; he seems happy with his life. He and Mira talked, and she promised to keep the secret of the mystical creatures. She still refuses to talk to me though. I'm not sure why her panties are in such a twist, but I still reach out to her every few weeks.

I don't mind it all that much. I have a lot going on most of the time. I patrol three times a week, when it's warm out I run swim lessons and act as a lifeguard, I've been doing some online classes, I have Lucas, training with Miss Lynn, and we are all gearing up for a war with the council.

It's been quiet on that front at least. The council hasn't made many moves against us, they've been keeping low and so have we. I'm sure they know we are gathering together, there's no way someone hasn't told them yet. Packs of shifters and covens of witches have uprooted. We aren't all here for a party.

We train silently, witches practicing their defensive spells, enchanting objects, and setting up wards. Shifters working on their fighting skills. The harpies don't train much, for the most part, they are just there and don't interact with us. I see them flying in the air sometimes, manipulating this way and that. There's only five of them, two couples and one child. They apparently have an even harder time conceiving than Empusae do.

Finishing my patrol, I run back to the section of wall that leads into my backyard. I shift and change back into my clothes before passing through. I'm greeted by Lucas, who is braving the cold and swimming. Stupid pure wolf who can handle extreme weather. Why couldn't I get that power? His face is dripping wet, hair sticking to his face. He steps out of the water, his abs flexing as he walks. And he's naked. Lucas has a thing for skinny dipping.

"Naked again?" I tease, eyes locked on his body.

"My eyes are up here," he jokes. I laugh and take a step closer, wrapping my arms around him. I don't care if my clothes get soaked, I want to touch him all the time. That hasn't changed a bit in the last four months. We are still madly in love and want to jump each other's bones 24/7. We've mentioned marriage a few times and kids, but we want to wait to find my dad to have a wedding. And the kid thing? We aren't trying per se, but we aren't using any protection. We figure it will be hard for me to get pregnant as it is- why would we try to stop it? If it's meant to happen, it will.

"I missed you," I say, taking a step back and walking into the house.

"I missed you too. How was patrol?" He asks, following behind me. His feet trail water on the floor, and I stare pointedly at it. Ignoring his question. He looks down and signs. "Sorry. I'll clean it up later. I'll be right back."

While he runs upstairs to change, I get out the mop and clean up his mess. I don't mind cleaning up after him, I just wanted to avoid the patrol question. He always wants to know how patrol goes, how I'm getting along with the pack. It just isn't progressing, and it makes me frustrated. Floor cleaned, I take a seat on the couch and look around. This is my home now. There are pictures on the walls, mostly of me and Lucas, but some of his family. We have a larger tv than before, Lucas insisted since there are now two of us. I guess two people watching tv at once, means a larger one is needed? I shake my head and snort. Lucas is full of shit.

I relax against the couch cushions and look at the pale blue walls. I much prefer the blue and gray color scheme to the red and gray, this is much more relaxing. We have a beautiful leather gray sectional, light gray wood throughout the house and blue accents. Our kitchen is all slate gray and much bigger than any other kitchen I've been in, even bigger than Lucas's family home. I've taken to baking in my spare time, and share pastries with the pack. They won't befriend me, but man will they take that apple pie I baked.

Lucas comes downstairs, fully dressed this time. What a shame. He's wearing dark jeans and a black button-up shirt, typical for him. He always has this casual-formal look to him that I love, and he still favors black more than any other color. He sits down beside me, throwing his arm over my shoulders. I curl into him, leaning my head against the crook of his neck and inhale deeply.

"You need to feed soon?" He asks, voice getting deeper. I swear he's insatiable! We had sex twice last night before bed and once early this morning. Which, yeah, was my fault... but still!

"Soon, but not right now. Maybe tonight?" I suggest. He lets me drink from him every few days and really he enjoys it more than I do. Twice a week we go hunting for wild game to satisfy my hunger for flesh. I'm still getting used to it, but it gets easier every time. Plus, there are some benefits from feeding on Lucas. It's very intimate and usually leads to sex if we aren't already having it. Sometimes, Lucas begs for me to bite him and I'm all too happy to oblige. And no more blood powder- though we do keep it around just in case.

"Tonight will be fine, whenever you are in need is fine by me," he says, smiling down at me and kissing my forehead. He's so affectionate with me. "Are you happy here?"

"What kind of question is that?" I ask, pulling away and looking at him. My face is scrunched up in confusion. I'm not sure where this is coming from, why wouldn't I be happy?

"I can feel your emotions Lyra. I know sometimes you aren't

happy here. I know you are happy with me and our home, but is this enough for you?" He asks, searching my face. I relax a little and smile at him. I place my hand on his cheek and lean in for a kiss.

"Of course this is enough for me Lucas. You make me the happiest girl in the world. I just have a lot on my mind. I'm worried about my dad every day, the council, the Empusae uprising, children, and the pack still isn't letting me in. They accept me, but none have reached out and befriended me. I don't know what else I can do! I did swim lessons and lifeguarding, I babysit, I bake desserts, I patrol and take extra shifts for people. Nothing is really breaking the ice. I want to be a part of this pack, not just in it."

"I get it. Maybe you should ask them directly? Say what you just said to me? You can also try asking one of them to hang out. They might not know how to interact with you, you are a lot to take in and people may need more time," Lucas says, rubbing my back. I know he's right, I just thought four months would be long enough. "Give it some more time. Once they really get to know you, they'll love you. Hopefully not as much as I do though. I'll fight them off!"

I laugh and relax into him. This moment is perfect. Just the two of us in our own home, being together despite so many odds against us. The only thing I would change is my dad being here. No matter how much I distract myself, my thoughts still drift to him. I don't even know if he's still alive, but a part of me feels him. I truly believe he's still out there and I also believe everything is going to work out alright in the end.

We sit in silence until Lucas's phone rings, jerking us out of our relaxation. Lucas walks over to the counter and picks it up, answering. "Yeah, dad, what's up?"

"We need you and Lyra at the front gate now," I hear through the phone, thanks to my super wolf hearing. I cock my head, wondering why we are needed there. I just did my patrol and everything was quiet. I stand up and Lucas hangs up, not bothering to ask what the problem is. We both know if he wants us there, he's not going to tell us over the phone. We jump into my new Toyota Highlander, Lucas insisted I needed a need vehicle and I must admit I love it and make the short drive to the front gate. Pulling up, we see many wolves surrounding it and Jon is nowhere to be seen. I park and we both jump out, looking around for him and the cause of the commotion.

"Dad is past the gate," Lewis says, coming up behind us. His face is serious, so unlike the easy-going guy he usually is. This must be bad. Lucas takes my hand, and we walk together to the wide privacy fence that swings open when people drive through. It's closed tight when we get to it and the guard on duty opens it up, allowing us to pass. We step out and see Lucas's dad and Leo standing a few feet away with a woman. She has light blonde hair, almost white, and pale skin. Her face is covered in blue tattoos and I instantly recognize her as the harpy who attacked me all those months ago.

"What's she doing here?" I ask, standing up tall. I might be scared, but I refuse to show it. Her head whips around to me and I notice she's wearing normal clothes this time. Blue jeans and a long sleeve red shirt, her feet remain bare though. She doesn't smile, but her body does relax as she stares at me.

"I need your help," she says. I give her a *what the fuck* stare. Why on earth would she think I would help her? "It's your brother. He's alive and you're the only one who can save him."

Well fuck.

Author Page

Sam Miller lives in Wisconsin with her family and cat. Of course, she has a cat, what female author doesn't? Kidding… But for real, her name is Aria, and she's a witch… with a B. Anyway! Sam enjoys writing in her free time and dreams of becoming a home-birth midwife. She is currently a stay-at-home mom and spends her days chasing after her toddler. Like this main character, Lyra, she is sarcastic and loves to read. Her current work-in-progress is the second book in The Greek Mystical Series, Ryan, which will be available by the end of this year. What to know when it's released? Like and follow her author page to keep up-to-date on the latest news and exclusive sneak peaks!

www.facebook.com/SamMillerAuthor/

www.ingramcontent.com/pod-product-compliance
Lightning Source LLC
Chambersburg PA
CBHW020258200626
46816CB00001BA/353